THE
FACTORY

AMANDA DACYCZYN

To my parents, who never stopped my creative thinking, as well as my sister who constantly made me want to do my best no matter what. And finally, to Mae, who told me to write a book about her.

***

Chapter One:

Gavin

Rocking back and forth on his toes, the town crier, Gavin, waited for the signal to announce the start of market weekend. In the cold of winter, the marketplace was open only on the days of rest, and therefore the announcement was vital to the entire village. About three dozen vendors, pulling their wheeled carts behind them, trudged down Market Street to mark their usual territory. There were grunts as some wheels sunk into the muddy ground, made soft by the mix of snow and constant moving of the merchants. Many yawned as they prepared their stands, placing tomatoes, carrots, some apples, along with wares such as bracelets, plates and other essentials at the front. There was the smell of warmth with stewed meats and veggies as two or three of the cart owners began to boil their soup to sell. Gavin became more anxious as the sun began to peak over the horizon.

He glanced behind him at the town, its small, mostly wooden buildings reflecting the golden light that eased its way into the sky. From the few trees that stood near the tattered gated entrance, crows cawed loudly, their wings spreading wide. The boy looked at the old rickshaw gate that was barely held together now, the latched gate blowing easily in the breeze, almost laughing at the thought that it could actually protect the people within the town. His thoughts were interrupted by another shriek of the crows. A shudder ran up his spine as they continued their calls. The crier never liked the sound of the black birds; their song reminded him of a cruel day. Not any day in particular, just a day that could quickly become unpleasant. Whenever he saw them, he took it as an omen—an omen one that would not be in anyone's favor.

His thoughts were shaken as someone grunted behind him. The lead vendor Dax, a scrawny old man with a grey beard down to the middle of his chest, stood there, looking down at the boy. His brown eyes almost looked black, the sun behind him casting a shadow on his leathery face. The bell heavy in his hand, the crier waited for instructions. Although he'd been working this job for the last year and a half, the old man peering at him always made him feel inadequate. Perhaps Dax knew Gavin always was anxious to shout and run around the town as fast as he could, which was why he was so curt toward him. There was a way of doing things, and it needed to be done right. The old man looked over his shoulder at the rising sun then back at the boy.

"Give it another thirty minutes. When the sun has risen completely over the mountain over there," Dax said gruffly, scratching at his beard. "Don't want to be bringing any angry customers here from the start."

Gavin nodded, and the old man ambled away. He dragged his way over to the nearby well station and sat next to one of the eight pumps that circled a great drain. A few droplets were freezing over, and he knew that if he didn't move the water out, it would remain frozen for the day. Actually, he now thought, with how cold the weather had been the past few days, the water might even freeze for a week. Sighing, he pushed his way up and pumped some water out of each of the spigots, passing the time.

He let his mind wander as he took in the village around him. The compact houses almost lay on top of one another, with a few alleyways sprinkled here and there. Some stood at a slant, while others remained straight and tall. There were a scattering of brick houses, but those were only for the powerful folks—the "richies," as he called them—and they were located right by the town center. People like the mayor of the town, and the head of the police were able to call that slot of rocky soil theirs. These wealthy villagers were able to establish their dominance here and also had the best view of the town. Even though that "view" pretty much just encompassed the pumps and the partially working fountain, it didn't seem to matter to them.

As the boy approached his last pump, he glanced at the Hall of Records—although "hall" probably wasn't the best word for it, as it was just a small five-sided wooden building. But it was important since it held the records of everything that had happened in the town from its beginnings. Birth certificates, marriage licenses, prison papers, obituaries—they were all stored here. And the hall also held the lists of certain dead people. Although these lists hadn't seen ink in thirty years, the mere thought of them terrified the townsfolk, so no one ever spoke of them. It was a distant memory—one that many never even had—but the tales were always there, like ghost stories told in the glow of a campfire. The only difference was these legends were true.

Lost in his thoughts, the boy almost didn't hear the stern call of the old man telling him it was time to start. With Dax's raspy blessing, it was time for Gavin to go. He forgot all about the lists and what they represented and began by walking around the open courtyard that led to the wide street occupied by the market. Slowly he rang his bell, softly at first, then louder and louder. He turned quickly, cupping his mouth and bellowing "Market open this weekend! Market open. Come getcha' fruits, veggies and needs! Market open!"

Through the soft light in the windows of the brick and wooden houses, shadows began to move about, some pulling shades back to peak at Gavin as he turned around the spouts. After making three laps around the pumps and the fountain, he headed down the street, where the cobblestones made his jog a bit more difficult. Spraining an ankle was the last thing Gavin needed, especially since his family needed to take care of his sister's illness. The money was the only thing that paid the doctors' bills, as the rest went to food for his kin. Gavin remembered this as he pushed his way further down the winding roads, yelling "Market open!" ever few seconds. Whenever he passed an alleyway, he'd poke his head in and let his voice and bell echo.

Gavin passed the line into the middle-to-lower-class area; these houses were made of wood, with thatch roofs covering them instead of the more upscale terracotta slates. As he hustled down the street, he noticed the

4

bookkeeper's apprentice hanging the OPEN sign on the old, weathered building. The young man gave him a wave as he walked back in, his dark and tall lanky frame ducking through the doorframe. The boy continued along, ringing his bell as he scurried by the town inn, The Blood Brothers Inn. Although it wasn't the prettiest thing to look at, with its rotting panels and a sign that was no longer clean enough to read, the place was always busy.

The sign hung low and Gavin glanced at it once more, seeing the E, R and S paint had completely chipped off. No one actually called it the Blood Brothers anymore, instead the Blood Broth. It was almost a joke to the town. Many villagers went there, not only for drinks but also for conversation, as the place also served as the town's meeting hall. When Gavin scurried by, he spotted the wiry white-haired woman who was always hanging around outside the place. Although she gave him a smile, nothing about it made him feel good inside. He continued to run until he was outside the pathetic gate, and headed towards the outskirts of town.

The boy reached the edge of the town entrance, knowing there was only one more place he had to go to make sure everyone knew the market was opening. *Up the road and at the fork, take a right*, he told himself. The left led to the farming sector and they already knew about market, since most of them were there. No, this was a solitary house—the last person in town. Gavin never liked going there, but it was part of his job.

After sprinting up to the fork, he made a quick right and raced toward the lot. Strangers who took this path into the village might not even notice a building was there, as it was covered from top to bottom with leaves and overgrown vines. But Gavin knew about it. Everyone in town did. There was a reason the house looked that way, but forgetting was much more comfortable. He stayed a safe distance away and rang his bell as loudly as he could, preventing himself from taking another step.

"Market open today and tomorrow!" he yelled, the wind pushing his words toward the mess of brambles and needlegrass. At first there was nothing, and Gavin wondered if the occupant was even awake, let alone hear him. He paused for a moment then shouted once more, louder than the last time.

A bit of quick movement flashed inside the house as a shadow passed through one of the few openings that the crier could see. A female, quickly rummaging for something, getting ready for the cold winter day. He stood for another moment as he watched her throw her hair together before disappearing from view. For now, Gavin's job was done. He could rest until it was time to make another announcement. He began to made his way back, jogging lightly as he went. Quickly glanced behind him and saw the girl running out the door, headed his way.

A few seconds later, Mae sprinted past him and into town.

Chapter Two:
<u>Mae</u>

Mae Fyez brushed through the throngs of people as she tried to figure out what to procure for the week ahead. She always planned, especially when it came to what she ate. Living alone at the edge of town, she was never quite sure when the best foods or items would be available, especially as the winter chill filled the air. Food in general was scarce, and when market days came, everyone tried to get there first. Therefore, when she heard the town crier yelling outside her house, she almost knocked him over to get there.

As she walked through town, Mae pulled her thinning woolen jacket closer to her. She wished she had grabbed some gloves or something to cover her now raw fingers. It had been so mild for the last few days, but now winter returned with a force. Other's in town had been more prepared than she was. Ladies in long pants, much like Mae's, trudging in what looked to be a type of boot. Other's wearing long woolen skirts and they shuffled along with their long jackets that almost touched the ground. Scarfs and hats nestled on their figures, making them look warmer than Mae felt. Men were wrapped up in leather and fabric jackets, their boots much sturdier than the one the women chose to wear. Their massive gloves, many which had been made by a family member, morphed to their hands. The drab mix of grey's, black's and browns were all Mae could see as she made her way deeper into town. No one could really afford colored fabric here. Not even a lot of the richies. And besides, colors were for spring. Darkness was for winter.

The bottoms of her shoes were worn through, and the stones and pebbles on the dirt roads and paths that lined the village poked the soles of her feet. As she weaved her way through the crowd clustered at the top of Market Street, a few people grumbled as she passed. But they quickly disappeared behind her. In the middle of the busy street, Mae slowed her pace, looking around to see what was open and which new shops might have popped up since her last visit. Her change purse hung at her neck, keeping the slimy urchins of the town from stealing her money. Although, in all honesty, she knew she would use little of the tins here. Stealing was how she got most of her food. Quick and nimble, she'd try to avoid the eyes of the vendors as she picked off the stands, preventing the involvement of the authorities, although she didn't worry about that as much as she used to. Not anymore.

Mae was able to pilfer so easily because no one wanted to acknowledge her presence. At one point, the other townsfolk had noticed her; they had seen her as the human she was. But things had changed in the last few years. They always do, and sometimes the way people see a person changes too. That was exactly what had happened to Mae. They once had looked at her, seen her as skin and bone, but slowly she had become almost transparent. As time went on, the townspeople looked at her less. Finally, she never even caught a passing glance. And now she knew she was invisible. In this town, this small town that she had once considered her home, Mae knew no one wanted to see her. No one wanted the reminder of her at all. And now, because of that, she used it to her advantage to survive.

A sharp pain struck Mae whenever she went into town. She knew why no one noticed her, why everyone quickly looked down when they accidentally made eye contact with her. It was because of what had happened. She was the reminder of the vile actions of the town and what the authorities had done to a family who had done nothing but love this charming yet run-down place. Mae was the tarnish that never would leave the minds of the people who remembered. And that was why they couldn't look at her.

There was a reason she lived at the edge of town and not right in the middle of it, like many of the villagers. She used to in her younger years. She had played in the streets with her friends, other small children whose parents worked as artisans, and bought candies from the old lady who sold them on the street. She went to school until the age of thirteen, when children were expected to find an apprenticeship. Mae always knew she would either work with her father, or hopefully find a rich merchant and stay at home like her mother. Mae had lived in an apartment above a bakery, and since her father was the town's favorite local leather maker, many times her family woke up to fresh bread, free of charge, on their doorstep. It was a good life, one that was burned in Mae's memory.

The news came when she was fourteen. A sickness—some called it a plague—was sweeping through nearby villages and taking out almost two-thirds of their populations. When one was infected, it was rumored, their skin would blister and puss; their ears and eyes bled; and every cough seemed as though it might be their last. Still it was nothing but a legend to her own village, and no one thought it would actually hit the town. That was until the traveler came, one no one knew, and he had the sickness. He stayed at Blood Broth, talking with everyone, no symptoms showing. But as he left, someone noticed it: the blisters on his back; the dried blood on his earlobe, which he had forgotten to clean. As he left, word spread: the village was now infected.

It didn't take long for the sickness to spread. But although many had feared it would be deadly, it was quite treatable. Children and young teens, for some reason, were immune, and only adults fell victim. Those who were ill were sent right away to the closest medic and usually returned home without any symptoms, free of the illness completely. The doctors had found some sort of root that settled the symptoms and calmed the blisters when mixed with a paste, allowing the treated to recover within a week, as their bodies became stronger. Those who waited a bit longer to seek medical attention had to stay in isolation houses for a few weeks. But otherwise, there was nothing to fear. The town seemed to have the sickness under control—that is, until Mae's mother and father fell ill.

Filip and Emi Fyez were among the last of the townsfolk to contract the illness. It started out as everyone else's had: a little fever, some coughing, blistering here and there, but nothing too worrisome. But then the symptoms didn't go away. Not even with the magical root soup and paste. Their coughing became deep and clotted; their fevers never stopped rising; and blood often poured out of their ears. Sometimes, when they slept, Mae heard their moaning and got up to check on them, only to find that the sheets were drenched with sweat, their blisters open and festering. When they sneezed, blood sometimes flowed for minutes at a time, and the color in their faces had vanished.

It was then that they decided to move. As Mae's parents were the only ill villagers, many townsfolk were worried they might bring the sickness back, only this time worse. Over time, the locals began to avoid the braided young girl, as she might carry the illness her parents were suffering through. The old lady with the candies quickly pushed her cart away whenever she saw Mae skipping toward her. The warm bread she and her parents had grown so accustomed to stopped coming, and Filip's shop had closed, since his getting out of bed was nearly impossible at this point. Luckily for Mae, as she was now the sole caretaker, her parents had set aside money in case of emergency, and she was even willing to delve into her dowry money to keep them going. Even in their feverish state, her parents knew that if they didn't leave, the villagers who had once loved them would chase them out.

On the outskirts of town, they found a small run-down house, which was practically handed to them, and for a while everything was as normal as it could be. Her parents' fever was still there, along with the coughing, but Mae felt better about her situation. She no longer felt like a pariah who scared the townspeople off. And there was a sense of calm since they were keeping the town safe. The most important aspect of this isolation, however, was that Mae was with her parents, and she knew she would be until their last days.

When Mae's fifteenth birthday passed, the illness began to take them further away from her. It was clear her parents had less and less time each day the sun dipped beneath the horizon. Doctors refused to see them, fearing another spread, and even the old herbal healers deep in the woods wouldn't step anywhere near their house. Mae watched as her parents withered away, their bones protruding in unnatural ways, eyes sinking deeper into their skulls, while their breathing was almost a whisper. As hard as Mae tried, they would not consume any food, even refusing to eat the simple broth she cooked for them. She sobbed at night as they hallucinated, calling out to the two children they had lost before her in birth, crying that they would hold them soon. Finally, it all stopped. The tears, screams, and moans disappeared with their final breaths, first her mother, then her father. Then there was silence, and Mae was alone.

That was part of why walking through town was so easy for Mae now. The guilt was almost too much for people to bear as they saw her walk by. They knew what they had done to Mae and her family, and they didn't want to remember, didn't want to recall how they had driven a sick couple—a dying couple—and their young daughter to their death house. A family that had done nothing to them but catch an illness. And Mae was a constant reminder of their evildoing. If she had died as well, they would be able to live with themselves, as the memory would fade over time. But she hadn't, so the town forcibly forgot her. As a result, it was just easier for Mae to accept her transparency and adapt accordingly.

Mae snuck past more people, moving from that old man Dax's bread stand, to the young woman, Reese was maybe her name, who sold sewing needles and thread. Whatever it was, her hand would find it, a carrot or pear no one would miss, and stuff it into the small satchel that was hidden underneath her jacket. There was always a chance that she might get caught, depending too much on her towns dismissal of her. There would always be a quick heartbeat, the small exhilaration and fear that a person might grab her hand and call the cops, but Mae knew she was smart enough to pick stands that were surrounded by the most people.

The smell of soup and hot meat pies steamed into her nostrils, and the yells of different vendors echoing through the tight space, screaming how wonderful their items were, vibrated through her ears. In spite of herself, Mae felt herself smile the smallest bit, looking at the scene around her. As she continued, the welcoming heat of the winter sun suddenly disappeared. She didn't realize how far into the marketplace she was—how deep she had gone—until it was too late. Mae didn't like it here; she never had. Even when she lived in town, this area made her stomach drop. She abhorred what made this shadow cross and tried to avoid it whenever possible. But almost as an instinct, she looked up where the sun once had been and saw the massive figure that blocked it.

It was a great iron building, the only thing in the village that didn't belong. The entire being of it looked out of place in this simple town, but it always had been there. It towered over everything, and Mae wasn't sure how far it went. No one did. But it was clear, from the forest that surrounded the structure in the extreme distance, the building stood well above the trees. The structure wasn't working and hadn't for a few years, at least for as long as Mae could remember in her last nineteen years. She didn't know how far back it went; all she knew was that it was tall and foreboding. And, most important, that four major chimneys stood on the right-hand side. Chimneys that once had brought smoke and fear. But Mae never glanced at those.

A shiver coursed down her spine as she looked up, and it didn't come from the chill of the day. Even before Mae had heard the stories of what had once happened in this building, she didn't feel safe around it. The iron and tall walls brought a sense of dread. When she was a child, whenever a ball rolled toward the building, she'd always halt and try to convince an adult to retrieve what she had lost. There was something about the structure that was dark. Darker than the shadow it produced when it took the light of the sun away. Sometimes Mae thought it was a reminder of the way things used to be. How that same building took away the light of the town and its people.

She looked down quickly and continued to push her way through the crowd, noticing that the market was becoming even more congested as people were stopping in their tracks. She took a few extra items, a small block of cheese, a few move vegetables and even a decent sized woolen strip of cloth with a bit more ease, as those around her weren't paying attention. At first, she relished this instant, but that moment slipped away, replaced with an unknowing fear. She didn't even get the usual side-glances of pity or discomfort. Not being noticed was always useful when she was picking, but being nearly invisible was something she wasn't used to. In her distraction, Mae bumped into a man, covered in fur and velvets, clearly one of the wealthier merchants who traded outside the town. She braced herself quickly, expecting him to turn and snap at her, push her aside in a rage, or even strike her. But he didn't do any of those things. In fact, it seemed that he didn't even notice that Mae had run into him. The man's neck was craned to the sky, his eyes wide and mouth open. Mae's eyebrows furrowed as she tried to understand, and then she followed the man's gaze.

And that was when she saw it.

Chapter Three:
<u>Javeen</u>

"That's too much," Ludlow Carten yelled, his round and red face getting too close to Javeen Nikilan's face, his spit flecking onto his cheekbones.

"All I'm asking for is five tins. That really isn't too much," Javeen said as calmly as he could, refusing to anger Carten even further. He dealt with this sort of scrutiny all the time; it was just part of his job of selling in the market. People claiming that his fruits and vegetables weren't good enough, swearing they would go somewhere else. And sometimes they did walk away, and Javeen would let them. But most of the time that wasn't necessary, as he was able to persuade them that the price was right, even if he had to go down a bit.

Ludlow looked over the tomato in question and poked at a section of it with his dirty finger. "See here? Right there! There's a spot!" He threw the tomato at Javeen, who examined it.

Yes, the man was right; there was a spot, but it wouldn't compromise the taste. The fact that he was even able to grow fruit and vegetables in the winter was something to be said. Thank the saints for the warmth of his small greenhouse that lay off the barn. It allowed him to grow a small plot, where his crops were thriving. Still, this yelling was creating a scene, and that wouldn't help business. Javeen noticed others gazing in his direction with looks of distaste. In order for anyone to win, he would have to come down a little on the price.

"All right, fine. Three tins then," he said, sighing loudly, so Carten thought he had become the victor. In actuality, it was Javeen who had won this battle. Just getting him away from his cart was a win in and of itself.

Ludlow looked him over, trying to keep his frown, but Javeen saw the pull of a corner smile. "It's still too much, but I'll take it." He grabbed the tomato with a meaty hand and threw the coins at Javeen. "Glad you saw it my way, boy," he snarled with grimy teeth before tipping his old winter cap and disappearing into the crowd.

Ludlow Carten would come back. They always did. The ones who made a stink knew they could because Javeen was fair. They understood the need for survival, especially in the winter, and so did he. Other vendors in the market overpriced their products and refused to budge, wanting to make their way into some of the brick houses in town. They thought it was the only way to ensure a better life for themselves. But that, Javeen had learned at a young age, was how you lost returning customers. Even the wealthier merchants came to him and gave him more than they probably should, because they knew his food wasn't only cheaper but also of a higher quality.

Javeen exhaled the deep breath he was holding and relaxed his shoulders. These types of confrontations always took a lot out of him, and sometimes it impacted his sales. He would lower his prices a bit in order to avoid another fight. There were even times when he lost money due to fights like this—after some sort of altercation, he always felt like packing it all up, trying again tomorrow and accepting the lost wages. Out of habit, he scratched at his hands nervously. It was this itch on Javeen's wrist that always changed his mood and brought him back to his cart. He touched the twine bracelet that rested there and nodded, reminding himself why he was at the market. If he didn't do this—deal with men and women yelling at him each time he put his goods out for sale—his family wouldn't survive. This was the only way.

Javeen, who was a month shy of twenty-two, was the eldest in his house. At such a young age, he should have had nothing but the world to look forward to. Normally a young man his age would be out and about, trying to find a girl to romance into marriage, traveling around to other places he'd never dreamed of. Even maybe, if he dared, visit the brothels or gambling houses in nearby towns. With his good looks, stature, and charm, Javeen could have become a traveling merchant. He should have been living his life. Just living. But he could never do that. He could never live like the other carefree young men in this town. Not when he was in charge of his family.

It all began when Chase Nikilan, Javeen's father, had walked out to enjoy his favorite pastime. A hunting trip, simple enough. It was what he liked to do most when he wasn't farming or selling his produce. And being at the marketplace was second best to hunting. People loved him, and his father knew it, just as Javeen knew they liked him now too. Javeen had learned everything about selling in the market from his father. How to charm people first before trying to sell them something and how to overprice an item before getting it down to the price you truly intended to sell it for. Above all, his father taught him that the people were just that. People. Javeen learned to actually know his customers and understand the lives of every person who presented themselves at his cart. Chase smiled at everyone, that charismatic grin that would pull people towards them. But not only that, he would talk to them, getting to know what their lives were like. Congratulating them on triumphs and consoling them on sorrows. That was the most important lesson Javeen had ever learned. These people who came to his cart weren't just a means to make money, though they did help produce some income. He knew, as a seller, you need your customers to trust you and to believe you're there for them. And then, by your treating them right, they would help you in return.

On the day of the hunting trip, Javeen had wanted to go so badly. His father had only taken him on a few trips, and they hadn't brought home an animal on any of them. Javeen wanted to experience what his father had called the "thrill of the kill," and so far, he hadn't had that luxury. This was his chance to go out and finally prove to his dad that he actually was a good hunter. So Javeen begged his father to take him. But he had said no; a winter storm was on its way, and there was a chance the trip would take more than one day. Someone needed to take care of the family, his mother and siblings, well as the farm while he was gone. And even at sixteen, Javeen, as the eldest child, was responsible for that—just until his father crossed the threshold again. Then he would return to his normal role in the family.

But that didn't happen. Javeen's father never returned from the hunting trip. He and his mother and his brother and two sisters waited for weeks, hoping he had just gotten lost in the woods and eventually would find his way home. The storm had been quite brutal, and it had made sense. Or maybe he had decided the trip would last longer than he had thought; perhaps he needed a break from the hectic market life. Javeen kept up with his chores and tending to the farm, hoping that when his father returned, he would be proud that his son had done exactly what he was told to do. He made sure that his siblings had enough food and were as happy as they could be while they waited for their father to come back. All in all, the gardens thrived, and the family was fed, but still, his father never returned.

They couldn't create a reason in their minds as to why their father would leave. Javeen always thought his father was content, and he seemed to love his home and family. So many questions kept Javeen up at night while he continued to wait for his father. Why would he just disappear? Did he actually disappear or did something else happen? Finally, after three months, his mother gathered the family in the forest and gave him a small funeral, knowing that, more likely than not, he had passed on. Javeen had stood at the makeshift cross, knowing his life had changed forever. Since his father never crossed the threshold again, he was now the man of the house.

In the early years, it wasn't too difficult. There were times when he wished he had paid more attention to what his father had said when it came to growing plants, but after a lot of trial and error, he was able to understand the ways of that world and became a decent farmer. Of course, he was nothing like the seller his father had been, but he remained one of the best in town. And the people at the market still loved him and offered their condolences to him. They mourned Chase for some time, and that was when selling seemed to be the easiest, which pained Javeen to know. People were buying his produce because they felt bad, but even as the time of mourning passed, Javeen held on to his salesmanship skills. Most important, he remembered to treat his customers as people, not a means to an end.

It was his home life that became difficult as the months passed and turned into years. His younger sisters and brother had a hard time understanding why their father wasn't coming home. Jiro and Mami, who weren't much younger than him, understood after a few months exactly what was going on and stepped up to take on more work in and around the house. Jiro helped more with the land and eventually became quite the farmer, while Mami took care of the cows, chickens and small amount of sheep they held. Asha, the youngest, took her father's disappearance the hardest and still gazed out the window every now and again, looking for his return. She had given Javeen the bracelet that he always touched.

"I know it's just twine," she had said, her little shoulders shrugging. "But it reminded me of you."

"How is that?" Javeen had asked, ruffling her hair and giving her a smile.

"Because it holds things together. You hold us together." And with that she skipped away.

Javeen felt as though he had been punched in the stomach when her little mouth had said that. He knew Asha was talking about the state of their mother, Tess. After they had held the funeral for their father, she never had recovered. It was as if her sorrow had completely consumed her. Her once happy and motherly attitude towards the children was gone. To this day, she sat in the corner of the living room and swayed back and forth in her rocking chair. When any of the children tried to console her, she'd stare out the window that faced town, comatose to the world around her. The only time she moved was when she needed to relive herself or when it was time to eat. And that was by merely turning her body to take the broth or small bits of meat that Mami or Asha brought her. Javeen knew that he was the only reason that none of the children had run away. He always attempted to bring the light his father once had back into their home, trying to make his siblings laugh, smiling even on his darkest days, and bringing surprise gifts every now and then. Even when the dark sullen figure of their mother loomed in the corner.

Javeen's thoughts were shaken as he saw a hand glide over a carrot, grab

it, and disappear into the crowd. Infuriated that someone would take advantage

of him once more, he was just about to run after the thief when he spotted the

two blond braids the body was attached to. It was Mae, the girl the villagers

called the "Unseen Reminder." Everyone knew what ultimately had happened

to her parents; even so, they chose not to look upon the girl who had suffered

the most from the plague, even though it hadn't infected her. The townsfolk

could easily live with their shame, as long as they chose not to remember it.

Javeen watched as Mae continued through the crowd.

He always let her take a little something from his cart, since her living

conditions were far worse than his, and even those weren't ideal. Her thin frame

showed that she ate very little, so letting her have a fruit or vegetable every now

and then was an act of kindness on his part, even if she thought she was stealing

it. Still, there was another reason he was being generous: he felt a strange

attraction to her. He wanted to talk to her, wanted to know if there was anything

she needed to say. He wanted to say something to show her she wasn't invisible

to at least one person in this run-down place. But every time he thought he

could approach her, he froze. Something about Mae scared him, made him

nervous when he tried to go toward her. And he knew it was the fact that she

was so independent.

Mae had been living on her own for so long. Since the age of sixteen,

she had to become an adult faster than anyone else her age. And she didn't seem to care what people thought about her or her past. She was able to walk through a town that had done everything but destroy her birth certificate in the Hall of Records, as though it were something that didn't even bother her. Nothing seemed to put fear into her clear blue eyes. Even grabbing that carrot and just walking away. Javeen could have run after her, could have demanded she give it back or have her thrown in jail, and still she had done it. Javeen felt a pit of envy and anxiety as she walked away knowing that someone could be that strong, when he was frightened every day.

As he watched Mae walk deeper into the throngs of customers, he once again felt a need to talk to her. Enough was enough; he had to try to follow her or he'd never be able to find her in this crowd. This time, Javeen was determined to actually go up to her. Maybe he'd say something about the carrot, a smart comment that would come off as a joke rather than a threat. Then perhaps they could talk…about nothing or maybe everything. It was an act of courage in his eyes. But maybe, just maybe, something would happen.

He covered his produce with a heavy wool blanket and put a sign on the cart, promising his return, then followed the direction Mae had taken. Javeen knew it would take him a while to find her, as the market was infested with people today. Market days were important in the winter, but this was the busiest he had seen the street in a while. Everywhere they pushed and shoved him, and he heard a few grunts from men as he pushed back. Farming had made him strong, and he wasn't about to be shoved around by some rich merchant types.

Javeen was on a mission, and if that meant throwing his muscle around to get there, he would do it. He was just about to give up hope when he saw Mae's blond braids in the middle of the path.

Now was his chance.

Javeen's heart lightened when he looked at her, the sun radiating off her face. It was now or never. He began to move forward through the crowd, suddenly no longer having to push himself through. When he was about ten feet away from Mae, he suddenly realized the swarm wasn't moving at all. They were completely still. No one even swayed as an icy gust of wind barreled through. As he circled around and looked at each person, every single face held a terrified expression. When Javeen glanced at Mae and noticed her head was craned up to the perfectly blue sky, he looked up as well.

Now it was clear why the whole town was standing still in horror. The perfectly blue sky was becoming contaminated as four chimneys expelled billowing clouds of black smoke.

Chapter Four:
The Factory

The chimneys hadn't been lit in more than three decades. It had always been considered a sign that all was well in the village. The skies had remained clean, and the people had lived in peace and without fear. Therefore, when the black smoke rose from the cylinders, the townspeople had stopped and gaped in dismay. Many thought that they'd never again see the dark clouds ruin a perfectly good sky. That their children would only know such a fear as a mighty legend, not something they would ever experience in their lives. But on this day, every single person who remembered, who hoped it would never happen again, was proven wrong. The dark, populating skies only meant one horrible truth. The Factory had awakened.

The Factory was a relic of the past, of the way life used to be. It was the presence of fear, of a structure that couldn't be broken. Mostly it was a memento, a reminder of way the people never wanted life to be again. They didn't want that ongoing terror of not knowing who might be next. That anxiety about the future. However, with the darkening sky, they knew the past had returned. The furnaces had been started, and the process would begin anew.

Dread spread as dirty smoke filled the once clean, clear sky, and the stories of a previous lifetime were retold.

***

Centuries ago, this village, like many around it, had been in a thriving region of the United States, but after the nations of the world had passed the Technology Termination Agreement, everything had changed. Governments believed technology had brought nothing but havoc on the world, as many countries had dropped low grade nuclear bombs, as well as used electronic drones to destroy whoever considered the enemies. Therefore, technology had to be abolished altogether, as countries, including many "modernized" countries, were only using their technological advancements to better place themselves on the top of the horrific game they were playing. Though the announcement brought many a rebellion, as governments went about to destroy everything from modern weaponry to lightbulbs and generators. The world needed to revert back to the time of its early civilized ancestors. The earth had become a simpler, more peaceful place due to lack of extreme weaponry, and the town had to resort to its now meeker standings. Gas lamps, fireplace heating, and an agricultural lifestyle that dominated the economy, was the new world. The Factory remained the only reminder of what the industrial past had been like.

No one in town knew who had built The Factory. Over time, the builders were lost, and the ways of their creation were lost as well. It was the only building in the village that was made of steel. Clearly it didn't belong, but nevertheless The Factory wasn't leaving. Whoever the builders were, they obviously didn't want to be remembered for their deeds and either had hid themselves away after constructing The Factory or perhaps had gone down with its last nail. No one could say when it was built, as those who remembered were nothing but dust by now. The village only knew *why* it was built, why someone would put such a large, imposing building in a fairly remote village.

There was a time, the elders said, when The Factory was opened three times a year. Once at the winter solstice, once at the first flowers of spring, and once at the summer solstice. These were the easiest times of the year to track, and therefore everyone knew when this unstoppable fate was coming. The Factory was mainly used during the time of the Great Numbers, when the world's population was still too large after the end of technology. Though the threat of overpowering technology was gone, a vast amount of people remained on earth. Cites had become overgrown; rivers and lakes were polluted; and the ground had become barren. Illnesses of the long-ago past, including the plague and other mutant diseases, raged through the most heavily populated areas. Other sicknesses had wiped out hundreds of thousands of animals, especially livestock. Civilized society had all but become extinct.

The townsfolk began to become weak, both mentally and physically, as they had little grain and produce with which to support themselves. They tried to farm on the dry land, but nothing came, so they ate their scant sources of meat. Eventually, meat became so scarce that the townspeople resorted to feasting on anyone else who fell due to illness. Through all this, the town's population still grew. People had children as a reminder of hope, as a way to show that life kept going. But in the end, it all became too much. And that was when The Factory appeared.

The Factory was created to reduce the number of people in and around the village. In this way, it would stabilize the population, and the townsfolk could live prosperous lives once again. Through a simple list, one hundred people were chosen to enter The Factory. Over time, as the population began to reach the desired number, whoever was in charge changed the number to fifty. Originally there were no age restrictions, and many a time an elder or a toddler made his or her way through the large iron doors. However, as fewer and fewer people walked in, the small and the elderly were excluded. Some said people had spoken up, and those in charge of The Factory had heard. Eventually, it seemed only those between the ages of fourteen to fifty-five made their way into The Factory's large courtyard.

The age range and the number of people who entered were the only aspects of The Factory that changed over the years. Once everyone whose name had been called was inside, the doors were closed for two weeks, and at points sometimes longer. No one in the outside world knew what happened behind those iron doors and steel walls; they only knew that what was going inside was a gamble. They would either see their loved ones in the flesh once more or receive a notice that a funeral must be arranged. They also knew the smoke in the chimneys would continue to burn. For every one hundred—then later, fifty—people who went in, only six were released back into the world. Six people, to remind the village that even in times of horror, life could continue. That is, until next time.

Those who survived refused to reveal what had happened inside the iron structure. It was clear that some sort of physical action was needed in order to return to the light, as those who came out were always littered with some sort of lacerations, bleeding, and in some cases missing eyes or fingers. They eventually became known as the Leavings, since they were the only people who left The Factory. A few went on as if nothing had happened to them, as though they'd never stepped foot inside the steel hell. Others would sit and stare and never speak again. The Leavings became a sad type of celebrity in town, and since there was no money to be won by surviving The Factory, the townspeople collectively decided that those who lived would never have to pay for almost anything in the village. It was considered a small token for whatever had happened to them in The Factory. The villagers thought it would help them return to normal living, ease them into the lives they'd had before, but usually it didn't work. A large number of the Leavings didn't make it to a natural death. Whatever they'd seen in there had driven them to madness. As these people didn't want to haunt themselves with what they'd witnessed, they ended their lives before their rightful time.

There were others who lived full lives, accepting their past but looking toward a future. Still, they never spoke of what they saw in there. And this always brought more questions. At first, many wished to know and pestered the survivors. What exactly did they go through? Why was it so difficult for the survivors to talk about what they had done? What *had* they done? What happened to the remaining people in that building? Above all, what had the survivors seen? But after a decade or so, those who wanted answers seemed to realize the mystery was for the best. Living in ignorant bliss was better than understanding what had happened to more than ninety percent of the contestants of the names that were called.

Then one day it stopped. The doors didn't open, as they always had on the shortest day of the year, as everyone waited for the names to be read. And then, when the trees sprouted their leaves, the doors still stayed closed, but the villagers remained on edge. It wasn't until the long sun of summer passed that the residents' hope began to stir. Was this the end of The Factory? The smoke was still pouring from the chimneys, so perhaps it was too good to be true. When the doors stayed closed for another year, everyone thought that perhaps it was over. Whoever was in charge of The Factory probably felt as though the population was where it needed to be. During the third summer, the final smoke from the smoldering coals burned out, leaving the chimneys barren for thirty years.

In those thirty years, the town had prospered much more than it had when The Factory had been in operation. Crime was at its lowest, and there were little to no quarrels as the tension and the anticipation of death dwindled. Most important, the townspeople began to live once more. Instead of dreading the winter and summer solstices, they held parties in celebration of the new lives they'd been given. In the spring, the blossoms of the flowers brought smiles to the children and blushes to the ladies being courted by men. After some time, people ignored The Factory altogether, and those who did remember what had occurred eventually died off or began to forget in order to live their lives anew.

After so many years, The Factory not only was a reminder of a terrible time, but it also didn't belong to the simplicity of their lives. It was too modern looking, too industrial. Many wondered if there was a way to destroy it, but they had no idea how they could possibly get over its high steel walls and doors to take the building down. In the end, the townspeople left it there, not as a reminder, but as an object that refused to be forgotten.

What they didn't know was that a slumbering giant was beginning to wake. The flames of The Factory weren't completely extinguished. There was a flicker, a small ember, kept lit in case the time came. In case the people needed to be reminded about The Factory and exactly what it could do. And on this day, oxygen was given to that small ember, that tiny reminder of the past, and it started to grow. Slowly it began to ignite, grabbing the other cold coals around it and covering them in flames—flames the villagers would soon see, soon feel. And as that one ember began to gain strength, taking the black coals with it, smoke curled its way up the chimney, releasing itself once more into the blue winter sky. And in that moment, that black ringlet told everyone what they had dreaded and forgotten for years.

Death was on the horizon.

The Factory was open again.

Chapter Five:
<u>Javeen</u>

Panic ensued immediately after everyone registered what was happening. People pushed their way out of the market, with mothers grabbing their children as quickly as they could and some little ones being dragged on the ground. Men skidded in the mud, some falling and crawling, attempting to get back up in the chaos. Many villagers were stepped on, as others wanted to leave at all cost. The other vendors in the marketplace began to close up their shops, some not even securing their goods as they fell off their carts. Normally, villagers would race to pick up any objects or food that had fallen, but in this moment of panic, no one noticed. They trampled over everything, breaking or burying whatever they stepped on.

Dread swelled in Javeen's chest as he looked up. However, he knew that if joined in the madness, he would be consumed by it. He had to stay calm and work his way back to his cart and keep his goods safe. He looked over to see Mae still standing there, staring up at the smoke. She looked mesmerized by it, her eyebrows meeting in the center, showing her confusion. *Doesn't she understand what's going on?* Javeen thought. *What this means*? She put her head down and looked his way. As they made eye contact, Javeen inhaled sharply. Her eyes were actually filled with fear, something Javeen never thought he would see in her. He wanted to walk over to her and see if she was okay, but then he remembered his cart—and his family—and pushed those thoughts away as he trudged along.

When Javeen reached his cart, he was surprised to see that it wasn't a complete mess. In the chaos, some people had taken the opportunity to grab a few items, but nothing major. And the wheels were still there. Some of the vendors had left their carts, not because they wanted to, but because they couldn't push them back on two or three wheels. At least Javeen could get home and bring his cart back tomorrow—that is, if anyone actually decided to come tomorrow. Now that he thought about it, he doubted anyone would show up, but knew he would come regardless.

Walking home seemed to take longer than usual. Javeen and his family lived beyond the farming community, owning a chunk of land that was larger than anyone in that commune would. His journey was always about a quarter of a mile longer, as the borders of town is where he called home. The cart was still heavy, but not as much as the thoughts in his head. Why was The Factory opening again? Javeen always had thought the town was rather small, but had the population grown too large again? There was a little more than 750. Well, 778 if you really wanted to be specific. But was that really enough people for The Factory to wake up? As he reached the top of the hill that led to his house, he looked back up and saw the smoke again. He didn't know how he would tell his family. They would have no idea, unless a neighbor had told them. He hoped he could get to them first.

When he finally got home, he realized someone had gotten to them before he had. Before walking into the house, Javeen heard the hysterics coming from the house and watched his brother's shadow pacing back and forth. As Javeen ambled through the door, Jiro came running toward him, while Mami and Asha remained stock-still.

Jiro's lumbering figure almost mimicked that of Javeen's. His dark curly hair was a bit more unkempt though, and his skin tanner, weather ridden from the last years of working the fields. Beyond that though, many thought that they were twins, which made some sense, as Jiro was less than a year younger than Javeen. They both had wide shoulders, muscular arms, and a strong core, all due to their constant work in order to keep the farm running. Yet there was one distinctive feature that made the two different. Their eyes. Javeen had inherited his father's distinctive green eyes, while Jiro's were the hazel hue, the mixture of his mother's brown and father's green. It was those eyes that glared at him, as he walked in the doorway.

"Is it true?" Jiro demanded. "Is The Factory opening?"

Javeen strode past him, not wanting to answer. Jiro was always one to jump to conclusions. He was about to tell his younger brother to shut his face and just wait, but he saw the scared look of his sisters' and sighed. "Look, the chimneys started smoking again. It doesn't mean that it's going to open, but it doesn't mean we're safe either. In fact, I don't know what it means, but perhaps we should prepare ourselves in case it does…" Taking a deep breath, he added, "…and one of us is called inside."

He heard Mami's and Asha's shocked gasps and knew they were hoping it wasn't true, but actually hearing the words made Mami sink into a chair. Her hair fell all around her shoulders, and in the light of the day highlighting the slightly red hue that buried inside the almost chocolate majority. She clutched her chest while trying to control her breathing, her thin fingers gripping her dingy white blouse and wrapping around her knuckles. Jiro's face went pale, knowing what Javeen already knew. He was almost twenty-one, a year younger than Javeen, and he knew their chances were higher than some of the others in town. Mami was eighteen, but the history records showed that more men had gone into The Factory than women. She had a chance. And Asha was only twelve. If she went in, Javeen would be stunned.

He looked at Asha, and even though she was young, his sister was older beyond her years. She was on the taller side than most twelve year olds, but her eyes told a different story of her wisdom. Beyond those green eyes, the ones she shared with Javeen, Asha had been through more than anyone near her age. Her hair, cut about to her shoulders, was lighter than them all, the color of tree bark, unlike Javeen and Jiro's night black color or Mami's mixture of dark brown and red. She was a thin little thing though, and Javeen wondered now, if she did for some unknown reason get called in, could she fight like they knew might happen?

Javeen turned to Jiro. "Go get four pieces of paper." Jiro, stood still, his eyes

blank, as if he weren't understanding. The possibility of what was going on seemed to be far too much for him. Javeen walked up to him, their faces just about at the same height, and stared into his brother's hazel eyes. "Listen to me," he whispered. "I don't want Mother to hear this, but we need to prepare wills in case we're called. We don't know what's going to happen." He backed off. "Get some paper."

Jiro nodded, his face still stone, and raced up the creaking stairs to their small room in the attic to get the paper and pencils. Javeen heard a sob behind him and looked at Mami. She was still in her chair, and Asha was now consoling her, but she continued to let out gasps of air. Javeen knelt to her level and put a comforting hand on her shoulder. "Mami, it's going to be okay. Breathe. Just try to breathe. You probably won't be picked, but we need to do this. Everyone in town needs to be ready." He flashed a weak smile toward Asha, who looked just as white as Jiro had. Although she was young, she'd heard the legends of The Factory.

"But what if..." Mami hiccupped, looking over at their mother. Javeen sighed as he watched her rock back and forth, the creaking continuing at a constant rhythm. Her once vibrant red hair was greying, fading out into an almost rust color. Her hazel eyes stared out into the distance and she moved, and Javeen looked at the wrinkles that buried deep into her skin. His mother looked much older than the forty-odd years that she was. Javeen knew wasn't always like that. Once she had been young and alive, her smile and laugh was contagious. But that all changed, and there was nothing left but sorrow and misery left in her soul.

"Mama isn't going to be picked," Javeen said. "I have her under disability." Mami and Asha looked at him as though he had lost his mind. "She's barely moved from that chair for six years. I signed papers saying I was head of the household and taking care of her. They don't choose people who are incapacitated. Mama is safe. She can't go in."

Mami nodded, her breathing getting steadier. But then Asha spoke up. "What if you go in?"

Javeen looked at up at his sister, her large green eyes filling with fear. She knew better than anyone else. He couldn't leave this family. She reached out and touched his twine bracelet. Mami reached over as well, trying to comfort him too, but her eyes couldn't meet his. If he was called in and didn't make it out, then there was nothing holding the family together. They might just fall apart, turn on one another, or even leave the farm entirely.

Javeen sucked in an uneasy breath and smiled at his youngest sister, then squeezed Mami's hand. "We won't worry about that until the names are called. We can't say what will happen, and there's no sense worrying now. If worse comes to worst, Jiro will be in charge. And you know he's just as capable as me." He stood up, looked down at his sister, and winked. "Even if I'm smarter."

As he said that, Jiro returned with the paper. He nodded toward Javeen, as if saying he understood what he'd just told their littlest sister. Jiro's face showed no anger toward his brother's last comment, as he knew Javeen was just trying to make the air less tense. The two of them took one more moment and looked at their mother, who continued to rock in her worn-down wicker chair. It was the only noise they ever heard from her, the back-and-forth creaking. The back of the seat was beginning to fall apart, therefore Mami and Asha made her a cushion to rest her head. Even now, she continued to remain expressionless as her head rested on the padded surface. In this, a most dire moment, they still couldn't reach her. Perhaps Javeen had done the right thing by registering her as disabled, for if she went in, he knew they'd never see her again. Jiro sighed with Javeen and headed toward the table.

As they all sat down around the rough-hewn wooden table, Javeen quietly explained that writing a will didn't mean they were going into The Factory, but they ought to be prepared, just in case. He instructed them all to write down the things they owned and who they wanted them to go to. Then, at the bottom they would each sign their name, and someone else at the table would sign as a witness. They all nodded in understanding, but Javeen noticed how Asha's and Mami's hands shook as they began to write. Still, they scribbled away on their slips of paper in silence.

Although the farm did make money, Javeen knew there wasn't too much to put down. They were nowhere near the richies in town when it came to their possessions. Therefore, it took only a few minutes for them to write their wills, as none of them had much to give away. Asha and Mami were the quickest to scrawl down what they were to give away their pencils not even needing the knife to sharpen them. The only things of value they owned were a few pieces of jewelry, as tarnished as they were. The only piece of Mami's that had worth was the now dirty necklace she refused to take off. They gave them those pieces to one another, and the few clothes they had they wanted sold so the family could have a bit more money for the farm, though Javeen knew that half those clothes were second hand and would get little to no money. Jiro bequeathed his favorite leather gloves to Javeen, and all the money he had saved up from his side jobs around town, like re-thatching houses and bricklaying, would go to the rest of the family. Javeen gave everything—including the farm and the house—to Jiro. They all signed each other's papers as witnesses and placed the wills away in the old dusty drawer next to their mother's chair. No one would think that an old decrepit woman would have anything important sitting next to her.

Mami quickly made up a sad chicken soup, stirring the worn seasoned spoon in an old dented pot, as none of them had time to prepare lunch due to the news of the day. The soup, just like the few burnt rolls being thrown back in the oven, were left over from the night before. As Asha placed the scraped and chipped ceramic plates on the table, Jiro and Javeen tried their best to find some utensils that weren't already used, or rusted and glasses that were a bit transparent. When lunch was ready, Asha brought a bowl to her mother and whispered to her as she fed her the soup. "Mama," Javeen could hear slightly, "Mama, it's time for lunch. Come on Mama. One bite at a time." As they sat eating, Jiro finally asked what everyone in town probably was thinking as well. "So…what do you think actually goes on in there?"

Javeen shrugged as he slurped his soup. "Honestly, no one knows. The Leavings never told anyone. Or they didn't live long enough to tell. So really, it's anyone's guess."

Mami placed her spoon down and put her head in her hands. Staring at the table, she murmured, "Earnest Cane told me they keep the furnace lit by…those who don't make it."

Javeen didn't want to talk about anything that had to do with The Factory, but he'd heard the rumor too. Everyone in town claimed that those who hadn't been released had fallen into some sort of fire pit. That was why, they said, the chimneys never had stopped smoking in the past; they were constantly fueled by dead bodies. The coals were the remains of people who didn't finish what The Factory had wanted them to do. And with forty-four corpses three times a year—and at one point, ninety-four—then it would make sense why it had burned for so long. Yes, it was a rumor, as no one knew what really had happened, but one that many accepted as the truth.

"You also have to wonder how they get into the fire. I heard they put everyone in a room and wait for them to go crazy," Jiro whispered. "And then sometimes they give weapons to a few people—just a few—and order them not to tell anyone. Then at night…"

He crossed his thumb past his neck and continued to eat his food. Javeen glanced at Mami, who looked as though she were going to lose whatever was in her stomach. He then quickly turned to Jiro, whose eyes fell down.

"That's enough," Javeen hissed at him. "We don't want her hearing any of this." He nodded toward Asha, who continued to urge their mother to eat. "I know Asha has heard the stories. Everyone hears them when they're around her age. But even though she knows about the place, she's still too young to understand what might be happening."

Mami nodded, but Jiro shrugged. "You don't know that she won't be called, Jav. They might have lowered the age restriction and—" But another look from Javeen silenced him. They continued to eat as the ticking of their mother's rocking and Asha's whispers filled the room.

Jiro took another gulp of soup and finally said, "On a happier note, a lot of crazy things will be happening in the next couple of days. It'll be so entertaining." Javeen looked up at him, his eyebrow raised, as if questioning him. Challenging him. Jiro ignored him and continued. "Oh, come on!

Everyone now knows this is the time to do stuff. Anything you want. Think about it. The odds aren't the best, seeing as our town only has about seven hundred, plus a little extra, people in it, and if we're called, that could be it. Now's the time to do whatever we've always wanted to do." He looked up at the ceiling. "I'd like to buy one of Ms. Hurma's chocolate pies. And then eat the whole thing. I wouldn't even care if I threw up. Or just go kiss some gal 'cause I could. Something like that."

Mami giggled as she stirred her soup. "That's so childish, Jiro. You'd go buy a pie just to get sick. But you do make a good point." Her brown eyes seemed to drift. Mami was the only one in the house hold who had gotten purely her mother's eyes. "I'd finally tell Colby Martin that I think he's so handsome. And even if he didn't reciprocate, I wouldn't care. And I'd give him my poems to remember me by."

"*Poems*?" Jiro spat. "First, you wrote poems about Colby Martin? That ginger kid who looks at bugs all day? And second, what if *he's* going into The Factory? He doesn't want poems to remember you by, you dink. He wants to remember you with a big wet one on the lips. That's what'll keep him fighting…that is, if he even likes you."

Mami's face went red. "You don't know that! He could be a very cultured person and love my poems! Not everyone is as animalistic as you, Jiro. And besides, you don't know that he doesn't like me. In fact, he could very much…Javeen where are you going?"

While the two of them had been arguing, the thought had hit him. He knew what he would do. Javeen quickly pushed himself from his chair and ran to grab his coat. He threw it on and rushed toward the door. "You two got me thinking. I've gotta get some fresh air and think about what I might have to do. Also, I'm headed to town to get that pie. You made it sound so good." He winked at Jiro, who scowled at him. "I'll eat it all myself." He dashed out the door and slammed it behind him.

"What was that about?" Jiro asked, his mouth full of food as he glared at the doorway. "And he'd better not be getting that pie. Seriously. I've been thinking about it for weeks." Mami laughed and threw a burnt roll at him, shutting him up as Jiro shoved it into his mouth.

Javeen, however, wasn't headed for town. If they had followed his shadow, cast from the full moon, they would have noticed he was headed toward the only other house on the outskirts of the village. Jiro was right. This was the time to do what he'd been afraid to do for so long. What if he was sent to The Factory? He thought about the words he would say as he pushed his way toward Mae's house.

Chapter Six:
<u>Mae</u>

Mae waited until almost everyone had left the market. This was the best time to grab any leftovers forgotten during the panic. Luckily for her, some of the vendors had left some food on the ground or had abandoned their carts completely. Because of that, she was able to snag a few items that would get her through the next four days—the four days before the names were called. Even though The Factory had been closed for thirty years, everyone knew the rules. Four days after the announcement was when the stage was put up to call those who went into the gates. And with the black soot making the sky almost turn into night, the announcement had clearly been made. Mae knew very few vendors would show up at the market tomorrow, and prices would skyrocket, as desperation on both ends would be at its height. Farmers needed to protect their families if they went in, and those who bought needed to stalk up in cased loved one's didn't return. This was her best chance to collect as much supplies as she could.

Mae grabbed a few more carrots, along with some beets, a head of broccoli, and winter squash. She was even able to get her hands on a loaf of bread. It had been in the dirt for a bit, but at least it wasn't soaking in the mud.

Most important, it was edible. Finally, she snatched up a bundle of potatoes before noticing something she'd never thought of grabbing in her life. Slowly she lifted it, making sure no one saw what it, but there wasn't a soul around her. She cradled the glass bottle in the sack of potatoes as she walked out of the marketplace. In one moment, the busiest place in town had become deserted.

As Mae began the uphill trudge back home, she noticed the tall dark-haired young man she had made eye contact with earlier. He was pushing his cart back up the hill, ahead of her, near his farm. It wasn't too far from her house, and sometimes Mae heard them calling out that dinner was ready or heard them playing in the summer. She felt a sting of regret. Mae stole from him all the time, but he never went after her. She wondered if he ever noticed she was stealing from him. Then she realized he probably didn't, as everyone in town pretended she wasn't alive. Still, that burn of shame in her resurfaced as he turned his head and looked up at the smoke once more. Then he continued on.

Mae shook off her feelings and dragged herself home. When she arrived, she let out a frustrated sigh. The house was nothing to be proud of, and a person would have to really look in order to see it. It was overgrown with the plant life that Mae had no desire to keep up with. There were a few holes in the sagging roof, but she had worked it so that the rain or snow was caught, a system of creating a gutter in the open areas of the roof to run the liquids into a large bin. After boiling the water, Mae used it as drinking and bathing. The house itself look ragged and run-down when someone was able to approach it. The trees were over grown, along with the grass, and vines were beginning to cover up the exterior walls. Mushrooms had started to grow out of the holes in the outside paneling years ago. Had anyone actually seen past the wall of sticks and trees, they would have thought the whole structure would have fallen in days. Or more importantly, that no one lived there. However, there was one exception to the house's decaying façade. Mae always made sure the door was secure and strong. Although she understood she was a figure no one wanted to see, protecting herself was important. The door had sturdy locks, and the windows were booby-trapped. And Mae always slept with her father's rifle, in case a drunk ever decided it was time to see what she was all about.

When she went inside, she smiled at the prospect of making a late lunch. The cupboards were always so barren, so the fact that she had a choice tonight excited her. A hunk of bread, potatoes, and carrots, and she'd have more food in one meal than she'd had in weeks. She chuckled as she ripped apart the bread and happily shoved it into her mouth. There were some nights when she was so close to starvation that the bugs in the corner of the room almost looked appetizing. But she never had stooped to that level. This meal this late afternoon, though, this was meant for a king.

Or as a last meal before her death.

Mae's stomach churned as she remembered the smoke rising from the chimneys. When she had craned her neck to the sky, she felt as though she were living in a dream. At first, she thought that it had been a mistake, that something had caught on fire and perhaps The Factory itself would burn to the ground. She had waited, as she now thought others might have, for it to burn to ashes and for everything to carry on as usual. But the longer she stood there, watching the dark smoke continue to rise from the chimneys, the more she understood the truth. Mae had stood and stared for so long, wondering what this would mean for the town. What it would mean for her.

Sudden thirst attacked her as she shoveled more bread into her mouth. That and the fear of The Factory had made her mouth dry up quickly. As she got up and collected melted snow water to wash down the bread, she thought maybe The Factory opening up again was a good thing for her. Perhaps her stomach ached from the natural human fear of death, but she decided to shove that away. She knew now that there wasn't a reason to be nervous. If she wasn't on that list, if she didn't go into The Factory, then nothing would change. Her life would remain the same. But did she want that anymore?

If Mae was chosen, however, perhaps this was her chance. Yes, it was true; she didn't know what happened in The Factory. No one did. But she felt her street smarts could get her through it. If there were fights, Mae was sure she could muster the strength to take a few people down. She might be one of the six who made their way out of those iron doors. And if she did that, then people would have to notice her. This was her opportunity to actually become someone in this place—not to be remembered as the poor girl who had been pushed out of town, not to be shunned. She would be someone who had survived The Factory.

The more she thought about it, the more her fear of the name call disappeared. As she crunched down on the carrot she had stolen from that young farmer, she looked around her. All she could see was the rotting wood panels, the furniture falling apart, and the sound of mice running through the house, looking for a small bite to eat. Half the ceiling was sinking in, and Mae couldn't even make it to where her parents old bedroom was. What she called her bedroom now was the open living space that connected to the unusable kitchen. Was this really worth anything to her? She didn't have anyone left, no one to tell her to worry or reassure her that she wouldn't be chosen. She sat alone in a cold, dreary house, heated by a small fire she was only able to muster through sheer determination. Would dying in The Factory really be any worse than this? And if she was as determined as she knew she was, then maybe she wouldn't have to die at all.

Mae shivered as a cold draft ran through the house. The fire was warm enough, but she knew she would need all her blankets, even the moth-eaten ones, in order to stay somewhat warm tonight. She began to beat herself up, knowing before she left this morning that she should have grabbed a few logs from the pile under the tree and brought them in. But no, she had to sprint to the market as soon as she woke up. And now the wind was blowing so loudly, her bones ached at the thought of even stepping outside. Mae could see the small layer of snow atop the logs and sighed, her breath fogging in front of her. That was when she remembered her treasure.

The dark bottle was strange, with its thin neck connected to a fat, curved bottom. Mae had left it in the corner near a small pile of snow she used to chill things. She'd overheard people say wine was very good cold, although she'd never thought she'd actually get the chance to enjoy it. Some of the richest merchants in town even had a hard time getting it, but there it sat, staring at her. She'd also heard that many men at the The Blood Broth would walk home in the bitter cold, not feeling a thing due to alcohol. Perhaps it was what she needed. The bottle was small, probably not enough to get her drunk, but maybe it would be enough to keep her warm.

With confusion, she stared at the top of it. She tried to pull out the cork, but her frozen fingers couldn't get a good grasp. There was no opener in the house, so Mae banged the neck of the bottle over the mantle of the fireplace. The glass shattered, and she tossed the shards into the fire, watching the flames dance off the deep-green fragments. She grabbed a heavy brown mug and poured the white wine into it. It was one of the few objects she had left that had belonged to her parents. After Filip and Emi had died, Mae needed to make some money in order to survive. She had tried to get a job, but doors were locked and hired signed disappeared as she walked towards the stores. Eventually, money became so tight Mae began to sell most of her belongings to passerby's who were willing to take it. From her parent's bed, to her own jewelry. The chairs, table, and all of her father's leather work were sold for much less than what they would have ever sold at market. Still, she couldn't let go of everything, including the large cup. This was the mug her father drank his one glass of ale a week out of. It was quite large, and as Mae held it, she could almost see where his fingers would have lined up. She wondered if her father would have been proud of her at this moment, then brushed it off and took a swig.

The first trip down was the harshest. It burned her throat, and she erupted into a coughing fit. The next sip was only slightly better, the coughing reducing slightly. Slowly, though, warmth filled her chest. As Mae nursed the mug, the heat of the wine began to take over her body. Every now and then, she sipped the water next to her, letting a snap of coldness filter back into her body. She couldn't let her guard down or let the wine jumble her brain. People did crazy things before they thought they might die, and Mae had to have her wits about her.

As if on cue with her thoughts, she heard a knock at the door. For a moment, she looked at her glass and thought it was the wine, or even the wind. But the door was sturdy, and she knew it wouldn't make that noise unless someone had knocked. Visitors never came to see Mae, so immediately her chest tightened. Perhaps someone was here on a dare, a challenge to see how close they could get to her house. Or maybe someone had more threatening ideas. Slowly, Mae got up and walked toward the door, grabbing the rifle and holding it to the side of the door so whoever was out there wouldn't see it. She unlocked the bolts and creaked the door open, ready for anything.

But nothing was there. Mae opened the door wider and poked her head out a bit. There was no sign of anything, just the wind blowing the dead leaves and loose snow that was falling around her house. Mae took a daring step out to the porch and saw that the overgrown yard and sad excuse for a garden were empty too; she must have just imagined the noise. She looked over her shoulder at the bottle of wine and shook her head. Perhaps it was time for her to put it away. It was playing games with her mind, and she had the next three days to finish it off. She shut the door and locked it back up, setting up her nightly traps as she did. She knew she wasn't going anywhere. She pinned back the string across the windows that rang a serious of old rusted forks she had stolen when her desperation was at its highest. Then she moved to the entrance and back entrance, flipping six wooden panels over at each point, leaving long jagged nails to stick up in the air. In the light of the late afternoon light, they were obviously there, but at night, no one would know. As she headed back to the fire, she realized not only had the wine muddled her head, but she also felt her eyes drooping. Mae took another swig, knowing she didn't want to wake up until the morning.

Mae lay down on her straw-filled mattress and rolled over to the cracked mirror next to it to get ready for bed. She sleepily undid her braids and brushed out her hair with a makeshift comb she had made with a tree branch. They were her signature look, even when her parents had been alive. Her mother always had loved to braid her hair, and when Mae was old enough, she had learned herself. It was easier to control her hair that way, and after her parents died, she thought it was the only way to remember her mother. Every morning she put her hair back into its twisted state as a reminder and a testament to the woman who had raised her.

While she was brushing her hair, she looked around at the few clothes she owned. She knew she needed to pick out some smart clothes for the name call. If your name was called, you went in, no matter what you were wearing. She decided that her gray pants and a simple white cotton shirt would do. She would wear her jacket there, but if she was called in, she would toss it as soon as she found fit. The slip-on leather shoes her father had made for her before he had fallen ill would be perfect as well. If she needed to escape, the shoes would be simple enough to get out of if she had to tread quietly, and since her father had made them, the quality was better than that of most shoes in town. No matter how much the townsfolk ignored her, they still knew Mae's father had been the best leather maker in the village in more than forty years. She glanced at the belt and decided to wear it too, as it had belonged to her father. Mae figured that if she was going to her death, at least she would have some part of her parents with her as she did.

Her eyes began to close, and when they became harder to open again, Mae knew she had to sleep. The next few days would be long and difficult, so perhaps a nice tipsy slumber was what she needed. She grabbed all her blankets and walked over to sad excuse for a mattress. As she curled up, she reached under one of the pillows and pulled out a ragged doll, one that she and her mother had made together. When they had put it together, the doll smiled back, stitched on crooked as Mae first learned to sew. Her mother braided the yellow yarn, as Mae attempted to sew in the button eyes. Now, it was nothing but a ball connected to a loose rag. The smile and eyes were gone, and only a few strands of white yarn remained. Mae almost saw it as a reflection of her life. A sad reminder of what was, and how it could never be the same. She brought it close and inhaled the smell, hoping to catch some sort of familiar scent of her parents, but there was nothing there. She placed her head down and let the remainder of wine inside her and the embers of the fire warm her as she drifted off to sleep.

***

Among the crooked oaks and leafless maples, Javeen stood watching Mae's house. He wished he had been brave enough to face her. But at the last moment, he had walked away, worried she would reject him. That she would see him as inferior, and that when he confessed his feelings, ones he'd been holding for a while, she would laugh at him. And so, after that knock, he had run away. But he stood in the trees and watched as Mae made her way to sleep. After a few more moments, he hung his head down and sulked back to his house. He had lost his chance to see her one more time. One more time before the name call of The Factory. Before everything changed.

Chapter Seven:
<u>Mae</u>

For the next four days leading up to the calling of the names, the villagers acted in strange ways. Although Mae didn't know it, what Jiro had said was true. The smoke rising in the sky had prompted people to try to fulfill their dreams. Men proposed to women whom they had loved for so long, while mothers and fathers held their children closer than ever. And for the first time in almost twenty-five years, the practically empty church was filling up with people, to the point where there was a line outside day and night. It was time to repent for one's sins before possibly being called to an almost certain death.

When the day of the names call finally arrived, Mae woke up early. She slipped on her comfortable, formfitting pants, knowing that if she was indeed called, they would be easy to move about in. They had almost felt like a second skin to her for years. *Ready for anything*, she thought, as she continued to dress. She looped the belt around her pants and had to poke a few extra notches in it in order to make sure it fit her properly. It wasn't an easy task, as she tried to keep her fingers from trembling. Her top was a simple one, but a strategic pick as it clung tightly to her figure, with no stray fabric to catch onto anything. She didn't know what would happen in The Factory, so she prepared for the worst. She looked in the broken mirror, and was surprised to see a ragged looking, freckled faced and scared girl looking back. Her hair was disheveled from constantly running her fingers through it, and her breathing was heavy, shirt quickly rising and falling. Mae could see her eyes watering slightly, knowing this might be the last image of herself she could see. But quickly she rolled to shoulders and regained herself. Then, with less shaky fingers, began to work on her signature hairstyle.

Mae had debated whether to go with a long French braid in the back or the two French braids everyone in town knew to avoid. Instead, she'd had an epiphany, an idea for a style that would make a statement. She pulled her hair up into a ponytail, something she hadn't done in years. Then she separated the ponytail into six different segments and began to braid each one. At the end, she secured them with a few short ties. With the final product, she looked harsher than she usually did, her hair pulled back tightly and pulling her face with it, but her updo made statement.

Six braids, six people who would come out of The Factory. And if she were called, she was determined to be one of them.

The walk toward town felt longer than ever. Mae dragged her feet, trying to look at everything she passed, taking it all in, preparing for the possibility of being chosen. The pebbles in the dirt road that were surrounded by a small layer of snow. The houses, some with cracked windows, others with leaky roofs. She even gazed at the The Blood Broth, a place where drunkards went in and women of the night followed them out. A few of the men had stumbled out and tried to make a move on Mae in the past, but she had fought them off. In this moment, however, she couldn't help feel a pang of pain, wondering if she'd ever see the place again. Eventually, Mae was standing within the crowd, right in front of the tall iron doors she had feared for so long.

The mob huddled closely, with the smallest whisper here and there, perhaps a child whimpering, but otherwise there was nothing but the sound of the wind. They looked at the platform at the side of the doors, waiting for the names to be called. Although no one spoke, Mae felt the tension. The villagers were all on edge, waiting for something that hadn't occurred in three decades. Hoping their names wouldn't be on the list.

Slowly an old man, Alton Channon, was helped by law enforcement up the stairs then made his way up to the platform. It was customary for the eldest member of the council of the mayor to read the names of the doomed. His hunched-over body couldn't hide the fact that this wasn't something he wanted to do. Each of his age spots seemed to have told a story. Thin lips pushed even tighter together, the pressure making them white, as his hands with the paper shook. What was left of his thin white hair, pushed away from his balding scalp in the wing. It wasn't an honor, but a heavy burden to call out the names. And Alton's face showed it this was not a weight he wanted handed to him. In the middle of the stage stood podium with a large megaphone. As Alton made his way over, Mae heard the breaths of the people around her hitch. Suddenly she realized her own breathing was becoming staggered and shallower than usual. Taking deeper inhalations, she tried to calm herself and remain strong.

There were no ceremonies as the large doors creaked open, just more silence from the crowd as the rust from thirty years fell off the hinges. There, in front of them, was the only glimpse of ground inside The Factory they had ever seen. The large gates were a smaller version of The Factory, forged in impressive iron, but somehow the beauty wasn't welcomed. Although it shone slightly, there were hints of rust in some places. Still the gate held strong. The crowd stepped back as the doors opened slowly, but there was no need to. The doors opened inwardly, not toward the crowd. The public was retreating because the farther away they were, the less harm could be done, or so they thought. If The Factory wanted someone, it would get them.

With a deep exhalation, the old man on the stage took a piece of paper held by the sheriff, and with trembling voice into the coned megaphone said, "These names have been chosen at random by the eldest and highest ranking officials in town. When you are called, you must enter The Factory. Anyone who refuses to do so will be brought in with force, or shot on the spot if non-compliant. Let that be understood. The names are finalized." With one last inhale, Alton closed his eyes. "Taro Jinken." The first name.

Slowly, a man in his late thirties, wearing a tattered tweed coat, walked forward. Before he got too far, a dark-haired woman grabbed him and gave him a long kiss, knowing it might be the last they ever shared. He trudged his way through the crowd, pushing at first, but slowly a pathway opened for him. As he walked, the second name was called. A plump, red-faced woman in her mid-forties began her march too. Her grown children wept as she moved toward the gates.

As more names were called, Mae kept count of them in her head. Kemp Teplar was number ten, a burly man who looked no older than twenty-five. Felta Prie was number twenty, a skinny thing Mae had seen earlier this week begging for money, as her parents had kicked her out of the house for having attacked her pregnant mother in a state of drunkenness. She was no older than fifteen. With every name, Mae felt a bit lighter. For even though it was cruel to think it, each name that wasn't hers meant she was safe. Though a part of her was hoping maybe her name would echo out…after all she wanted to be remembered.

The thirty-fifth name called was Raya Grogan. Mae looked up and around. She was trying to look at all the faces that went in, wanting to know who they were, even if they didn't want to see her. Raya was young, perhaps Mae's age or a few months older. She was shorter than some of the people around her, and her flaming red hair was tied up in a bun as she marched forward, making her stand out from the crowd. Her calf high boots crunched loudly on the gravely soil as she made her way, but Mae couldn't stop staring at her face. A nasty scar ran from the corner of her left eyebrow to her chin line. A deep white line, with the edges of the skin looking slightly inflamed.

Although she clearly had suffered the injury her years ago, it hadn't healed properly and gave the girl a sinister look. Mae was intrigued by this girl and wondered if Raya wore her hair up and away from her face, like Mae wore her braids—to make a point.

She was so distracted by Raya walking into The Factory that she missed the next few names. She quickly reminded herself that she had to remain completely alert. It wasn't until she heard name forty-three that she focused once more on the old man at the podium.

"Javeen Nikilan."

There had been other cries for loved ones as they were called to their fate, but the shriek that followed the call of Javeen's name turned Mae's blood to ice. She turned toward the noise and saw the tall farmer from the market that she had made eye contact with four days ago. He looked terrified, and his face had gone pale. A small girl clung to his leg, refusing to let go, screaming while tears streamed down her face. Another boy, most likely his brother since they were about the same in looks and age, held her by the waist, while a younger woman, another sister perhaps, was speaking to the little girl. Alton froze on the platform, and stopped calling names as the family tried to pry the little girl off the young man's leg. Eventually they coaxed her off, and Javeen lowered himself, giving her a kiss and pointing to his wrist. She nodded. He kissed the other young woman and hugged the young man before turning toward the doors.

Mae felt something as she watched the family grieve for him: an emptiness she had tried to fight for years. If her name was called, there would be no cries of horror or pain. No one would hug her or wish her luck. Instead, the people of this place might smile if her name echoed out. The thought was too much to bear. Mae's eyes stung with tears, but she quickly wiped them away, knowing this wasn't the time to show any emotion. She suppressed her feelings and opened her ears, knowing there were only a few names left.

A few moments later, she heard it.

"Mae Fyez."

Her breath caught in her chest. *Forty-eight.* Of course she would be one of the last ones. The people around her all gazed, and this time she felt as though for the first time in five years that they were actually looking *at* her. They separated as she made her way through the crowd, but she again felt that wrench of a void. There was no one there to say goodbye to, no one to give her a few words of advice. She was going in alone and unprepared. But before she began to pity herself, Mae put her chin up and marched determinedly toward the gates. These people had to stare at her, but she had no reason to even look at them. *They will remember me*, she thought, as the crowd continued to let her through. She would be one of the six. These people would see her again. And then they couldn't ignore her.

As the last two names were called, Mae had made her way past the gates and into the courtyard. When she craned her neck to see who the final two were, she collided with a wall. At least that was what it felt like as she tried to regain her balance. When she looked up, she saw the tall farmer standing—no, towering—over her. This large man was the one the little girl had been clinging to. Ja…something. In her panic of coming in, Mae had forgotten what his name was. His broad shoulders, as wide as a house, tensed up as he slowly turned around.

His curly dark hair moved in the winter wind, and Mae almost shrank back when his green eyes narrowed and looked down at her. They were full of anger and rage, perhaps a few drops of fear, but if it was there, it only amplified the other emotions. His jaw clenched even tighter when he locked eyes with Mae, and his hands clenched into fists. Slowly he let out a growl and spat, "Watch where you're going." He looked her up and down. "Pox Face."

Mae tried to steady herself. She looked back at him, trying to match his ferocity. Fighting back wasn't the best option, but she wasn't going to let the first person she talked to in here push her around. "They're called freckles, you literal giant ass," she hissed, hoping he was too tall to hear her. She tried to move past him, but as the mountain lowered himself to her face, she knew he'd heard her. He looked her up and down before returning an intense gaze.

"Listen to me. I can make this easy for you in one of two ways. Once you're in there, I can help you get out." The words seemed kind, but the tone was harsh and violent. He paused, his eyes on fire. "Or I can make sure you don't get in there in the first place."

Mae was scared of him. He was huge, and she had caught a glimpse of his hands. True to his trade, they were farmer's hands. Dirty and rough, large and strong. They could easily wrap themselves around her throat and end her oxygen supply or snap her throat in two. Once they were in The Factory, she needed to make sure she stayed away from him and never spoke to him again. But she surprised herself when she heard her hard voice reply, "I'd love to see you try."

He was about to respond when a loud noise filled the air. A shrieking sound, but not something any human could possibly make. The farmer stood up, looking over her shoulder, the strength in his eyes disappearing, his shoulders slouching. Others looked over their shoulders as well, while the older villagers stared forward. They knew what was happening; perhaps they'd seen it occur long ago to others in the past. Mae understood what the noise meant and knew it was nothing good. But she figured she should watch this, as it could be the last time she ever saw her little town.

The gate to The Factory was closing. Behind them, the people's faces weren't as happy as Mae would have thought. After all, there was a chance they would finally be rid of her. Many people, family, children, lovers and friends, looked terrified and some turned away. Some pulled their jackets closer, as though the temperature had dropped drastically. There were a few waves and shouts from loved ones or family, but nothing that could stop the gate from closing. Finally, with a demanding *thud*, it closed, vibrations traveling through the bones of everyone in the courtyard. A second later, there was a click, followed by many others. The locks. There was no turning back now.

It was time to find out what The Factory had in store for them.

Chapter Eight:
Javeen

Once Javeen heard the gate close, he immediately regretted how he'd spoken to Mae. He looked back down to apologize to her, but to his dismay, she had moved away from him. His stomach curled as her braids moved farther into the crowd.

With a boiling rage, Javeen mentally berated himself. He hadn't meant to lash out at Mae. Being called into The Factory was stressful enough, and when Asha had grabbed his leg, every measure of his strength drained from him. Still he had moved forward, focusing on taking one step at a time. When he had crossed the threshold, he knew this wasn't a dream and his chances of returning home were slim. That was when he felt someone bump into him. Thinking it was someone trying to establish dominance, he tensed up, determined to fight back, to show he was tougher than this fool. A huge thug or a brawler from the inn—that was what he was expecting. But when he turned around, he saw Mae.

He had watched a figure, now he knew Mae, as she stormed her way towards the gates. Shoulders back and chin jutted forward. Javeen noticed she didn't make eye contact with anyone around her, even though the whole town was watching her. Mae's blue eyes were focused, looking through everyone that had been herded into the courtyard, and was looking straight at The Factory. To Javeen, it looked as if Mae believed there were only two people in this game they were about to play. Her and The Factory. And she would be damned if she didn't come out as the winner. Then she ran into him.

Javeen's anger rose faster than he ever imagined it could. Not because she had run into him, but because she wasn't supposed to be here. How was this possible? It was as if their worlds had collided in order to make his life even more hellish. If he was in The Factory, then Mae would be safe. That was what he had told himself. Mae was supposed to be safe because Javeen was taking her place, even if that logic was flawed. Nearly anyone could be chosen for The Factory, but for some reason he had convinced himself of his theory. Now that she was in here with him, he would have to do everything he could to save her. He needed to make sure she was one of the six to leave. No matter what.

His rage, however, had overpowered him as he had looked down at Mae, and he snapped. Javeen couldn't stop the crazy things that had rolled off his tongue. He had called her Pox Face and threatened to kill her. But he also had said he would offer his help. Perhaps he could try to let her know he meant it. Maybe, if he apologized and told her he really would help her get out, she would agree, making his mission easier. But was it too late? Had he already established himself as an aggressor, only out for himself? And if Mae did decide to trust him, could he trust her? After all, she was much more independent than he was and, therefore, probably could fend for herself.

Javeen shook his head, trying to clear it. He had to focus on what might lie ahead. Instead of worrying, he had to mentally prepare himself for the competition. After all, this had to be some kind of a challenge, and it was one he was planned to win. He looked around at the people standing in the courtyard with him. As he'd expected, there weren't many elderly folks. He spotted a few younger ones—maybe fourteen or fifteen years old—and felt relieved knowing that Asha and Mami weren't in the throng with him. Still the group was quiet, the loud cawing of crows high in the sky the lone sounds around them. The fog of their hot breath in the cold air was the only thing that proved human life existed here.

The courtyard was large, but not too spacious. It reminded Javeen of some of the busiest days he had seen at market. There was enough room to get from one side to the other, but one would have to push or squeeze through another person in order to get there. Still, on this day, no one really moved. Every now and then, Javeen saw someone rocking back and forth on their heels, or looking around like he was. But mostly, the people stood still, with their necks bent, heads looking up. Javeen own eyes trailed their glances, and understood. Everyone was looking up at the large structure, and for a moment Javeen did too, seeing as this was the closest he had ever been to The Factory.

The building was much taller now that he was standing at the base of it. He could see the iron panels, much smoother than the ones the blacksmith in town made, were held together by massive nails. Around the edges of the nails, there seemed to be some rust, but not enough to affect The Factory in anyway. There were no windows or doors making him wonder where the light would come from. In the distance Javeen could hear a roaring of some sort. Not the sound of any animal he had ever heard before, but the sound of many different metals clanging together. He continued to look up, and noticed how many different sections this place actually had. There were walls that jutted out towards them, while others receded inward. Some of the tops stopped short of the highest point, and Javeen was shocked that a building so massive and well put together unsymmetrical. He also noted that there were no gables or peaks at the roof of The Factory. Just a flat surface that only a bird could see the top of. And from there, Javeen saw the chimney's, covered in soot, and still smoking. Quickly, he dropped his gaze and began to look at the crowd once more.

He wanted to know every single face and gauge who he would be up against. A scraggly older woman, her hair thin and brittle, stood staring at the ground. He had noticed her outside the The Blood Broth a lot too and knew why she practically lived outside the old place. She was one of the local prostitutes. An enormous man a few feet away from her was the bouncer for the local pawnbroker, who needed protection due to his slimy dealings with the villagers. Javeen wondered if he could win in a fight against him—maybe, but maybe not.

Then there was the bookmaker's apprentice, Sadler Alim, scrawny yet sharp, scanning the faces around him, a calculating look in his eyes. He too seemed to be memorizing every face, or maybe measuring them up. Javeen couldn't really make out his character from here, but maybe that was Sadler's intentions. Stay as neutral as possible. Javeen then noticed the red-haired girl, the one with the scar on her face, standing in the middle. The mark was a thick ugly line, but she seemed to wear it with pride as she stared forward at The Factory, not up like many of the others. Her eyes looked dark and meaningful as she took deep breaths.

"Don't do it, kid."

Javeen jolted at the sudden noise and quickly turned to the man next to him. He was an older fellow, with a roundish belly, but with arms that showed strength. His brown beard was coarse, as if he had refused to shave since the first day of the smoke, and judging by the bags under his eyes, he hadn't gotten much sleep lately either. His skin was tanned and wrinkled, making him look as though he'd spent much of his life in the sun. But the most striking features were his ice-blue eyes. Not the kind someone would compliment, but something to be feared. Ice-blue eyes with no feeling or emotions behind them. The man was facing forward, his terrifyingly fascinating eyes watching Javeen from the side, his brows tight in the middle.

"What are you talking about?" Javeen spat. After his encounter with Mae, he wasn't in the mood to talk to anyone.

The man's eyes narrowed even more, as if challenging him. "You'd better listen to me, kid. Don't try to get to know these people. Forty-four of us are going to die in the next week or two. If you see them as people, the weaker you'll become."

"How so?" Javeen asked, his voice trying to challenge Ice Eyes' in return. He didn't like the man's tone, and more important, he didn't like that he was making sense.

"Because you'll feel for them and see them as human. You'll want to help them, and you'll show compassion. None of us are human anymore. From the minute we walked through that gate, we lost that right. Now we're all pawns in a sick game. So, stop looking around and seeing them as people. If you do that, in the end, you'll go wherever they store the dead ones."

Javeen was taken aback by the man's blunt statements. But he tried not to show it. "And what makes you such an expert?"

The man shrugged, his eyes still digging into Javeen's soul. "Everyone's out for themselves here. Remember that. You think they're humans; I can see it in your eyes, boy. But they aren't. They'll kill you in a second if they think you're weak. You'll become an easy target. Don't even think about wanting to know who they are. And whatever you do"—he stepped forward and poked Javeen in the chest—"don't get any of their names."

Javeen was about to shove him off, tell him he knew nothing. Then something happened as the man's finger buried itself in his chest. There was a flash in Javeen's mind, and he saw this man, but not standing in the courtyard. He was somewhere else, somewhere Javeen couldn't place. There was a haze around it all; the image wasn't completely clear. At first, he thought he might have seen him at the market, but those blue eyes would have made an impression if he'd seen them that often. No, he knew him from another place. He turned back to ask, but when he looked up, the man had disappeared into the crowd.

As the wind picked up, Javeen rubbed his hands together to stop his fingertips from going numb. He didn't think they'd be standing outside as long as they were, but there had to be a reason for it. Perhaps they needed the townspeople to return to their homes before whatever happened in here commenced. While he tried to keep himself warm, he looked around again, but not to memorize the faces of the people around him. He was trying to find Mae. He needed to make sure she was safe. *No matter what happens*, he kept reminding himself. He stood on his toes and saw her, with her six braids, looking straight forward, just like the girl with the scar. Her face was hard and determined, as if she were trying to prove something.

He considered going over to her to apologize, to explain why he had lashed out at her, when there was a small ping, and a voice traveled through the courtyard, making everyone freeze. The fog from the crowd's exhalations disappeared as they waited, holding their breath. If a pin had dropped in that courtyard, it would have sounded like an explosion.

"Welcome to The Factory," a cheery female voice said, loud enough to produce just a slight echo in the courtyard. Javeen wondered if anyone outside of The Factory could hear it. The voice continued, "You've all been chosen as members of your community to make the ultimate sacrifice in order to preserve what is right and pure. In these next two weeks, you'll undergo a series of trials that will test you physically and mentally. Stages that will challenge your morals and your judgments. Six stages to be precise. In the end, six of you will walk out of The Factory, as a reminder to the villagers outside these walls that there is hope in this world, and even after terrible events occur, there is always something good worth living for."

As the crowd stood still, another surge of irritation flowed through Javeen. The voice had made it sound as if each person here was doing something for the greater good. As if those who died in this place would be heroes, not people who had been placed in a terrible trap. Javeen knew better. What would happen in these next six stages would bring out the worst in everyone, perhaps even him. In life-or-death situations, humans deserted their normal train of thought and became the animals they once were. In order to keep what was "pure," as the woman had said, this crowd would have to sacrifice the goodness of their human souls and become rabid creatures.

"And now," the voice continued, "Stage One will begin."

Chapter Nine:
<u>Mae</u>

Mae looked forward as others around her began to hyperventilate. Her own breathing was coming and going more quickly too, as the reality of her situation set in. This was it. The Factory was becoming more and more real the longer they stood there, but until the announcement had been made, it still could have been a dream. Once that woman had spoken, everything became a harsh reality.

"Stage One is quite simple," the voice said. "Fifty doors will appear in a few moments. When they do, please choose a door to enter The Factory." There was a click as the last syllables of her voice echoed in the stale winter air.

A second later, another loud noise filled the courtyard. This time, it wasn't the voice of the mysterious woman, but a different noise, one made by a machine. It was the sound of metal shifting, first in and then pushing itself out. In the back of The Factory, there was loud roaring noise, and puttering noises. The crowd around Mae began to cluster closer together, and now a tall man stood in front of Mae. She stood on her toes to see what had happened, as those around her inhaled sharply. Looking at the once-smooth facade of The Factory, she noticed fifty door handles sticking out, waiting for everyone to choose an entrance. Mae couldn't help but gasp in amazement at what she was looking at. Only seconds ago, there had been no sort of entrance into this horrible place.

Just some dingy metal staring back at her and the few heads in front of her. The only things that here exposed to the air was the bolt type things that held the place together. Now, there were doors. *Is this what technology used to be like?* She thought to herself still staring at what really was a door, *One moment there is something, and then it just changes in an instant?* Mae began to understand now why society must have been so afraid of it. *So why is this place still here?*

There was no rush. In fact, no one moved at all, afraid that this was some sort of trick, that perhaps the first person who entered would be the first to die. Slowly, however, people inched their way toward the doors. After all, this was the only way to get into The Factory, it seemed. And no one wanted to find out what might happen if they refused to enter, so they marched forward. At first it was like a herd of cattle running toward one small gate, as everyone thought there were a limited number doors. However, that changed when they realized there were enough doors for everyone. They began to spread out evenly, and the crowd quickly thinned as they walked toward the entrance of their choosing. Mae waited a moment for the crowd to disperse even more before she too headed toward one of the entrances in the wall.

Feeling something odd, she suddenly she stopped. Although her shoes were made of tough leather and had withheld years of wear and tear, the bottoms were worn, due to her constantly running in and out of the market. Because of the thin soles, Mae was able to feel something that didn't make sense on this blistering cold winter day. Heat. As she made her way toward her chosen door, the ground below her was heating up, as if someone had spilled a very large hot drink. Had it been snowing that day, it surely would have melted the instant it hit the ground.

Mae's brow knitted as she considered what this meant. In her gut, she knew something wasn't right. The ground shouldn't have been warm, especially since the ground had been covered in snow for the last three weeks. It was only yesterday that the sun had broken through the clouds, melting most of it. But still she remembered walking here this morning and curling her toes under the frost that had covered the dirt road from her house to the village. Only moments ago she had berated herself for not bringing gloves, as her hands were freezing up and turning a blistering red. A theory about the heat struck Mae, and she decided to test it.

Ever so slowly, she stepped a few feet to the right, making sure no one around her noticed. As she moved, the ground began to cool, and soon her feet were begging for her to step back over to the heat. She listened to them and once again felt the warmth underneath her soles. Once more, she stepped to the right, and again the chill of winter surrounded her feet. Mae looked back at the warm area and the door in front of it. Although she loved the heat that filled her body when she was standing in front of the other entrance, she knew something was wrong with that comfortable feeling. *The Factory doesn't want anyone to feel comfortable*, she thought. She looked in front of her, at the door in front of the cold area, and saw that the door was still open in front of her.

Mae walked toward it, then felt as though someone were watching her. She glanced to the left and saw the farmer boy standing in front of a door, watching her. His eyes had softened, and they looked almost happy. He gave her a nod, as if telling her she was doing the right thing. Mae glared at him, wondering if he'd seen what she'd done. If he had, she must have looked like a spectacle, moving back and forth like that. Mae felt the color flush to her cheeks as she turned to face the door. She didn't like how close this boy was to her, both physically and now mentally. Was he trying to get into her head and mark her moves? It was almost as if he were following her, watching her every move.

When she turned, she almost walked right into the door. She stood there for a moment, contemplating whether to go in. Mae had no idea what lay before her and wasn't sure she wanted to know what The Factory had in store for her. She glanced around the courtyard and the closed doors while others made their way inside. What would happen if she decided to stay outside? Would someone come and dispose of her? Or would she just be left here to freeze and die from lack of food and water? It wasn't as if she could climb over the walls and get out. As she pondered it, her hand instinctively went to her braids and she froze. Six braids, one for each of the six people who would leave The Factory. Mae remembered her promise to herself. She would be one of those six people, and refusing to go in would ensure that her promise would never be fulfilled. Closing her eyes tightly, she grasped the knob and went inside.

She had barely stepped inside when the door slammed shut, almost catching her heels. Hearing the distinctive click of a lock behind her, she understood that she was in here for better or worse. There was no turning back now. As she slowly opened her eyes, she realized she was standing in complete darkness. There was no light from the outside world, as the doors were windowless. Blindly she moved her hands around her to feel out the room. It was small, as though she were standing inside a tall, thin closet. There was just enough room for her to slightly reach around her, elbows bent. Her breathing grew ragged, and she let it this time. No one was around to see her fear, and if this was the only moment of solitude, she would take it to allow herself to fear. *Only now*, she reminded herself. *Only now.*

There was an echo, just as before, when the voice had spoken. "Stage One is complete." And then an alarm chimed once.

Mae waited for something to open up in front of her. But it didn't. After the woman's voice disappeared, she saw a small gap by her feet, then an orange glow from the room to her right. And then the screaming began.

Chapter Ten:
Javeen

Javeen *had* been watching Mae, and he was ashamed to admit it. Although

watching her made him feel like a creep, he wanted to make sure she figured out

the key to this stage. There *was* a difference between the doors everyone was

choosing. He had felt it the moment he had taken a step. He wasn't as cold as he

had been before the voice had come. He no longer needed to rub his hands

together in order to stay warm. Javeen had actually been quite content standing

there, even with the blustering winds. That was when he knew something was

wrong. When everyone began to move, he had pretended to tie his boots and

placed his hand on the ground. It was hot. Not a burning sensation, but like the

heat that comes when you stand at a perfect distance from a fire. He looked up

and saw a door in front of him. That was when he put it together. The furnace

wasn't a myth.

Out in the open like that, Javeen knew he couldn't go up to Mae and tell

her what he had discovered. One, because then he would be showing attachment

toward another person, but more important, she might defy him out of anger or

spite and choose the other door. Instead he had found two doors next to each

other without heat rising in front of them. Watching Mae dance from side to side, her face twisted in confusion, he couldn't help smirk. Even in this extreme situation, he didn't attempt to stop feeling a strong pull toward her, and though she didn't know it, he would do everything in his power to make sure she stayed protected. When she walked toward the door that was next to his, Javeen had felt the knot in his stomach release. Then she made eye contact with him, and he gave her a nod, telling her she had made the right choice. Still, she glared and faced the door in front of her. Javeen didn't blame her, after the way he had treated her earlier, but he would make everything better. Perhaps because they had chosen doors next to each other, they might be together in The Factory— that is, if he was right about this stage.

Javeen went through the same steps as Mae. He heard the door slam behind him, heard the lock click, then felt around to estimate how large the room was. Even though he was glad to know that Mae was next to him, he beat himself up. She didn't even know him, and even if she did, now she knew him as a tyrant. What was the point of retaining these feelings for her? Although they had haunted him for years, why hold on to them now? When his life could hang in the balance? When Mae might die? But he didn't have time to ask any more questions, as the woman's voice returned. After she announced the end of Stage One, Javeen thought that the underworld had come alive next to him. In the room to his left, he felt a blazing heat and heard the panicked screams of a woman who had chosen the wrong door.

At first Javeen wasn't really sure what had happened. The door had closed behind him and he waited so see if he had made it. Once the voice echoed out of his ears, Javeen heard a heavy clang next to him and the sound of a door slamming open. That was when the heat came, and Javeen knew the fires had opened up. In a panic, the woman next to him sounded as if she had tried to throw her body into the wall, but it didn't work. The whole floor must have opened up, as he heard the sound of nails scratching down the wall, and finally latching onto something.

Whoever she was, she was desperately trying to hold on. As the fire blazed, sweat formed around Javeen's eyebrows. He stepped away, as close to the wall on the other side as he could, but he couldn't ignore the sounds in the other room. The woman's cries lasted longer than they should have, and at one point, he saw her fingers latch onto the small opening that led into his cramped quarters. He heard her wail for help and the continuing sound of her scratching at walls. The screams weren't ones of sorrow or fright; they were desperate shouts of unearthly fear. A fear Javeen never wanted to know.

He closed his eyes and tried to drown out the noise. This wasn't the time to panic. "Don't get to know these people," the familiar man in the courtyard had said. Javeen knew he was right. He tried to—no, he *had* to—think of something, anything that could divert his attention from this moment. Maybe a better time in his life, something that would relax him before he went into the heart of The Factory. It came to him slowly, like morning haze on a summer day. He began to see the outlines of the memory, and the more he concentrated, the more the mist disappeared, and he could see clearly.

***

It was a summer day, when he was almost ten and an almost nine-year-old Jiro was following him. Mami was six and clung to her mother, who was rocking on the porch with newborn baby Asha in her arms. As Mami swooned over the infant, their mother laughed, her vibrant brownish red hair flowing around her. Mami always did everything she could to help her mother with her baby sister. Even though this was only a memory, Javeen felt a pang of sadness, knowing he had to search so deep in his thoughts in order to remember a time when his mother had been happy. He shook his head, the screams continuing, and began to think harder.

Javeen and Jiro were running, very fast it seemed. But toward what? His father, who had brought them presents. He had promised them he would, as he did every year around this time. Javeen and Jiro were born almost a year apart, give or take a few days, so when their birthdays came around, their parents always made sure they received gifts at the same time. Although they didn't have too much, they had enough to give each of their children a birthday gift. Javeen and Jiro knew today was present day; in the evening, they would enjoy a birthday bread pudding, as cake was too expensive.

Their father, a stocky man who always kept a beard and mustache, headed toward the house from the field, as the road to town hadn't been established by their constant traveling yet. Javeen was the first to notice him. As they got closer, Jiro tripped in the field, taking his brother down with him. Javeen, knowing they were both too excited to care about scraped knees or dirty pants, helped Jiro up, and they continued toward their father. When the boys reached him, he embraced them, his arms big and strong enough to take them both in his grip. He gave them a shake as they both laughed. "My boys! My big boys," he bellowed. "How was the farm while I was away today?"

"Great!" they both squealed as their father still held them. He released them slowly before getting down on one knee so he could make eye contact with them.

"And your mother? You've been taking care of her?" he asked, his face stern, although he knew well enough that his boys were helping their mother and the baby. They nodded, though Jiro admitted that Mami was helping more. Javeen elbowed him in the ribs, hoping his honesty wouldn't cost them their gifts. It wasn't their fault Mami was overjoyed to have another girl in the house and was willing to do most of the work.

Their father belly laughed at Jiro's honesty and Javeen's fear of losing his birthday gift, then placed his hands on their shoulders. "I'd expect that from her. Don't worry, boys. I know you work hard and love and watch them while I'm gone." He glanced toward the porch, his face full of affection for his wife and two young daughters. "As long as we take care of our girls, and each other, then we'll always be happy. Isn't that right?" The two boys eagerly nodded.

Javeen's father stood up and put his hands on his hips, a smirk dancing on his face. "Now I know you two didn't run all the way over here just to see your old man."

Their faces flushed; they knew their father had seen right through them. Normally, they waited until he was halfway through the field before rushing to meet him. But not on gift day. They protested that they had no idea what he was talking about—of course they were running just to see him—and again their father laughed. "Sure, sure," he said as he made his way toward his cart. He reached in and brought over two boxes and handed one to each boy. "Happy birthday, my two troublemakers," he said, ruffling boys' dark curls.

Jiro was the first to rip open his gift. Paper went flying as he tore the lid off the box and tossed it behind him. He gasped when he saw the leather gloves inside. But they weren't just any leather gloves that could be bought in town. They were almost exactly the same as his father's. Custom made, just for Jiro. They were a rich, dark brown and smooth to the touch. From where he was standing, Javeen saw fur lining in the gloves and wondered whether his father was lucky enough to have his gloves lined with such warm material.

"That leather maker in town knows what he's doing," his father said, then added proudly, "And that fur is rabbit. I trapped it myself!" He winked at Javeen. "So that way, when you help me chop wood or go hunting with me this winter, your hands won't get numb." Jiro was always whining about how his hands went dead whenever they chopped wood, which left most of the work to

Javeen and their father. These gloves might actually help him stick with it, allowing the work to get done faster. As Jiro looked them over again and again, his father quickly added, "They're a little big, but you'll grow into them."

Jiro couldn't contain himself. He took the gloves out of the box, and although it was a hot summer day, he pulled them on. He gazed over them in amazement, then wrapped his arms around his father's wide waist, exclaiming, "Thank you! Thank you!" In the next moment, he was running back toward the house, his glove-covered hands flying over his head as he screamed, "Mama! Mama! Look what Papa got me!"

Javeen looked down at his box, knowing he wouldn't be getting leather gloves. He'd gotten a pair of gloves as his winter solstice gift last year. He had no idea what his gift was, and that thought thrilled him. Javeen tore off the paper and, with shaking hands, went for the top of the box. As he slowly pulled off the lid, his eyes grew wide. The gift wasn't new, but it held so much more meaning than any shiny present. In the box was his father's hunting knife.

Ever since he was little, Javeen had told his father how much he liked his knife. It was a wooden-handled switch knife with three blades needed for hunting. The dark handle was so smooth; no matter how many times Javeen went over it with his fingers, he never got a splinter. At the base three letters were notched in: CRN, his father's initials. Although Javeen had begged him for the knife for so long, his father always had told him that when he was old enough he would get his own. He had thought that getting a new knife was probably his fate, and he would treat it just like it was his father's. But never in his life did Javeen imagine he would actually get the knife his father had used for so many years.

He looked up and smiled wider than he ever had in his life. "Thank you," he whispered, afraid to pick it up.

"Turn it over," his father said, a smile of great happiness creeping across on his face.

With shaking hands, Javeen turned the knife over. At a quick glance, he saw nothing, just the smooth black wood, until a glint at the bottom of the handle. He almost dropped the box when he saw three new letters there: JCN, his initials.

When he looked up, his father was back on one knee, smiling at him. "I want you to know that this is yours. It truly is. But I don't have enough money yet to get a new knife for myself, so you wouldn't mind sharing, right?" he asked.

Javeen nodded enthusiastically; sharing anything with his father was an honor.

His father stood up again and pulled the cart toward the house. Javeen followed in step, looking down at the gift he would treasure forever. When his father finally arrived at the house, he bounded up the stairs, grabbed Mami around the waist, and gave her a spin. He then walked over to his wife, gave her a kiss on the cheek, and played with the babbling Asha for a few moments while the boys showed their gifts to Mami. Suddenly their father jumped off the porch, grinning widely as he exclaimed, "I almost forgot something!" He went back to the cart and brought back a box tied in twine. Javeen and Jiro looked at each other, hoping perhaps it was another gift for them.

"Chase!" their mother exclaimed, clearly knowing what was in the box. "How could you—"

"Oh, Tess, it was an exceptionally good day at the market," he said, placing the box on the table outside, before giving her another long kiss on the cheek. "And besides, it's not every day your two boys turn nine and ten!" With that, he untied the twine and lifted the lid. Inside was the biggest, darkest-looking chocolate cake Javeen had ever seen. In all of Javeen's ten years, never had he had a birthday cake before. In all honesty, he didn't even know what cake tasted like. Or even if he would like it.

Jiro, on the other hand, didn't care if he liked cake or not as he nearly pounced on the dessert. They were lucky their father was so quick, or the expensive thing would have been destroyed in minutes. He wrapped his arms around Jiro's waist, then placed him as far from the cake as he could and told him he would have to wait. They all laughed at Jiro's groans, knowing how much he loved sweets and how torturous this was for him. Javeen went over to his mother and showed her his gift. Of course, she told him how careful he would have to be with it, but still it was something he was very proud of.

This was one of the happiest moments of Javeen's life, yet it had a connection to the saddest memory as well. His recollection of that warm summer day melted away, replaced with a later memory, from when he was sixteen. The winter chill rushed through the drafty house, and even in this memory, Javeen felt himself shiver. He clearly remembered this moment, as it had haunted him for so many years. He was standing at the door with his father, the clouds outside dark and ominous. He should have seen it as a sign.

"I want to come!" Javeen had whined. He would have stomped his foot, but he was trying to prove that he was old enough for the trip.

"Someone has to stay here and take care of the farm and the family," his father had said, slinging his rifle over his shoulder. "And don't say Jiro can do it. He isn't old enough yet." Seeing the hurt on his son's face, he spoke more softly. "I promise. I promise, Javeen. Next time you can come with me. But it's going to be bad weather; I can feel it. I could be out there for several days, and that isn't safe for you. Not yet. It's not a good time. I promise I'll take you out when the weather is clear." He ruffled his son's hair like he always did. "Stay warm here, with the family. I'll be home in three days. Four tops." Javeen nodded.

There was a sound outside, someone calling his father's name as a figure stood in the doorway. Chase turned towards the shadow and said something, though Javeen couldn't remember what he had said. He really couldn't remember anything about that doorway, guilt eating away from the memory of anyone else in his father's hunting party. All he could recall was his father turning toward him with an outstretched hand, and then Javeen handed over the knife they shared. He didn't want to, out of spite, but he knew that wouldn't get him that trip his father had promised him. So Javeen turned over the dark-handled knife with his and his father's initials on it. After goodbyes, and a few more hair ruffles, the hulk of a man disappeared into the rising sun.

It was the last time Javeen ever saw him and the knife again.

***

Javeen opened his eyes suddenly, unaware that the screaming had stopped. He blinked a few times, trying to remember where he was. He still felt the sweat around his forehead, but this time it wasn't from the heat. It was a cold sweat, from the memories of his father. The memories he had tried to push away for so long had come back, and Javeen's body and mind weren't ready for that. He had to shake his head to rid himself of the images, but still they wouldn't leave his brain.

It wasn't until the wall in front of him opened and let in artificial light that he remembered where he was. The Factory. His nightmare wasn't even close to being over. *Now's not the time to remember the past*, he told himself. The past was behind him, and no matter how much he missed his father, he wasn't coming back. Javeen knew he had to focus on two things: getting out of here and making sure Mae got out with him. Slowly he stepped into the light, not knowing what might come next.

Chapter Eleven:
<u>Mae</u>

The blinding light was so fierce that Mae had to shield her eyes and wait for them to adjust. When they finally did, she knew she was inside. She had made it past Stage One, and for a moment her heart was lifted. Somehow, she had made the right choice, and she was safe. But it immediately dropped when she understood how everything had changed. Mae was now *inside* The Factory. And there were still five more stages before she could possibly be free. She took a deep breath and walked toward the light.

She was standing in a black room the size of a very small bedroom, a space much different than the musty brown spaces she was used to at home. And although the walls were dark, the room had an air of cleanliness to it, as if someone had come in here and washed it until all living matter had been cleared away. The only object in it was a bucket—probably for relieving oneself, she thought—and even that looked as though it had been polished. As she looked up, she saw bright objects in the high ceiling that had almost made her lose her eyesight. She remembered reading once about these things. They were special lights, bright and powerful not like the gas lamps they had in town, which emitted a weak glow. They were run by some sort of electricity, like the lightning in the sky. Mae then recalled the roaring sound outside. It was called something. A gen...genar...she couldn't remember, but that loud noise it what created this artificial light. But the new objects in this room wasn't what caught her off guard.

This isn't a room, she thought. *It's a cage.*

The large black box was clearly a cell, with black iron rods surrounding her. They stopped high above her and made their way across, breaking up the light from above. Mae went over and touched the bars, hoping they would disappear, but they stayed solid to her touch, their coldness reminding her of the bitter weather outside. A few inches beyond the bars, black glass walls surrounded her chamber. She couldn't see anything beyond them and didn't know whether she actually wanted to.

Fear slipped in as Mae realized that, once more, she was alone. Her heart beat faster than it had in the last room, and her breathing quickened as the cage around her seemed to close in. She grabbed her head, which throbbed from anxiety and racing thoughts. She was in a cell, which meant anything could happen to her. And at this point, since she was alone, no one would actually know what became of her. The black walls could hide any sort of foul attack or trick from anyone else in The Factory.

That was when she began to scream. At first Mae didn't realize she was doing it, but suddenly she heard her own voice, shivering with dread, as she banged on the black walls surrounding the cage. She should have guessed that they would hold just as strong, that each pounding motion she made with her hands would do nothing, but panic was sweeping in, and she had no idea how to handle it. She hadn't been this afraid since the day her parents had died. When she was first truly alone.

Then she stopped, realizing her actions were futile. She was here, and there was no way to get out. As quickly as her panic attack had started, it ended. Mae took a step back, trying to compose herself. A few stray tears had settled on her face from her lapse of judgment, but she quickly wiped them away with the back of her hand. She wasn't alone. She knew that. The Factory was filled with people, and there was no way she was actually deserted in this place. Perhaps this was part of the game of The Factory, she thought, to make you feel secluded. That way, it would be easier to accept death. A death that was, more likely than not, coming for you.

As her breathing began to steady, she walked back to the center of the cell and heard a hissing noise. She turned quickly, expecting something devious to be headed into her holding, but the door she had entered through had closed, and bars now stood in front of it. The hissing came from the black glass surrounding the cage, which was now slowly rising into the ceiling. Mae continued her deep inhalations, afraid of what would be on the other side as the glass enclosure continued to make its way down. But instead of seeing some sort of monster or new challenge, she saw people.

Everyone else was in the same type of cell as Mae. All the enclosures were in a circle about two feet apart from one another, with a big open center that resembled some sort of blank stage for them to stare at. In fact, the entire room was a circle, with a few doors that led to who knew where. As she examined the cages, she felt as if The Factory were mocking them, as though they were all feral animals. *Perhaps we are*, Mae thought, surprising herself. The Factory might know more than she ever would about human nature and what people did in order to survive. Perhaps in its early stages, The Factory didn't have cells to keep the people in but had to add them later, for reasons unknown to Mae.

The other cages had the same black glass walls, all of which were receding into the ceiling as well, showing who, out of the original fifty, were left. A few people looked around and challenged the bars of their cages, pushing back and forth, hoping they would give. They eventually gave up and kicked or punched them in frustration. Others paced, like the animals Mae was worried they would become, in their small square boxes. Their arms legs flailed about, and they'd turn sharply on their heels, looking at the others or the ground. Finally, some stood and rested their heads against the bars, waiting to see what would happen next.

Just then, Mae realized what that last group was doing. They were looking around them, sure enough, but they were also speaking. As their mouths moved in quick bursts, Mae realized they weren't talking; they were *counting* those around them. Immediately she did it as well, calculating how many people she might have to fight in order to get out. She crawled along her bars, trying to get a better look at the people around her. *Ten... Move your damn head down!* she wanted to scream at the man two cells down from her. *Fifteen...* She caught sight of the girl with scar on her face, who most likely was counting too. They made eye contact but both quickly moved on; they were on a mission. *Twenty-five...or is it twenty-four?*

"Forty-five," she heard someone say. Mae wasn't sure where the voice had come from, but she trusted it.

It came back to her in an instant. The screams of the person who was next to her. She had almost chosen that same door. The five missing people were the ones who didn't make it. The ones who didn't realize their door was the end. Before, Mae had been so focused on just getting into this place that she hadn't really comprehended what had happened. But now she remembered it all so clearly. There was a wild noise, and orange and yellow illuminations had moved toward her feet. For a moment she had felt heat, the type of heat that rises when you take the lid off a pot of boiling water. Quick and then gone. But there also were screams—loud, terrible screams—and the smell of cooked flesh. She shivered at the thought and heard the voice again.

"So, I see you made it?"

She looked to the left, to where the voice had come from, and saw the farmer sitting in the corner closest to her cell. His back was facing the empty circular stage, and he was looking up, his green eyes glimmering at her. A small smirk crept across his face.

Mae couldn't stand it. It was just her luck that she would be stuck next to him. It was as if someone had planned it. She headed to the corner and glared down at him, her hands wrapped around the bars so tightly that her knuckles turned white. "Why? Did you think I wouldn't make it? Maybe you wouldn't have to kill me off then. Well, too bad." She started to turn and then added, "Oh, and by the way, I saw you watching me, you creep." She smirked back at him, knowing she had called him out. But he didn't falter. Instead, he got up and grabbed the bars of his cell.

They were only a foot or two away. If he wanted to, he could reach into her cell and tear her apart for what she'd just said. But he didn't. Instead he slowly reached out and touched her hand, not breaking eye contact. His voice was weak, as though he'd been through war and returned, only to enter back into it. His eyes blazed with a ferocity that was different than before; they held a hint of distress. "I know you felt it," I said. "I know you saw it and heard it. I know you felt the power of the furnace."

Chapter Twelve:
Javeen

The look in Mae's eyes was more than enough proof that she knew exactly what Javeen was talking about. The person to her right had gone into the furnace. He knew that, since Mae had almost chosen that door. He waited for her to open up to him, but she kept her eyes cold and dark as she stared at him. From the ashen look on her face, he could tell she had seen something, had heard someone die like he did, but she wasn't willing to give that information to him. Not yet.

"I have no idea what you are talking about," she spat, trying to pull her hand away from the bar and his grip, but Javeen held on firmly. He needed to show her that he was there for her, that the bully persona he had put on in the courtyard was gone. He wanted—no, *needed*—to protect her. She pulled harder, but his farmer's hands held tightly. Her bright-blue eyes looked afraid. *Of what, though?* he wondered. *Of the truth? Or of me?*

"I saw you walk toward that door," he said slowly. "The one to your right. And then you stopped."

Another smirk crossed Mae's face, but this time it wasn't as menacing; rather, she seemed amused. "Ha! You admit it. You *were* watching me."

Javeen nodded, once again feeling his face flush. "I...I wanted to see if you felt it too." She averted her eyes, and her smirk vanished. "You weren't jumping around to distract people. I know you felt the heat under your feet."

Mae pulled her hand away from his again, and this time Javeen let her. She clearly wasn't ready to talk about it. He told her his story—how he had known something was wrong and had felt the ground with his hand. He spoke about the screams next to him and the heat that had radiated into his cubicle. The whole time, Mae stood there, her eyes fixed on the floor, as though she needed to listen to his story, needed to know she wasn't alone with her terrifying experience in the darkness.

"I always thought it was a myth. The furnace, that is," Javeen continued. Mae's eyes perked up in interest for a moment, egging him on to continue. He let out a small chuckle and sighed. "My grandpaps used to tell me a story when I was little. He remembered how the smoke from The Factory's chimneys always burned. *Always*. And no one ever saw the funerals of those who didn't win. Someone just came out with a list of the people who had died, and everyone accepted it." Javeen noticed Mae was still staring at him, wanting him to go on.

"He claimed that one day in town, one of the neighboring families had lost a son or daughter—I can't remember—to The Factory. He went up to their home to say sorry or some kind words and asked when the funeral was. It wasn't a question most people asked, but he thought he'd buckle down and just do it. The woman he talked to, well, she laughed when he asked. Grandpaps said it was a chuckle that chilled his bones. She said, 'How can there be a funeral when all we got back was a pile of ashes?' And she wasn't even sure if the ashes belonged to her child. They were just ashes. Then the woman turned around and shut the door. After that, Grandpaps had this theory that everyone in The Factory who didn't make it was burned, that they used…" Now knowing the truth of what he was about to say, he took a deep breath and continued. "They used the bodies to keep the smoke rising. To keep The Factory alive. At first I didn't believe it. I mean, honestly, who could think the smoke rising from the chimneys came from actual human beings? You think a fire is just a fire, but it has to be fueled by something. When the smoke first came a few days ago, I thought it probably was from wood or coal. But you heard it; you saw it. And so did I. Haven't you noticed how warm it is in here? Don't forget heat rises. The furnace is real. Realer than I ever thought possible. And it's right under our feet."

A silence settled between them, but not one that indicated that the conversation was over. In fact, the conversation continued in the silence. Mae and Javeen stared at each other, their eyes wide as this new realization sank in. They had heard the tales, knew the legends, but those were just stories. In the end, no one could have prepared them for what they were now facing.

When a child hears a story about a monster, he or she is constantly reminded that monsters don't exist. The monster in the closet can't touch you, because it doesn't exist in reality; it just lives in our minds. But as these two stood staring at each other in wonderment and fear, they saw the facts. What do you do when a monster becomes more than just a thought in your head and has entered the reality of your world? The monster was The Factory, and it was coming out of the closest to get them all.

After a few moments, Javeen decided the silence was enough. The more thinking they did, the more it might unhinge them. Talking would be the only thing to keep them sane. He looked at Mae and gave her a small shrug. "Look, earlier, when we were outside. I'm sorry about what I—"

"Whatever. You said it. It's done," Mae said sharply, her hands covering her stomach. However, there wasn't any true anger or spite in her tone. She looked like she was going to be sick, the gravity of what was happening sinking in. Even so, Javeen felt a sting from her words, but he tried to shake it off. Mae was scared, and he wouldn't hold that against her. He was just as scared, not knowing what the next challenge might be. But he did know he had to win her over, show her he was better than the guy she had seen in the courtyard. Above all, he needed to prove they could work together and get out of this hellhole.

Slowly and carefully, he reached his hand into her cell. Although hyperaware that she most definitely could break his arm at any moment, he knew he was quick and could pull back if that was case. Although Mae shot him a suspicious look, her arms didn't move. She clutched her stomach tighter, as if protecting herself from his hand. Still Javeen kept his palm outstretched.

He knew what he was doing was wrong. He remembered the man with icy blue eyes staring into his soul. His dark, wrinkled face had scowled at him as he gave him the greatest advice he could have in this competition. *Whatever you do, don't get any of their names.* The man was right. A name was an ultimate connection to someone. It created a relation that would be disastrous in a place like this. A connection that, at any point for the next two weeks, could be destroyed and burn with the fires below his feet. And still, even after knowing all this, he still heard his voice, shaky and deep say, "My name is Javeen."

Mae glared at his hand, and for a moment he thought she might go after him. But instead she stood still, just looking. Javeen watched her face and noticed she wasn't angry at the proposition of an ally or a friend; rather, she was wary. And Javeen understood that. This wasn't the time or place to try to make new friends. In fact, this was one of the last places a person should try to establish any sort of relationship with a human. And besides that, perhaps Mae didn't trust anyone after her encounters with the townsfolk over the years. Slowly he pulled his hand back in defeat, trying to make eye contact with her, attempting to show the sincerity of his offer. But Mae's eyes darted to the floor, refusing to even glance in his direction.

Javeen, feeling beaten, slid down the bars. *What was I thinking?* he scolded himself. He had given her the idea that he was weak, that he didn't feel secure enough in his ability to get out of The Factory on his own. But that wasn't his intentions. He wanted to show her she could trust someone. And maybe have her see that she wouldn't be forgotten, even in a place that was meant to erase people from the world. But Mae was used to being alone. Going out of her comfort zone, especially here, was probably too much for her to handle. He rested his head, hitting it hard against the bars as punishment for being an idiot.

Then he heard the sliding of cloth against iron. From the corner of his eye, he saw that Mae also had decided to sit on the floor, choosing the corner of the cell closest to him. Still he looked forward, knowing she wouldn't to trust him, not after that show in the courtyard. *I deserve it*, he thought. With a sigh, he realized he'd have to start working by himself and try to get out of here for the sake of his family.

Then he heard it. If he'd actually been focusing on something, he might have missed it, as it almost came out as a whisper.

"Mae. My name is Mae."

Chapter Thirteen:
<u>Mae</u>

The time passed slowly, and Mae wondered how long they'd been there. She knew it was surely longer than a day, but perhaps they were sinking into the middle of two days. Three times a day, a meal would appear, rising up on a small platform from the floor in her cell. It wasn't anything special; dinner was just a piece of bread, a small slab of chicken, tomato soup, and a large glass of water. But for Mae, it was some of the best food she'd had in weeks. She tried not to show her enthusiasm too much as she attempted to slowly eat the food, but sometimes she couldn't stop herself and let out a small squeal. After dinner, the dishes would disappear into the floor, replaced almost immediately by a bedroll. This was how Mae calculated that the days had passed. Two times on a bedroll meant two nights sleeping in The Factory.

As the hours of the third day passed, Mae felt the tension growing in the large room around her. People were anxious, not knowing when the next challenge would begin. Some still continued to pace, perhaps the only thing keeping them sane as they waited, while others sat in the corners of their cells, fiddling with their hands or anything that was on or around them. Many Mae had seen before, including an older woman, one of the most notorious prostitutes in town. She picked at her nails, as her pale-blond hair fell in front of her face. Mae also noticed a Ridley Nadim who was dry heaving; he was the town drunkard. He must have been going through withdrawal, and it was taking its toll on his body and mind.

As Mae continued to look around, she noticed that the redheaded girl with the scar was pacing as well. Her hair, tightly wound in a bun, was fiery red with hints of yellow and orange. Every time Mae saw her, the girl's hair made her shudder, reminding her of the flames she had witnessed a few days ago. But that scar, that was a story Mae wanted to know about. She was determined to figure out how a girl with such beautiful hair and an attractive face had gotten such a nasty scar. It was raised on the sides, emphasizing the cut or burn had dug deeply into her flesh. As the scar-faced girl continued to pace, Mae decided to move on, not wanting to give unwelcome attention to someone who already got enough as it was.

Two cells over, she noticed a burly man she thought she had seen in the town's logging area. She couldn't recall his name, but his massive shoulders and distinctive beard solidified the thought that he indeed worked with the other lumbermen. He was sitting close to the edge of his cell, looking around, just as Mae was, when suddenly, his eyes fell on her. He was far away, but not far enough that Mae could avoid the power of his ice-blue eyes staring into her. No, not staring…boring into her soul. Mae crossed her arms to cover herself, feeling as though she were standing naked in front of him. She hated to show her discomfort, but nothing about those eyes made her feel safe. Although they were light colored, a darkness lurked behind them. Knowing he had affected her, he flashed her a crooked smile, then continued to look around.

Shuddering, Mae walked over to her usual corner and sank to the floor. She took deep breaths, shaking the fear the man had stirred up in her. As a chill ran through her, she rubbed her hands up and down her arms to create some friction and heat. She was finally able to get herself together when she felt a little shove on her shoulder. She almost jumped up, ready to fight, wondering if she'd missed the announcement of the Stage Two. But as she looked over, she saw Javeen sitting there, his green eyes calm and relaxed, a soft smile on his face.

"What's up, buttercup?"

Mae shook her head in frustration as she tried to calm her heart once again. He had been trying to talk to her the last two days, and she was trying to keep their conversations as short as possible. She knew that learning more about Javeen would be deadly. This wasn't the place to try to get to know him, and she'd already given him too much information by allowing him to know her name. She still sat next to him but refused to meet his eyes.

"Nothing," she said bluntly as she turned away from him a bit. She should have just gotten up and left, gone to the other side of her cage, but she didn't, and really, she wasn't going to. As much as she hated to admit it, she liked this corner because she liked sitting next to Javeen. He radiated a kind of happiness, a calmness she craved. He was the only one here who didn't seem to be losing his mind—either pacing or mumbling incoherently—and she figured if she stayed close to that energy, perhaps she would absorb some of it.

Javeen gave a heavy sigh. "You really aren't going to give me anything?"

"Why should I?" Mae huffed. "I'm sure you know all about me. I'm a freaking legend in this town. And not the good kind either. Although the villagers have chosen to ignore me, my history is infamous and gossiped about around the market. I know what people say. Every. Last. Word." Her confession stung because she knew it was true. She looked over at Javeen, hoping to see him look uncomfortable, but instead he just shrugged.

"I guess you're right." He turned his head toward her, and gave her a little smile. "But you know nothing about me. So, come on, we've got time. Let me tell you a story."

Mae closed her eyes. "Javeen, this isn't the place."

He pushed her words away with his hand. "Yeah, yeah, but if I don't talk, I'm going to lose it in here. Come on, let me tell you about my family."

Mae glared at him, questioning what he was doing. This was dangerous, and he knew it. Mae knew it too. Even so, he was persistent. "You aren't giving up, are you?" He gave a curt shake of his head, a smile still plastered on his face. Mae threw her hands into the air. "Fine! You got me. Tell me about your family."

Javeen's eyes lit up, and he turned his body toward her. "Really?"

Mae nodded and turned toward him as well, showing she meant it. She could tell he was excited. She felt the corners of her lips curl in a smile as well, but then she pushed them down quickly and tried to look annoyed. Javeen spoke in hushed tones so no one else would hear them. The large room was quiet, and others could hear them if they spoke at a normal volume. But their voices didn't echo too much if they spoke softly. Javeen situated himself to his liking and began his tale.

Mae learned he had a brother and two sisters. She had seen the older sister—Mami, he said her name was—in town. She sometimes came to the market with Javeen and helped with his produce cart. Mae always thought she was pretty, with her dark hair with red accents. Asha was the youngest, only twelve, and Javeen admitted he had been worried she might be called into The Factory, even though legend had it that she was too young to enter through its iron gate. Mae remembered the small girl clinging to Javeen. His brother, Jiro, although he loved him, tended to be strong headed, and Javeen couldn't help blame himself for that. Jiro was still young, and believed that whatever he said was true. Jiro needed to get out, Javeen told her, and see what the real world was like, and maybe get a bit of the bitter truth. He hoped, while he was in here, that Jiro would actually take care of the farm and go to the market so the family could stay afloat.

Mae noticed Javeen was scratching his wrist and, for the first time, saw something tied there. A piece of twine. She found it odd that a man of Javeen's stature would be wearing anything that might be considered jewelry. She leaned in closer and pointed at the twine.

"What's the story behind this beautiful artwork?" She tried to say it with scorn, but she could tell by the way Javeen played with it that he was deeply fond of the simple thing. She quickly gave him a small smile, trying to soften what she'd said.

Javeen's face lit up. "Asha gave it to me." A shadow crossed his once-happy features. "She...she said it was like me, because it holds things together."

Mae's brief happiness withered with him. She wanted to lighten the mood, to bring it back for both of them, so she made a joke. "Oh, so you must carry all the bundles of wheat and corn over your shoulders. No need for ties." She made herself big, bringing her arms out and trying to flex. "She must know you're that strong!" But the darkness didn't disappear from Javeen's face. He looked at her, his deep-green eyes filled with sadness.

"I hold my family together. That's what she told me. And damn it, that little girl was right." He shifted uncomfortably, and Mae wondered if he wanted to talk about whatever was bothering him. She was just about to tell him he didn't have to talk about it. She shouldn't care. She told herself she *didn't* care, but the pained look on Javeen's face made her want to comfort him, and it kept her silent. He continued anyway, without any sort of urging.

"My dad and I were pretty close when I was younger. He was training me to be a merchant like him, but he always told me that if that wasn't what I wanted to do, I just had to let him know. But I *did* want to do it. I wanted to do anything he did because he was my hero. He loved us all, and every night, even when the sales at the market were short, he made sure we had meat on the table. Even if that meant he went without eating it that night. My father was what I thought a man should be, and to this day, I look up to him as what I should strive to be like."

He took a shaky inhalation and continued. "When I was sixteen, my dad went on a hunting trip. He…he never came back. We don't know what happened, but that was when my life changed. I had to stay at home and make sure everything was taken care of—the fields and the family. I couldn't leave, even if I wanted to. I knew Jiro wasn't ready to take over like I had, and I didn't want him to. If anything, I want him to have the life I never can." His expression suddenly turned darker. "But it's my mother who worries me the most. Ever since we gave my father a funeral, she just sits in the corner and rocks in her chair, just getting up to go to the bathroom. She barely eats, and now it's like we aren't her children anymore.

"Jiro has accepted it…that our mother will never be the same again, and so have I. But it kills me to watch Mami and Asha try to get her out of whatever dark place she's in. So, that's where this twine comes in. I don't just provide for the family; I try to bring as much joy as I can into our house. Sometimes I bring my sister flowers, or my brother and I go to the Blood Broth to try and let off some steam that has been building up. Every night I make it mandatory that we sit at the table and talk, trying each night to get them to laugh or smile. If I didn't, my mother's sorrow probably would swallow us whole. If I wasn't around, Jiro already would have run away, and Mami would have been close behind him, dragging Asha with her. I try to bring the kind of happiness my father once brought into our home. But I know I can't compete with him."

Before Mae could stop herself, she heard herself say, "Well, maybe it's because you aren't your father."

Javeen looked up quickly, and Mae was afraid she had offended him, although his eyes were more inquisitive than accusing.

"What I mean is, your father sounds like he was a great person, and I'm not saying you aren't, even though I don't really know you. But you can't be him because you *aren't* him. You…well, you're you. You can't compete with your father because even though you strive to be like him, and you might be in many ways, you'll always be you."

As a moment of clarity passed over Javeen's face, Mae watched as his shoulders relaxed. It seemed as though a huge weight had been lifted off him, one he never even knew he was holding. He must have been carrying it with him ever since he knew his father wasn't coming home. He gave her a weak smile. "Thanks. Maybe I needed to hear that."

"It sounds like you're doing a great job with your family. They'll be so happy when you get out…yes, I said *when*. You're doing all you can, and they seem to appreciate it."

Javeen nodded and kept his gaze on Mae. She wasn't uncomfortable with it now, but a twist in her stomach warned her about the future. She didn't know if Javeen really would get out of here, and she shouldn't have listened to his story. She should have said no and moved to the other side of her cage. But now she knew him and all about his home life. If she got out of here and he didn't, she'd be haunted by the knowledge of his family, about how difficult his life had been outside these iron walls. She now had a connection, even though it was nothing more than a few words, and already she felt those walls she had built to keep her strong begin to crumble.

Mae quickly looked over at the corner of the room, feeling different than she had in years. She had to stop glancing over at Javeen. Her wall had always been equivalent to a fortress, and in a matter of moments, it was breaking. For the first time in a long while, someone was paying attention to her and looking at her. Not just through her. Javeen wanted Mae to talk, but she wasn't sure she was ready. Still, she had this feeling that she wanted to, because Javeen…Javeen wanted to listen. She could see in his eyes that he would be enthralled with whatever she had to say. And she even had the terrible idea that he might try and…comfort or help her. Her breathing quickened as she thought of another person besides her parents, actually caring for her again. She sighed the discomfort away and rested her head on the bars to calm her thoughts.

Suddenly there was a ring, the same familiar ring that had sounded in the courtyard a few days earlier. Mae and Javeen slowly stood, while the others gazed toward the ceiling, where they knew they would hear the dreaded voice.

"Stage Two is about to begin."

Chapter Fourteen:
Javeen

Everyone stood in silence as the voice from above paused. Javeen hadn't realized he was gripping his bars so tightly that his hands were losing circulation. They began to sting as he looked up to the ceiling. Another stage, another challenge. More important, another desperate attempt to stay alive and not become another victim of the furnace.

"In Stage Two, you'll each receive a pill. They'll arrive in your cells within the hour. This will be done in several intervals; therefore, not everyone will receive their pills at the same time."

Not really relevant, Javeen thought, but took it back quickly. Perhaps there was a reason The Factory was giving these instructions. There was reason for everything in this place. He waited to see if he could piece it all together.

"When the pill arrives in your cell, you are to take it," the voice continued. "When you do, the pill will affect you within ten seconds. After taking the pill, you will begin to hallucinate, but soon after, you'll forget that you're in a delusion and believe it is real. During this hallucination, you'll face your greatest fear. When you face your fear, there will be some sort of aspect that will allow you to recall that the event occurring is not in fact real. If you find this clue, you'll be brought back to reality, back to your cell. However, if you can't help yourself and allow the hallucination to overtake you, the pill will administer a lethal poison to your heart."

"Pretty blunt," Javeen muttered.

"Best of luck," the voice said, a little too happily for Javeen's taste, and with a click, she was gone.

No one was panicking this time around, at least not that Javeen could see. There was a tension, though, and people were clearly worried about what was to come, but he knew how they were feeling because he was feeling the same way. There was a lighter fear about this stage and for a reason. These people in these cells, these cages, believed they could control their own fates. They could try to find the clue that would release them back to safety, and no one else could control that. Javeen felt a sense of calm knowing that he would be in charge of what would unfold next.

In that moment, he glanced at Mae. It appeared that a stillness had come over her as well. Although he saw a slight fear in her eyes, she seemed, more than anyone else, confident that she would make it out. Javeen could only imagine why. She was always alone, and immersing herself in a challenge in which she wouldn't have to worry about the people around her, where she could stay invisible, would bring her a sense of empowerment. Javeen walked back to their corner, as he now called it, and called her over.

"Hey, Pox Face." This time he said it with a smile, and Mae gave him a small one back. "Come over here."

"Why do I always have to come to you?" she asked, staring at him, but Javeen noticed it was much more calculating this time. Stage Two had still put her on edge somewhat, and she was back to putting up that wall to protect herself from others.

"Please come over," he said, giving her a pout. Mae's eyes rolled, but he was happy to see that she was shuffling her way over. When she reached the edge of her cell, she leaned against the bars as one would lean against a doorframe.

"What do you want, Farmer?" She tried to say it as a jab; still, Javeen knew it would become their little joke. Pox Face and The Farmer. It had a good ring to it. Maybe those would be their nicknames in town…if they got out. He shook that thought out of his head.

"I need to tell you something. I don't know how long we have before this thing starts up."

"Any minute, it sounds like," Mae said, and as she did, a few lights in some cells grew brighter. The people inside them all turned to see a table rising up from where their food usually came from. Stage Two really was starting.

Javeen's heart raced, and he grabbed Mae's arm frantically. He didn't mean for it to come off as desperate, but did it really matter at this point? His cell could be next, and who knew if he'd be able to tell the difference between his mind's creation and reality. Mae looked at his hand then fiercely at him. "What do you want?" she hissed, her face now falling. The tension seemed to be rising between them.

"I want you to know we're getting out of here," Javeen said. Although he was shaking inside, his voice was strong and direct.

"Don't do that. Don't you dare. You can't promise me that. You can't promise me anything like that. So just don't."

Javeen shook his head. "Not in this stage, I can't. But I can with anything after that. Mae, if we work together—"

"This isn't a place *to work together*, Javeen."

"*If we work together…*" he nearly yelled, then brought his voice back down to a whisper. "Then we can get out of here." He gave her arm a squeeze, letting her know he was telling the truth. "At the very least, I can promise you I'll try my best."

The screams began, breaking their silence, and now Javeen understood why The Factory was giving out pills at different times: to terrify those who didn't have theirs yet. While he waited for Mae to reply, they winced at the deafening shrieks of those around them who were facing their worst fears. Out of the corner of his eye, Javeen saw bodies writhing around, others rocking back and forth. He wondered how long it would be before he felt the heat of the furnace again. Once more he looked at Mae.

Mae looked at him too, her eyes still wary but not untrusting. *How long before she has faith in me?* he asked himself. Maybe it wasn't that she couldn't trust him. Perhaps Mae couldn't trust anyone; maybe it was just in her nature. But finally, her expression softened, and she said, "Fine. I'll agree…to whatever crazy alliance you just thought of."

Javeen smiled and let go of her hands. "Not an alliance, but a determination to get our asses out of here."

Mae smirked. "That's called an alliance, idiot."

Javeen was about to say something witty when his room became bright. He looked around his cage, knowing a table would soon be rising and he would have to face his greatest fear. What that fear was, he wasn't sure, but he wasn't looking forward to finding out. He heard a hydraulic noise but didn't see a table rising from the floor. It reminded him of the noise that Javeen had heard outside when the doors had revealed themselves. When the sound stopped, he realized why the table that would hold his pill hadn't appeared.

The table wasn't rising in his cell. The light was in Mae's cell, and a table had brought her pill.

Chapter Fifteen:
Mae

She stared at the ebony table that held the pill. The table had a glow to it, as the bright light bounced off its dark finish. Mae wondered what might happen if she didn't take it, if she just left it sitting there. But she wouldn't dare. If she stood there and did nothing, The Factory probably would suck her into the furnace right then. No, she had to do this. With one last look at Javeen, she said, "If I get out, I'm holding you to your promise."

He gave her a quick nod. "I know you will." His green eyes were still striking, calming her somewhat. "But you'd better make it out. Be smart, Mae."

She looked back at the table and decided it was time to get this hell over with. *It's just my own min*d, she told herself. *All I have to do is focus.* On the table a red pill lay in a small paper container. Next to it was a glass with just enough water to wash the capsule down. Taking a deep breath, Mae picked up the pill and water glass and threw it back.

At first, she felt nothing. She glanced at Javeen, who was still standing there, looking to make sure she was all right. Mae gave him a shrug to tell him that she felt fine, that maybe the pill wouldn't work on her. But slowly Javeen began to melt away, the walls of her cells dissolving as other colors made their way into her vision. At first it was a mixture of browns, greens, and blues, but slowly the picture began to come together. After a few more hard blinks, trying to adjust her eyesight, Mae saw she was standing in front of her house on a lovely spring day.

Mae was confused. The house was similar to the one she was familiar with, and still run-down, but it wasn't as dilapidated as it had been when she'd left it a few days ago. The roof no longer had holes, and the outside panels were clean and healthy looking wood. The garden looked a little unruly, but it was still maintained. The old oak that had fallen over in a summer storm the previous year was standing tall, its new leaves swaying in the soft wind. The scent of lilacs from the nearby meadow breezed past her.

It was a beautiful scene, something she was happy to be a part of. The Factory must have been a dream, some sort of long-lasting nightmare that had been in her mind for no reason. Mae was convinced she had just fallen asleep in the meadow and dreamt the whole thing. This was clearly her life and her home, not that horrid memory. Inhaling the wonderful sweetness of the air around her, she hurried to her house, feeling a lightness in her step, knowing everything would be all right. She reached her door, the thick wood smooth under her fingers, and turned the iron doorknob.

The room inside was filled with light, with all the windows open, letting in the breeze. It was the brightest her house had looked in years, and a sense of pride ran through her. This was the house she knew—the clean, relaxing, homey feeling that made her want to return at night. The smell of cinnamon filled her nose, replacing the scent of the flowers outside, and even more warmth flooded through her. When she took a step into the house, however, her heart dropped when she saw what was perched next to the fireplace.

Two coffins.

She remembered them, the simple oak and walnut coffins with cream-colored bows and ribbons draped on the side. The tops were open, and Mae saw the name carved inside each lid: Mae Fyez. She had carved her name into the coffins in case her parents opened their eyes in the afterworld; then the first thing they would see was her name. That way they would never forget her. Slowly, ever so slowly, Mae walked between the two coffins and peered inside.

Emi Fyez looked beautiful and healthy, more than she had ever looked before her death. Her blond hair was flowing at her sides, curled in its natural way. Her lips were quite serious, in a straight line, which was nothing like her mother at all. She was always smiling, making sure her beam of light was contagious. Mae then turned to the next coffin and looked at Filip, his sharp distinctive chin covered in a dark beard. There were no bags under his eyes from the illness that had once taken over his body, and just like her mother, he looked healthier than ever. His large calloused hands were crossed over his chest, reminding Mae of his years of hard work. She eased her hand into the coffin to touch his skin, to remember him one last time.

That was when his eyes opened.

Mae jumped back, knocking into her mother's coffin. She turned to steady it, only to see that her mother was sitting upright, staring right at her. Mae let out a horrified scream as she backed away from her parents, who were now both climbing out of their caskets.

All the warmth left her body as fear settled in fast. She had to run to the door, but just as she turned, she saw it slam shut, shaking the house. There was a click from the outside, indicating the lock had latched. That was when Mae knew deep in her heart there wasn't a way to leave. The room turned dark, as if a storm were headed their way, and wind blew furiously into the house, sending Mae's braids flying in all directions. She felt as though a twister were forming right inside her house.

When she turned back, her parents were slowly moving toward her, their faces stern and angry. Her father pointed a finger at her, a now bony finger, one that shook uncontrollably.

"You did this," he said, his voice louder than it had ever been when she was a child. "You did this to us."

Her mother nodded, her face now full of sorrow and pain. "Mae, why? Why did you let us die?"

Mae backed up to the wall, not realizing she had cornered herself in. She was too upset by her parents' words. She tried to find her voice but was almost sure she had lost it. Her parents were getting closer, asking the same thing again and again. Mae then heard herself cry out, "I tried. Please know, please! Mama,

Papa I tried. But no one came. I tried…" Teardrops fell onto her open palms. Unaware that she had been weeping, she moved her hands to her face to find that it was soaked.

"You didn't try hard enough," her father bellowed, his voice shaking the room. As her parents moved in closer, their healthy figures began to waste away. Their cheeks become hollow, and their eyes darkened with the shadows of illness. Their once pure, soft skin was infested with blisters, some oozing puss almost immediately. Her mother's ears bled, staining her golden hair, while her father's suit shrugged off his shoulders, and his bones started to poke out.

"You could have made them come, Mae. You should have dragged the doctors to us, told them they had no choice!" her mother wailed, a clotted noise coming from deep within her throat. Mae knew that noise, and her mother began to cough violently, her frail body shaking each time. Still she walked toward her daughter, her husband in tow.

They were almost in front of Mae now, and she tried to push herself deeper into the wall. She felt the wall panels under her skin begin to shrivel up from years of neglect, and she heard the cracking of the structure around her. Even the house was starting to take its present form, a home that was falling apart, just like Mae was in this moment. She kept ramming her body into the wall, hoping the rot would allow her to break free. Perhaps the termites had done enough damage for her to get out. But it stayed firm as she threw herself into it multiple times.

"You murdered us," her father screamed, making Mae cover her ears and fall to the floor.

"No!" she yelled, rocking back and forth. "No! I didn't! I promise…" Although their shoes were right in front of her now, she no longer worried what would happen if they got to her. Whatever they might do wasn't worse than knowing they knew her dark secret. Her father had said what Mae always had known: she had killed her parents by not trying hard enough to save them.

"I never thought my daughter would be the reason I died," her mother whispered, standing right above her. As she coughed again, blood spilled from her lips. It continued to flow, and Mae felt the flecks splash onto her face as her mother coughed once more. She wiped them away, along with the tears, and watched as the blood flowed down her mother's beautiful yellow dress.

Her yellow dress…

This place isn't real, Mae suddenly realized. It never was. She remembered now that she was supposed to be looking for something, and this was her clue. Her mother never had owned a yellow dress. She had said that in all her years, she'd never let that color touch her skin. The only yellow she needed was from the golden waves of her hair. Once, her father had bought a yellow scarf and tried to convince her to wear it, but she had demanded that he take it back to the shop. "Yellow isn't my color," she'd told her husband, who had looked insulted, but he forgave her, as he always did.

This wasn't real. This whole thing wasn't real. Mae stood up forcefully and pushed herself toward her parents, facing her father straight on while her mother loomed close.

"You aren't real," Mae said, her voice shaking, and her father stopped in his place, tilting his head slightly to the side. Her mother also stopped moving toward her. Mae looked at both of them, a smile on her face as she realized the truth of the matter. "You aren't real!" she screamed in delight, and in an instant, they were gone.

The house and everything around her exploded, and Mae felt as though she'd been ripped back by the collar of her shirt. She was moving quickly, the world around her spinning in different directions. Then everything stopped suddenly, and she found herself on all fours, back in her cell.

She was breathing heavily, her shoulders rising and falling as she tried to calm herself. *None of this was real*, she told herself. *None of it. It was all a lie. Breathe.* After making it through that horrible hallucination, she was actually glad to be back in The Factory. If she hadn't been completely winded, she might have even kissed the ground. Never in her life did she think she would have to face that deep fear, one that had lingered within her, and now that she was back in her cell, she never wanted to go through it again.

"Mae!" she heard, and turned her face to see Javeen. He looked worried as he clutched the bars of his cell tightly. Mae wondered if he'd been shaking them.

"How long was I gone?" she asked, surprised that her voice was so hoarse. Sweat dripped off her chest and forehead as she crawled to the corner, where sat back, finally catching her breath.

"Not even four minutes."

Mae nodded and wondered what she had been like in that state. She looked at Javeen, who seemed shaken up. He must have witnessed whatever fit she had gone through, and it wasn't pretty. Javeen looked concerned, as if Mae had harmed herself. She scanned her body and noticed she had a few fingernail marks on her hands, and her hands were slightly painful as well. Clearly Javeen hadn't taken his pill yet, and after enduring her own hallucination, Mae worried about him. This wasn't a physical challenge, something he might excel at. This was all mental. *Will Javeen be strong enough for this?* she wondered.

There was another loud hydraulic noise, and Javeen's cell grew bright. Mae knew that sound and felt a tug in her heart and stomach. It was Javeen's turn to take the pill.

They quickly looked at each other, and Mae gave him a half smile. "Get through this, Farmer. I can't sass anyone else here without getting killed."

He winked at her as he walked over to the table. "Okay, I'll do it for you, Pox Face."

Chapter Sixteen:
Javeen

Standing in front of his table, Javeen worried what would happen when he took the pill. He wasn't certain what his greatest fear was, but after hearing and seeing Mae scream—and the tears spilling from her eyes—he definitely didn't want to know. But he did know he had to keep his head together and try to find something in the hallucination that didn't fit. If he kept his wits about him, he could get out. Javeen couldn't let this dream world overtake him and deliver him to the furnace. With a shaky hand, he picked up the pill and swallowed it.

What happened next was abrupt, and nothing Javeen could have prepared himself for. There he was in his cell, and then, in a moment, the world spun around him, quickly and violently. The bars surrounding him vanished, and he felt as though he were in the middle of a horrible twisting storm; even his hair was moving around his ears. Wind rushed through his ears, blocking out any other sound. As he wondered how long he would be stuck in this spinning agony, it all stopped. With a jolt, Javeen staggered into his hallucination and fell to his knees.

After his eyes had adjusted, he saw that his hands were pressed against newly tilled earth. The smell of the beginning of spring filled his nostrils. The scent of flowers coming to bloom, fresh air that somehow had a hint of rain in it, even the dew that rested on the early morning plant leaves. The odors brought a sense of relief. Right away he knew the soil he had landed in and grabbed a handful of the dark, rich dirt. Around him were his fields, and although they weren't looking their finest, they were still quite healthy, the majority of the plants green, their leaves flowing in the wind. Although the sky was gray, the sun was trying to peek through the clouds as they passed over it. Javeen looked up to see his wooden house in the distance, the same old structure with the rickety porch and slightly slanted windows that always infuriated his father. He felt relieved as he inhaled and exhaled deeply, letting all worries and fear cascade from him. Javeen was home. The nightmare he had been imagined was gone. He was safe now.

Standing up, Javeen brushed the dirt off the knees of his pants and clapped it off his hands. He took in the sweet aroma of the crisp air and the smell of manure and dirt mixed in with it. Although many might have found this scent too strong for their taste, Javeen couldn't help smile. It was a smell he had grown up with, and no matter how putrid the manure was, even in the heat of the summer, it always brought him home. He breathed deeply and headed toward the house, beaming the entire way.

To the side of the house stood his cart. Delight swelled through him, as it was full of fruits and vegetables. Looking up at the sun, he calculated that it was about seven in morning. That meant either Jiro or Mami was going to the market, even when he wasn't there. Although they should have already been there, Javeen felt touched that even in his absence, his brother and sister were trying to keep everything as normal as possible. How surprised they would be when he walked into the house, unharmed and alive. Javeen had made it through The Factory without even a scratch. He couldn't even recall what had happened, but that didn't matter; it was all over now. He jumped up on the porch, which moaned under his weight, but he didn't care. He was home.

With a wide swing of the door, he stepped in as loudly as he could. "I'm home!" he called out, and waited for echoing screams or heads popping out from around corners. Javeen knew Asha would be the first to race over to him, followed by Mami. They would both cry, of course. And Jiro would probably bound in behind them, his goofy smile lit up, and give his brother a bear hug. His siblings would him close and cry, remembering how they'd almost lost their oldest brother, but then rejoice that he was home. It was what Javeen was expecting, but the moment passed and still there was silence.

"Hello?" he said, quieter this time, slowly walking deeper into the house. Something didn't feel right. The cart was out front, which meant at least one of his siblings was in the house. Asha stayed home every day to take care of their mother, so she had to be home. But everything was completely silent. No clang of dishes being washed, no giggles from one of the girls. Not even a creak of footsteps from the small upstairs quarters Javeen and Jiro shared. He was just about to look in the loft where Mami and Asha slept, wondering if perhaps sleep had gotten the better of them today, when a dark, distant-sounding voice came from behind him.

"I didn't know you'd be returning so soon."

Javeen froze as a chill shot up his spine. That voice. It had been years since he had heard it. His mind strained, trying to remember when it had last drifted through his ears, but it was so long ago. Almost six years, if he was correct. Back then, the voice had been happy, full of life. Not the way it was speaking now. Now it was haunted, off in a different world. He turned slowly and whispered, "Mama?" before taking a step toward her.

There his mother stood, her small figure hunched over. Her diluted reddish brown hair was disheveled, her face sullen and gray, her eyes glazed over. Javeen tried to take in this woman as his mother, but he couldn't see her. She looked as if something evil had possessed her as a shadow passed over her face. She stared at him in confusion, as if he were a figment of her imagination, not as though she were seeing the son she thought might never return. But that wasn't what made Javeen halt in mid-step.

It was the bloody hatchet in her hand.

Silently she stood there, the weight of the weapon pulling her shoulders down. She was breathing heavily, her head down. As Javeen followed her gaze downward, he realized her entire outfit was covered in blood. When he looked down at the hem of her dress, he mustered all his willpower not to shout in horror. For that was when Javeen saw the three bodies on the floor.

Jiro was on his stomach, his dark hair covering his face, his back littered with slices and deep wounds, blood pooling beneath him. Mami was lying chest up, and though Javeen couldn't see her face, as it was turned toward the wall, her front was blooming with blood. However, it was Asha who made his stomach curl in terror and guilt. Her little body was riddled with cuts, the deepest at her throat, her white dress stained a rusty red. Her large green eyes, wide open and staring right at him, made his blood freeze. They looked as if they were pleading for Javeen to save her.

Javeen glared at his mother, his voice shaky. "Why?"

"I didn't want them anymore," she said simply. "They were a problem."

"They're your family!" Javeen bellowed, his fist tightening, his anger and sorrow rising. "They took care of you. They watched over you when you were sick."

His mother shrugged, as though she had thrown out an old dress she didn't like. "I didn't want to look at them anymore. They were too happy."

Javeen moved toward them, wanting to hold them and cry in sorrow, when suddenly his mother hoisted up the hatchet, the sharp bloody edge near her face. He stopped in his tracks as her glassy eyes fell on him. As he realized what was about to happen, fear overtook his need to embrace his dead siblings, and he tried to figure out his next moves.

His mother took a step toward him. "You were gone. You left them alone. You weren't here to protect them. And now you're back…." She looked at the hatchet and sighed. "My son, you picked the wrong time to come home."

It all happened so suddenly. Javeen's mother sprinted toward him, faster than he thought was possible for her. Considering all the years she'd spent in that damn chair, he thought her body would be frail, but she moved as quickly. Luckily, Javeen ducked as she swung at him, feeling the rush of the blade past his left shoulder. He ran toward the kitchen, knowing there would be some sort protection there; perhaps he could make it out the back door. As he dashed out of the room, his mother shouted, almost jeering, "Get back here, Javeen! You need to be with your siblings."

As Javeen raced into the kitchen, he knew his mother was too fast—no way would he reach the door in time. He frantically looked around the room, searching for anything he could use as a weapon. He had to defend himself. His mother had gone insane and no longer could live. Even if he did want her to, she was trying to kill him. Javeen saw the long bread knife on the counter, grabbed it, and turned. He jumped back, hitting the counter hard with his back, as his mother was now standing in front of him.

She gave him a sneer when she saw the knife in his hand. "Going to kill me? I figured this would happen. Been waiting a while to do that, haven't you?" She raised the hatchet and sighed. "Not if I kill you first."

Javeen tightened his grip on knife, ready to plunge it deep within his mother's belly. He felt an ache, a severe pain in his heart, as he prepared himself for the crime he was about to commit. It was the pain of knowing he was taking his own mother's life; he was sure of it. He looked at her one last time and then at the weapon she was wielding. That was when he noticed the silver handle of the hatchet. Letting the knife hit the floor, he stood straighter, no longer in a defensive position. He creased his eyebrows, the pain lifting from his chest.

"We don't have a silver-handled hatchet," he whispered.

His mother stopped mid-swing and looked at him, her face filled with horror. "What are you talking about?" she gasped.

"Our hatchet has a wooden handle," he said with a smirk. "We don't own one with a silver handle."

In a moment, everything around him changed. His mother let out a terrifying shriek, and with a pop, she disappeared. Javeen peered into the main room, and with another bang, his siblings' bodies vanished. The house began to get sucked into a vortex around him, and again Javeen was in some sort of microburst of a storm. He felt his body swirl, his stomach swishing its contents around, his eyes not knowing where to look as the area around him moved quickly. Then, with one more push, he saw the black stone floor of his cell under his hands, the coldness of it bringing him back to reality. When he looked up and saw the bars, he knew he was back in The Factory.

Mae was sitting where she had been before, staring at him with worried eyes. She moved toward the bars and began to open her mouth, but Javeen held his hand up.

Before he could even ask how long he'd been out for, an unpleasant feeling surged through his body. Everything he had seen had been too much for him. Along with the movement at the end of his hallucination, he couldn't keep it in anymore. He pushed himself up, ran to the opposite corner of the cage, grabbed the clean bucket that was sitting there, and threw up whatever was left in his stomach.

Chapter Seventeen:
<u>Javeen</u>

Javeen crawled back over to their corner, leaning against the icy bars, trying to cool the back of his neck. He felt as though he had a fever and was still trembling. He tried to shake the images from his mind but couldn't. The bloody hatchet, the bodies on the floor, his mother's glazed-over eyes—they wouldn't escape his head. They were permanent images, and even if he did see his siblings again, he was sure those hallucinations would remain. He looked up and saw that Mae was sitting with him.

"About four minutes," she said, and there the conversation ended.

The screams around them didn't stop, and Javeen shut his eyes hard as he tried to drown them out. People were sobbing and yelling through gritted teeth; he heard a few thuds and gasps and knew that some of them had fallen and weren't getting back up. Then he saw the flash under his eyelids as the furnace took the bodies it needed. When he opened them, Mae was flinching as another body fell into the heat and light. He wanted to reach out to calm her, but he stayed still, his body not reacting to anything around him.

Finally, he looked over, knowing conversation would distract from the others who hadn't gotten their pills yet. There were only a few, but the noises echoing through the room were so unsettling. Mae looked forward, not meeting Javeen's gaze, her expression stern and stony. He wasn't sure she would tell him, but still he asked, "What did you see?"

"None of your business," she spat.

He had expected it to be like this. Whatever she'd seen must have been terrible. After all, he never would have imagined he'd get the vision The Factory had given him. Yet it was still there, burning in his mind. Mae clearly didn't want to talk about whatever she had seen, and he respected that. It was personal, after all. But he couldn't hold it in anymore. He had to tell her what he had seen; maybe it would alleviate his pain and sorrow. Perhaps his mind would free itself of the images.

"My mom killed my family," Javeen said, his voice shaky.

Mae's head tilted in his direction, but she didn't say anything. Still he went on.

"She was standing over my siblings' bodies with a hatchet. She said she didn't want to see them anymore. They were too happy for her." He took a gulp as he realized what his true fear was. "My mother told me I wasn't there to protect them."

The screams continued as they sat there. The two of them rested a little longer, and then Javeen continued, looking at his feet. "She came after me. Said I shouldn't have come home and I should have been with them. She was trying to kill me too. I grabbed a knife from the kitchen, and I was about to stab her, to end it all. I didn't want to, though. I could feel it inside me. My heart, it hurt so much…" He paused, thinking about that moment. It really did hurt, in a painful way, not in a sorrowful way, as he had originally thought. It was a heavy feeling that he'd never felt before, even when his father had vanished. His head shot up as he finally understood.

It was Mae who said it. "The pill was going to kill you if you stabbed her." Her voice was hollow as she realized how close she had been to losing her newfound alliance.

Javeen nodded, shaking harder. He had been so close to death without knowing it. Was he truly that naïve? He thought he was feeling pain for almost killing his mother, when in fact he was in pain because he was killing himself without even knowing it. Javeen hit his head against the bars, letting the physical pain sink in with everything else he was feeling right now. He was truly pathetic, he thought, and almost too weak to pass Stage Two.

"How did you know?" Mae asked quietly.

"The hatchet," Javeen said. "The handle was made of silver. Not even the richest merchant in town could own a silver hatchet."

Mad nodded and waited. She knew Javeen had more to say, but she didn't want to push him, and he appreciated that. So, slowly, he continued. "I didn't know what my greatest fear would be when I went under, but I've figured it out. I was afraid that if I wasn't there for my siblings, I would destroy my family." Rubbing his nose with his thumb and index finger, he shut his eyes as tightly as he could. "I just didn't know how bad it might get if I weren't there. She could kill them."

"That would never happen."

Javeen's gaze snapped over at Mae, who was now looking in his direction. Her eyes were hard but not angry. They seemed as though they were looking at her so he would understand what she was about to say.

"Just hear me out," she continued. "Those pills were supposed to show us our worst fears. They dug deep and made sure we were afraid of the most terrible thing that could happen. That doesn't mean it will happen. If fact, I'm sure it won't. Your mother would never do anything like that. And even if she wanted to, she already would have done it by now." She nodded to herself, as if agreeing with what she was about to say. "Like you first said, your fear is that your family will fall apart if you aren't there. Not that your mother will kill them."

Javeen was about to argue with her, but after thinking it over, he realized his mother wouldn't kill her children. Javeen had left them plenty of times with her, and if she had wanted them gone, she would have taken those moments to do it. He felt a sense of relief. Mae was right. The Factory wanted him to terrify him so that he might die. He nodded and inhaled deeply, his shaking finally subsiding.

"Mine was that my parents called me a murderer," Mae said.

Javeen turned his head toward her. "What?"

She told him the whole thing, about the coffins and her parents lumbering toward her, telling her she had killed them. She described the coughing and the blood and finally her realization that her mother would never wear a yellow dress. As she told the story, she looked at the floor, refusing to make eye contact with him. When she was done, she took a heavy sigh, and Javeen realized she actually believed what they had said.

"Mae, you do realize that's a bunch of bullshit, right?"

Mae glanced over, and he could tell she was both relieved and confused. "You don't understand. I don't think anyone could. When the doctors and healers pushed me away, I didn't try. I just walked away, letting my parents get sicker with every step I took. I could have tried harder. I could have made someone come see them, but I didn't." Her head sank lower as she whispered, "Maybe I did let them die."

Javeen shook his head. "Mae, come on. I remember when all this happened. I was just starting in the market by myself. You went to every single medicine person on that damn street, pleading with them to just look at your parents. Anyone who saw you in town knew how hard you were trying to save them. No way could anyone say you didn't try to help them. That's why the town doesn't..." He paused, realizing what he was going to tell her the truth.

"That's why they can't look at me," Mae finished for him.

"Exactly. It wasn't you who let them die. It was the town. They pushed them away, and they didn't even try to help. I remember the doctors' wives talking about how guilty they felt. And yet they still said it was a good thing no one went to see your parents, so the disease wouldn't spread again. You were the only one who cared. Remember, The Factory showed you your worst fear. It's only a fear, and often our fears aren't true. And yours definitely isn't."

Mae nodded and whispered, "Thank you. No one has been willing to tell me that. Actually, no one has been too keen on telling me anything for the last five years."

After the last of the screams ended, Mae tugged Javeen's shoulder. It was time to count and see how many people remained after Stage Two. They looked around and saw that only five people hadn't been able to figure out the hint. Forty remained now. As they gazed around the room, Mae stopped and nodded at the scar-faced girl.

"We need her on our side," Mae said.

Javeen furrowed his brow. "What?" Why would Mae want to forge a connection with anyone else? Making one with him was hard enough for her; he could see that. Seeing she was serious about the proposition, he decided to press. "And *why* do you think that?"

"She went under after right after you did. I watched her the whole time. When you were in your trance, you were yelling and screaming. Slamming your fists on the ground so hard, I thought your hands would break. There was a second you actually hit your head against the floor, and yelled so loudly that I thought you were dying."

Javeen remembered how Mae had acted. Her screams were a mix of shrieks and sobs. She was shaking, yelling things Javeen couldn't understand. At one point, it looked like she was convulsing. She clawed at the floor and yelled for someone, anyone to save her. He wanted to go in and be that hero; that was why he had been at the bars when she had come out of her trance. To be as close as he could to protect her. Still he shook his head. "What does that have to do with her?"

Mae looked again at the girl and jerked her head back toward Javeen. "She didn't scream. Not once. She just sat there in her cell; she wasn't on all fours like everyone else. There were tears—I could see them from the light in her cell—and she was muttering to herself, but she didn't make any noise beside that." She moved in closer to him and whispered, "She was out in less than two minutes."

Javeen shook his head. No way could that girl have gotten out so quickly. It had taken him forever to figure it out, and some of the others had been under for five or six minutes. Still, as he glanced at her, he realized she looked solid, mentally and physically, as if nothing had phased her. He wasn't sure how he felt about making any kind of alliance with her.

"Whenever we get out of these cells, I'm getting near her. I want to see what she's about," Mae said, looking deep into his eyes, perhaps for his approval. Even so, she was determined.

Slowly Javeen nodded, but under his breath, he muttered, "Just be careful."

A few moments later, their bedrolls came up, and the two went to their respective spots. Whoever was in charge of The Factory liked things to be clean, because as they were talking, Javeen's soiled bin had been removed, replaced by a new bucket. He carried his bed to their corner, as did Mae, and closed his eyes, hoping this sleep would be one in which he remembered nothing.

***

Dreams didn't keep Javeen awake; rather it was the mutters and screams from those around him. Still he was able to get a better sleep than he'd expected, though the image of his mother's bloody hatchet popped up every now and them, jolting him from his sleep in a deep sweat. Even so, he was able to put his head back down. Soon enough the lights came back on, telling him and the rest of the survivors it was time to wake up.

As he was eating breakfast—oatmeal with some toast—Mae was rubbing her eyes. It didn't look like she'd gotten any sleep, and Javeen wondered if perhaps she was still haunted by thoughts of her parents. What she had told him sounded terrifying, and he knew that if he had seen it, the memory might haunt him as well. He munched on his toast as she gave him a weak wave. Although it wasn't a grand gesture, Javeen considered it a major breakthrough. Her walls of distrust were to beginning to crumble, which was exactly what they needed in order to escape this hell.

Light suddenly filled the entire room, not just the cells. Everyone stood and waited for the familiar ping. Once more, the too-cheery female voice came on, signaling what they all already knew.

"Good morning. Please prepare for Stage Three."

Chapter Eighteen:
Mae

"The rules of Stage Three are quite simple and are as follows. Momentarily, forty levers will appear, and your cages will rise. You are to select one of these levers. If you choose the correct one, your cage will reappear." There was a pause, and Mae wondered if the woman would tell them what they already knew. What would happen to those who didn't choose the right lever. But she continued, passing over that crucial detail.

"Only thirty levers are correct. Therefore, you must choose wisely. Your cages will recede into the ceiling after I'm finished speaking, and once everyone is free, you must make your way to the center of the room. From there, Stage Three will begin. Best of luck to all of you." And then there was a click.

Mae hated when that woman, whoever she was, wished them luck. That woman knew what was about to happen. Ten people were going to die, and everyone would be able to see who they were this time, as they'd all be wide-awake. Mae suddenly regretted having looked at all the faces in the room. By the end of this, she would know who hadn't made it.

But first she had to be live. *Survive first; grieve later*, she told herself.

Once again, her stomach twisted as the bars of the cages receded into the ceiling. This was a game of chance, just like the doors in Stage One had been. But this time, Mae wasn't sure she had enough time to figure out what kind of trick The Factory had in store for them. As she glanced around the room, she noticed many puzzled looks. Then again, others, like the man with the icy eyes, wore an expression of sheer determination. Mae was worried what he might do if she tried to take the lever he wanted.

The bars were now up to her shoulders, and she looked at Javeen. Maybe he would protect her. Maybe. That was what he had promised only yesterday. Still, she had a feeling that he'd do anything to save himself and get out of here in order to be with his family. She saw how the last stage had rattled him to the bone, and she wondered whether he really meant to keep her safe or if that image of his mother holding a hatchet would make him forget all about her. Javeen glanced at her and gave her a thumbs-up. She didn't know exactly what that meant, but she returned the gesture anyway.

When the bars were gone, they walked toward the center of the room. Javeen got close, his shoulders almost touching Mae's, and whispered, "Game of chance."

Mae shook her head. "No. There's has to be something. Some sort of clue. Like the doors and the heat on the ground. We just have to keep our wits about us." She paused for a moment then said, "If I figure it out, you'll know."

Deep within, she told herself she didn't want to help him, even though she had promised to. What did she owe to him? But for some reason she'd said she was going to help him, and she felt she would keep that promise. Was it because they'd spent so much time together these past few days? But that was involuntary. Or maybe it was because she had admitted her greatest fear to him, something she had done with no one. Perhaps it was something else, something she couldn't figure out, at least not now. Mae couldn't say what it was. All she knew was that she had promised him help, and for now, she would have to stick to that.

Javeen nodded, but as they moved into the crowd, everyone began to push, separating the two of them. Everyone was clustered together, and soon Mae felt as though being in the middle of the crowd wasn't the best idea. She tried to elbow her way out, but she was surrounded on all sides. A bit of dread reached her as she was pushed deeper, almost to the center of the throng. How would she get to the levers first if she was stuck in this mob? She might even get one of the last ones, a doomed one. Then she heard the smack of metal hitting the ground, and the hydraulic noise they'd grown accustomed to. Over one man's shoulder, Mae saw the levers lock into place in the floor.

Everyone stood waiting for the signal, and then the cheery female voice said, "Begin."

Once the crowd had dispersed, Mae saw that the levers were scattered throughout the room in a ragged circle. Looking around frantically, she spotted a lever to her left and ran for it.

She was gaining on it, her hand almost clasped on the deep-orange handle, when someone shoved her to the ground. A large man—the first one called to enter The Factory, she now remembered—had thrown his shoulder into her. She landed on her back, her head spinning from the impact. She quickly glanced up at him, afraid he might just kill her. Instead, he gave her a weak but mean sneer as he pulled the lever.

A large square tile beneath him opened up, and suddenly he was screaming. As a blazing heat emerged from the hole in the floor, Mae watched as gravity took his hulking figure into the flames. The man's cries still echoed as others raced past her. Still on the ground, Mae pushed herself away and watched as the tile closed and the lever disappeared into the floor.

Quickly she jumped up, knowing she had no time to worry about the man or even feel angry toward him for pushing her over. In fact, she was almost grateful, as that could have been her falling below. She looked at the other levers around her. *There has to be something about them*, she told herself. The lever she almost pulled was deep orange…but weren't they all? Suddenly she saw a flash of white hair. Mae watched as the prostitute from town ran and grabbed a lever and heaved it toward her. When she let go, the red handle disappeared as a cage closed in around her. That was when Mae figured it out.

Red handles meant safety. The orange ones brought you into the flames.

This wasn't just a game of chance or a physical challenge; this was a mental challenge. The two colors were so similar. One would only notice if they stopped and looked at them. But in their state of panic, few people seemed to have the energy or mental ability to examine the color of the handles. In their minds, this was a survival game, all based on chance.

Mae looked around carefully, trying not to show that she understood. She tried to appear confused as she circled the room. That was when she caught sight of the scar-faced girl running toward a red lever close to where the prostitute was. However, Mae noticed that another person, Ripley, was stumbling closer to it than the redhead. Mae watched in awe as the girl, showing no fear, took four large strides toward the staggering man. She advanced on him and reached for the lever, but the feeble old man pushed her back. Not hard, but enough to make an impact. The girl rolled her typically intense eyes, then planted her foot and swung her fist at him. Mae's eyes widened as the old man's head turned for a second before he hit the ground. With a kick to push his body over, the redhead pulled the lever and a cage formed around her. In one last moment, as the man got up and swayed toward another red lever, Scarface spat on him.

Thankful once more that she wasn't anywhere near that girl, Mae tried to shake off what she just saw and questioned what else she might be capable of. *Stop it! This isn't the time!* she reprimanded herself. She looked around the circular room for another red lever. As she turned, she saw one right next to the cage Scarface was in, making her stomach drop slightly. *Just my luck*, she thought. But if Mae was right about the colors, then maybe she'd have a chance to talk to the girl within the safe confines of a cage. With a deep inhalation, she slowly maneuvered toward it, hoping no one would notice, then sprang forward. Her feet pushed hard, the leather slipping a few times on the smooth tile floor. Still she was able to regain her balance and felt her heart leap as the red handle became clearer to her.

Suddenly a lanky teen, a few years younger than her, jumped in front of her, heading for the same lever. Mae drove harder, but the teen's legs were longer than hers. If she didn't take drastic measures, she wouldn't reach her goal. Easing her way to the side of him, Mae began to bow out, knowing what she was about to do was either a stroke of genius or the dumbest—and last— thing she'd ever do.

Just as the boy was taking his last strides, Mae made a final advance forward, pushing her legs hard, then quickly drew her body back and let her feet slide in front of her. She slid effortlessly in front of him, her skintight pants gliding on the tile, and quickly propped herself up. With two hands, she pulled the lever hard toward her and, with a sigh of relief, heard a resounding *thunk* as a cage surrounded her once more.

The teen only looked at her for a moment, and Mae flashed him a sly grin. She could tell from his baffled expression that he couldn't believe she had beaten him to the lever, but he quickly pushed that thought aside as he turned to find another handle.

Mae rested her head on the bars, imagining what might have happened if the boy had gotten to the lever before she had. She might have gotten under the bars, but perhaps only half of her. She might have been sliced in two and begged to fall into the furnace. The chance she had taken was a huge one, a dangerous one, but it had paid off. A sense of calm rushed over her; even though she was back in cage, she was safe.

As she looked up, that calmness disappeared. Javeen was still out there, and he looked more panicked than ever. His body had gone rigid, and he kept running his fingers through his hair in frustration. His head was turning wildly, and Mae knew he had no clue what to do. Javeen thought this was still a game of chance, or at least his mind had told him that. She watched as he made his way toward an orange handle.

Mae froze, knowing exactly what would happen if he pulled that handle. Then, without warning, that unsettling feeling of being alone in this place came back, which was the last thing she wanted. That emotion bubbled over, and before she could stop herself from showing any sort of weakness, she screamed, "Javeen!"

Chapter Nineteen:
<u>Javeen</u>

Javeen had no idea what to do or how this stage worked. All he knew was this game of chance was much harder than he'd imagined it would be. He watched as people threw each other to the ground, men being pulled back by their shirts and women screaming as they were pulled by their hair. Some tripped others in order to reach the lever they wanted. The scene in front of him reminded him of what the cages represented. All the survivors were becoming feral, and they'd been left in their cages in order to become even more rabid. Now that they were free, they were like a band of wild animals that hadn't been fed in days, and they wanted blood.

When the voice above had announced the beginning of Stage Three, Javeen had remained in his spot. He thought that would be the best plan, to calculate and see whether he could tell the difference between the levers or find any clue that might save his life. He watched as some were put back into their cages, and winced as a tile opened up, releasing the heat of the furnace. He tried to figure out the difference between the levers, but the possibility of knowing he could cause his own death from a simple slip-up had fogged his mind. When he was finally able to clear his thoughts, only a few levers were left.

Now or never, he told himself. He glanced at the closest lever, one with a deep-orange handle, almost blood orange, and shakily started toward it. His throat became dry the closer he got, knowing this simple lever would determine his fate. He was almost there when a voice from across the room grabbed his attention.

"Javeen!"

He whipped his head around after hearing Mae's voice. What the hell was she doing? Everyone remaining—and even those in their cages—turned to look at him. Was this the moment when she would betray him? To distract him while someone else grabbed the lever? And yet, there was something in the way she looked at him, in the way she clung to the bars of her cage. Panic had set into her wide eyes, as if she wanted to do everything in her power to come out and help him. Her hands were braced with fear as they firmly clutched the steel bars.

Javeen blinked hard. *What is she trying to…?*

That pause was all it took. A body suddenly connected with his, clearing any thoughts. Javeen faltered, but balanced himself before he hit the floor, only falling to his knees. Quickly he turned to see a man with a grimy, toothless smile; pale, liver-spotted skin; and thin hair standing near the lever. *The town drug addict*, Javeen quickly noted forgetting his name in the moment, having seen the man pawn his belongings for money, only to spend it on medications the town healers "threw out." The man, a bony bag of skin, almost looked proud that he had caught a large farmer like Javeen off guard and now had the handle to himself. He pulled it with a wink.

It only took a second. The lever dropped back with a snap, and the man was still staring at Javeen when the underworld came to life. The gaunt fellow's eyes filled with horror, and an orange glow reflected off his face, his toothless mouth now emitting a scream. Javeen felt the raging heat of the furnace as the man began to fall. In a desperate attempt, the man's hand latched on to the edge of the floor, but finally his fingers could hold on no longer and he dropped.

In the moment the tile shut, Javeen swung back toward Mae's cage. He knew now that she was in fact trying to save him. He looked at her, throwing his hands up in the air, showing everyone who was watching that he had no clue. Yes, this wasn't the place to show weakness, but Javeen didn't know what else to do. More important, he didn't have anything to lose at this point. If he had to beg for her help in order to survive this, then damn it, he wasn't too proud to do just that.

And then she said it. Actually, she said nothing at all. As he looked at Mae, she mouthed, "*Red.*"

Javeen rotated around once more and took in the levers with a clearer mind. At first, they all had looked the same. But after Mae had said that word, he realized the handles were actually two different colors. There was that blood-orange handle, the one he had almost pulled. But there was another—a red handle—and that was the one Javeen needed to find.

Only nine levers were left. He was hopeful there would be more than one red lever, that he would have options, but reality set in as he saw twenty-nine set of eyes looking at him. There was only one red left, he now understood. As he scanned them, he spotted it. The last red lever.

It was over by Mae, a few feet over in fact, and he had to get to it. He didn't want to make a scene, though; he already had brought too much attention to himself. Javeen slowly backed up toward the lever, cautiously watching the few remaining people around him. He took ten more strides then turned. Then he started into a full-blown sprint.

As he ran, he glanced at Mae, who was nodding at him, giving him the confirmation he needed. This was how he would live; this was his safety. He just had to keep running and make it there. But when he turned his head back, he saw that he wasn't alone in his chase. Another woman, a waitress from The Blood Broth, who had been there when Javeen was shoved to the ground, was running next to him. She must have seen what Mae had mouthed and knew what to do. A feeling of alarm rushed over Javeen as he launched himself forward.

No way would he die like this, by letting someone outrun him. He was stronger than her, and his legs were longer. And Javeen remembered his promise to Mae. They were both going to get out of here, and if he didn't reach that lever before this woman, his promise would burn with him. The thought of Mae being alone, of her having to fight this place by herself, was something he didn't want to imagine. It fueled him with adrenaline, and suddenly he felt his hand grasp the cold handle. Anger, happiness, and guilt surged through him as he looked back. The woman behind him shrieked as she lunged toward him. Just at that moment, Javeen pulled the handle toward him. With a loud bang, he was once again in a cage.

The lights dimmed back down, and the remaining levers disappeared into the floor. Those still outside the cages now understood they had lost this wicked game. It was always a game in which the odds were stacked, but all of them had hope at one point. Now, as Javeen looked at the woman who had raced with him to the lever, he saw that hope dwindle, replaced with terror. Stage Three was over, and the furnace would take what rightfully belonged to it.

One by one, the remaining eight began to fall, and Javeen decided to look at the woman he had beaten and watch her go, so he could feel her pain, knowing he had sent her to her death. Her head was down before it happened, but when she looked up, an instant before the tile dropped, her face had changed once more. She no longer looked afraid of what was to come. Shockingly, she almost looked at peace. And for a moment, Javeen could understand why. Her worries and anxiety were now behind her. She had nothing to fear. She knew what her fate would be and had chosen to accept it.

In that last millisecond, she smiled at Javeen. A sincere smile, one of warmth and gladness, to which one couldn't help smile back—which Javeen almost did. The woman took a large inhalation, then let released it, as if letting out anything that had ever held her back in her life, and raised her arms in the air. She held them there, the entire time, even when the furnace took her. She was now free of something she'd never wanted, and for that Javeen felt a sort of happiness for her.

He didn't hear the cheery female voice tell them that Stage Three was over. As he backed up in his cage, he couldn't hear anything beyond the sounds of his blood pumping in his ears. Sweat dripped off his brow, and a bead of it ran down his back. His breath was ragged, and he struggled to keep it calm. This was the second time The Factory almost had gotten him, the second time he had cheated death. When he felt the steel against his back, he slid down the bars and looked around to see who was left. Among them were the town drunk, Ripley Nadim the prostitute, and the redhead, who was sitting right next to Mae's cell.

When his eyes fell on Mae, who was a few feet away from him, she looked at him, her breathing almost as shallow as his, even though she had finished this challenge well before him. He realized she'd been worried about him. She flashed him a smile, a real smile, finally showing she cared about his survival.

Javeen gave her a grin back and another thumbs-up. He closed his eyes and rested his throbbing head on the ice-cold bars.

Mae had saved him. He had to protect her.

He owed her his life.

Chapter Twenty:
<u>Mae</u>

Since Stage Three had taken place in the morning, the survivors had the rest of the day to stew in their cells. Many of them just sat there, rocking and thinking about what had happened, perhaps wondering if they had pulled the right lever by chance and were now safe by pure luck. Others paced, trying to keep at least some part of their body busy. As the day went on and lunch came and went, the antsier everyone became. *Maybe The Factory will give us two stages in a row*, Mae thought. At this point, that wouldn't have surprised her a bit. But when dinner made its way into their cells, the tension seemed to dissipate a bit. Those who remained now understood they weren't going anywhere soon.

As Mae nibbled on a piece of bread, she glanced once more at Javeen's cage, where he was slurping down the watery chicken broth they'd all received. When he finished draining the contents and wiped the liquid off his chin with his forearm, he met Mae's gaze and wiggled his fingers at her. Mae let out a chuckle and waved back, remembering the brute she'd feared in the courtyard only days ago. That same mountainous dark figure had just given her the wave of a small child, a smile lighting up his face. She shook her head, smirking while taking another bite of bread. Then, as if a wave had crashed over her happy moment, a stab of discomfort shot through her body.

She had grown accustomed to having Javeen right next to her at all times. When she ate, wanted to talk to someone, or needed some entertainment, he was there. But now that wasn't the case, and Mae felt vulnerable. He always emanated a type of comfort, something she only noticed with his current absence. The feeling never disappeared whenever Javeen was near, even when she had tried to avoid being close to him in their previous cell arrangement. He was becoming her crutch, one she needed to stay sane and, dare she say, happy, in a place that was trying to kill her. Now he was on the other side of the room, his light too far away to shine on her.

The separation was causing her to collapse in on herself once more, as she was beginning to fear The Factory and her vulnerable position again. Anxiety rushed to her throat as she tried to breathe deeply. *Calm down!* she hissed in her mind. Showing weakness would do nothing to ensure her existence. But this was no longer just about her and surviving. That was clear after this last stage. She now also worried about Javeen and his safety. It also made her even more anxious to think that after all these years of neglect and pushing others away, she was beginning to care for people. More frighteningly, she was feeling for *someone* again.

"That was pretty stupid on your part," came a voice next to her.

Mae looked toward the source of the sound and saw Scarface eating on the opposite side of the cell, making slight eye contact with her. She violently ripped another piece of bread and dipped it into the broth. It was as if she were daring Mae to challenge her. The image of the girl punching the Ripley flashed through Mae's mind. She definitely had a chip on her shoulder, and Mae wasn't going to poke at it.

Mae tried to keep her composure. She didn't want to come off as too aggressive, since this was the moment she'd been waiting for. She needed to talk to this girl and convince her to join her and Javeen. Although Mae wasn't sure what that meant exactly, she knew this redheaded girl was key. Someone, especially a girl, didn't get a cut like that on the face and survive by lying down and doing nothing. With Scarface's grit, Javeen's physical strength, and Mae's sheer determination, they could do ensure their survival. But Mae had to win her over first.

"What are you talking about?" she asked without trying to sound defensive.

The redhead jerked her head toward Javeen while still looking at her food. "You trying to save your little boyfriend over there. You could have killed him."

"I saved him," Mae said almost proudly, then quickly added, "And he's not my boyfriend."

Scarface shrugged and stuffed the last of the bread into her mouth. "Could have fooled me."

Mae looked back at Javeen, who was glancing around the room. No, there wasn't anything there beyond pure survival. That was extent of their emotional connection. He was only paying attention to her because he saw her as an asset, a way to get out of The Factory. And Mae didn't mind being used if that meant she would get out with him.

"Why are you helping him then?" the girl asked.

Mae, still staring at Javeen, was surprised to find herself opening up to this stranger. "I don't know. I think…I think he can actually get me out of here." Honestly, Mae did think that, but she also needed to put a seed in this girl's head. When she turned and looked at her, that horrid scar gazed back at her. She lifted her shoulders before adding, "Maybe I just don't want to see death anymore." She sighed. "Or maybe I don't know why I'm doing it."

The girl swayed her head side to side, as if considering Mae's words, and nodded. "I get it." There was a subtle kindness in her voice; then her tone turned harsh again. "It won't happen, though, because people are going to die. That's the point of this place. But still, I get it. Even so, you know the rules of The Factory."

"Don't make friends in here, you idiot."

Mae and the redhead looked up and saw the white-haired prostitute, kicking her empty bowl across the floor, in a cell diagonal from them. Her thin, frail body leaned against the bars, and her arms were crossed. She wore tight black pants with a dirty tunic over it. The sleeves were ripped in places, and the thing looked too loose. Almost as if she had stolen it from someone twice her size. Although the woman wasn't facing them directly, Mae saw her looking out of the corner of her eye at them and a sneer plastered on her face. Mae remembered her name because of how stupid it was: Medusa, as she claimed she could turn men to stone. She always added a wink to that, so whomever she was addressing could interpret it however they wanted.

The redhead girl next to Mae rolled her eyes. "I'm sorry. If we wanted your disease-ridden opinion, we would've asked." She flashed her teeth in a wicked smile that would have made milk curdle.

Medusa turned toward them, unfazed. "You're an idiot, you know," she drawled, looking at Mae, her expression almost bored. "You shouldn't be getting to know him." She glanced at Javeen. "No matter how...well, look at him... I wonder if he's huge anywhere else." She gave Mae a cheeky wink, then bluntly added, "He's probably going to die here anyway." Her eyes darkened as her eyebrows creased. "End it."

Mae finally spoke up, her initial shock at this woman's innuendo disappearing. "You're disgusting," she spat. "Do you think of anything else? We could all die in here. None of our lives is guaranteed. None of us has a free pass out. And you don't know that he'll die. Ja...He could outlive us all. Just walk away while you turn to ash."

Medusa let out a strange laugh, her body language now trying to test Mae's will. She turned herself towards Mae, her hip dropping as she placed her boney hand on the other side. Medusa tilted her head, her face full of false pity. "You think that, huh? Honey, let me tell you something. Six of us are leaving this place, and here's what's going to happen. Either Mountain Hunk is going to die in here, or he's going to leave you behind because you helped him survive. There's no other alternative." She brushed her brittle hair behind her shoulder, trying to appear superior. "I know a lot about men…"

"Well, no shit," Scarface snapped from her cage, but Medusa continued, as if she hadn't heard what the girl had said.

"And if I could tell you anything, it's this. Even in the outside world, men are only out for themselves. They use people around them they think will give them the advantage they need. But men never want someone who might be better than them. The moment that kid tires of your help, well…" She gave her nasty smile. "I hope you like the heat."

Scarface finally had enough, and Mae jumped as the girl quickly stood up in her cell. "Look, you chlamydia-infected sack of skin, anyone can use anyone. This isn't happy teatime or the spring solstice celebration. This is a war. And in any war, the goal is to live. It's all about survival, and people make their own choices in order to survive." She pointed to Mae as she continued. "She can do whatever she damn well wants. You just back off and worry about how you're going through the next stage."

Medusa looked hard at her, as if she were trying to examine every aspect of this young woman. "You got a pretty loud mouth. You might want to try to keep it quiet and not bring unwanted attention to yourself."

Scarface moved closer to the edge of her cell. "Is that a threat?"

Medusa shrugged. "Just a suggestion." She looked at Mae. "That goes for you too, Plague Girl, and your mountain man. You don't want people noticing you either. Don't think we haven't seen your little friendship. See, you two are like the legs of a table. All we have to do is knock off one of you, and the other one will fall. Makes you an easy target." She gave Mae one last hard look. "It's like getting two for the price of one." Then she went back to the farthest corner of her cell and sat down, coughing deeply as she did.

The redhead went back and sat near Mae. "Goddamn it," she growled. "I hate her."

Mae let out a snort. "Thanks for that," she said, but the girl didn't respond. She just sat there, staring at the corner. Mae knew right away that Scarface was doing the same thing Mae had done to Javeen earlier. Putting up a wall. That way, if you survived, there'd be no guilt. Even so, Mae continued to look at her, trying to figure her out. There was a crack in nearly every wall, and she had to find it. Scarface sat rigid and hunched over, as if she were protecting herself. That was when Mae really looked at her face. Her eyes lingered on the scar, how deep the cut was and how raised the skin around it had become. The wound looked inflamed and infected, but she could tell it wasn't. Just bad stitching.

She must have been looking too long because suddenly, without moving, the girl murmured, "Dog got me." She looked over at Mae, her hazel eyes hard. "Don't ask."

"Wasn't planning on it." Mae sighed, looking away and resting her head against the bars. She knew what it was like to try to avoid a subject she didn't want to talk about, and when people pestered, it only made her mood worse. Besides, Mae could tell this girl wasn't to be messed with, and she kind of liked that. And it was clear she would be a valuable addition to whatever she and Javeen were calling their bond. She took the same chance Javeen had taken with her. She leaned her head slightly toward her and whispered, "You want out? You want to be a Leaving?"

The girl looked at her, then back at her empty food bowl, and shook her head. "Don't make promises that are too hard to keep." She pulled her knees closer to her chest and rested her chin on them.

Mae nodded in Javeen's direction. "Look, he and I working together— you got that right. But we can't do it alone." She turned her body and confronted the hard-faced girl, prepared to tell her the truth. "Six of us will leave. That's a fact we're all aware of. But who those six might be, we have no idea. The plan is simple. If we work together, we can be three of them." At first the girl didn't say anything, so again Mae took a leap. "My name's Mae, by the way."

"I know your name. I just don't know your intentions," the girl snapped. Mae could see her barrier break just a bit. She slowly lifted her head, loosening the grip on her knees. "How do I know you won't ditch me?"

"Because what do I have left?" Mae answered. "If I leave here and don't keep my promise to you two, I'll live with that guilt for the rest of my life. And guilt is something I'm already living with; I don't need any more names on my ledger. I have enough demons keeping me awake, and letting either one of you die would haunt me. I'm not in the mood to live with that forever. And getting out of this hellhole with you two…well, I could be leaving with worse." Mae gave a weak smile, trying to warm her up.

"How do I know you're not lying?" It was a fair question.

"I don't lie. I *can't* lie. It's a personal problem of mine. I have tells, like not looking people in the eye when I do try to make something up. And besides, you know I'm loyal. You saw me yell to save him, attracting everyone's attention," Mae said, pushing her head toward Javeen. "That's how this conversation started in the first place. I could have just let him die, but I didn't. And I would've done the same for you and still will. We only have three more stages, and I'll keep you as safe as I can. That is, if you're willing to do the same for me."

The girl inhaled sharply then sighed. "My name's Raya." Her head quickly snapped in Mae's direction. "That doesn't mean I trust you," she grumbled, "or that I'm agreeing to whatever you two have planned, but…that's just my name."

Mae smiled lightly, and Raya returned it with a wink. Something had given with this girl, but she wasn't sure what that was yet. Even so, Mae felt that whatever happened, things would get better. Raya had the necessary wits to survive, which was exactly what Mae was hoping to add to their alliance. They could get out of here with that alone. But Javeen needed to trust both of them, and Mae wasn't sure if he'd be as willing as she was to believe in Raya. Still, this alliance had to be made in order for them to leave The Factory alive.

Medusa's raspy voice jolted Mae from her thoughts. "Can you two dumbasses shut up? I need my beauty sleep."

"Oh, yeah, that'll definitely help your looks." Raya sneered, rolling her eyes. "Listen lady, I might have to kill you if you don't stop talking to us."

With a final cough, Medusa glared at them before turning around. Her gray eyes were hard and cold, as though she no longer felt any emotions, especially for Mae and Raya. Although it kept her quiet, her stern look didn't make Mae feel as though she had won. Soon the bedrolls appeared in their cages, telling them it was time for sleep.

Mae went over to her roll, hoping Raya would align herself with her and Javeen. Deep in her gut, she knew this was the last piece she needed to ensure her safety, and she almost had it. But then she remembered what Medusa had said about her alliance with Javeen, and it shook her feeling of security. *Will he actually be willing to help me if I really need it?* she wondered. *And if it comes down to it, will I be able to face him if he goes after me?*

As others around her turned in for the night, Mae was beginning to see why the Leavings never revealed what went on in The Factory. The screams and moans of those around her kept her from shutting off her mind. Others were shaking, either crying in their sleep or fighting demons only they could see. Mae knew that she when she eventually fell asleep, visions of what happened today would haunt her dreams. Still, sleep was something she needed, because a little more energy, no matter how little sleep she could muster, could be the difference between life and death.

Raya was lying perfectly still, twitching every now and then, but sleeping all the same. Javeen was tossing and turning, but still his eyes were closed. Mae decided it was time for her to face what she dreaded every time she saw the padded rolls. As she closed her eyes, the orange tint of the fire covered her eyes as she tried to drift away.

Chapter Twenty-One:
<u>Javeen</u>

Javeen had watched as Mae talked to the scar-faced girl. They had spoken in soft tones, and at one point, the redhead had gotten up to say something to the sickly-looking prostitute. When she sat back down, she was closer to Mae this time. There was something about her that Javeen had to admit was admirable, but would she be willing to help them? Or did she plan on using them and then literally throwing them into the flames as she walked out? This uncertainty made him uneasy and unsure whether he could trust her.

When he turned his head, the bedrolls were back up. He crawled his way over, as his legs were still aching from Stage Three. When his body hit the soft cushion, he lay there for a moment and closed his eyes. In his mind, he kept replaying what had happened. How he almost had died again, how he kept cheating death, how the only reason he'd been able to lie down on this sad excuse for a mattress tonight was because of Mae.

They'd become closer recently, and Javeen wasn't opposed to it. In the beginning, he'd just needed someone to talk to in order to stay sane. Then he actually began to enjoy their conversations and was happy she had chosen him when she needed someone to talk to. He felt honored that she had confessed her greatest fear to him. Although, perhaps that might have something to do with their cages being situated next to each other. Even so, she had told him. But Javeen couldn't lie to himself about what constantly bothered him. Mae was perhaps too independent, and at any moment, she could back out on her promise.

It was always in the back of his mind, and he tried to push it away, but before Stage Three had begun, Javeen somehow knew this would be the real test. Mae had every opportunity to let him run around like a chicken, holding the ax in her hand as she watched. That was why he didn't run toward a lever right away. He wanted to try to figure out the challenge on his own, just in case she decided to turn on him. If that happened, he could be self-reliant and forget her and their promise. But this last challenge was much more difficult than he'd expected. *If Mae hadn't yelled my name...*

When the cage slammed around Javeen, he knew Mae was there for him, not just for herself. He took that moment to trust her because he had nothing left to lose. But when the steel bars surrounded him, he wondered whether she really wanted to help him or if it had been a moment of weakness. Or perhaps, just maybe, she thought she couldn't get out of The Factory without him. Even with that ghostly "what if" locked in his mind, Javeen now felt confident about Mae and their...well, she had called it an alliance, meaning it was just an agreement. He now knew it was much more. It was a relationship driven by the resolute desire for survival.

That was why he was wary of the redheaded girl and didn't want to trust her. Was she willing to band together with them to get out? Or did she have her own motives? Javeen still was hesitant, no matter how much Mae wanted to trust her. There were so many people in here who would put on an act in order to make sure they survived, and it seemed the redheaded girl not only knew the game but also owned it. This girl needed to prove herself to Javeen and their mission.

The room around Javeen began to spin, and his head sank lower into the mattress. His thoughts and worries could wait until the morning. Slowly his eyes closed, and when he felt a pressure lift from his chest, he knew he might actually sleep well tonight. There were no images of the woman as he drifted off, and the light of the furnace didn't glow behind his lids. Instead he fell into a deep darkness. But as he began to dream, that blackness morphed into the darkness of dusk.

He was in the woods, it seemed, judging by the trees that slowly formed around him. As he stood on the snowy ground, a slight mist rose up to his knees. The sunlight was nearly gone, and everything around him was black and white. Suddenly Javeen forgot this was a dream and believed he had become completely blind to colors. Hearing the crunch of snow behind him, he quickly turned to see a shadowy figure standing between two pine trees.

The figure took tentative steps toward him, as if advancing on a diseased animal. It was clearly a man, with a large fur jacket draped over his shoulders.

He must have been hunting—he held a matching hat in his hands, and a rifle was strapped across his back—yet he displayed no type of aggression. It was almost as if *he* was afraid to face Javeen, not the other way around. When the figure stepped into the fading light, Javeen noticed the man's long, unkempt beard.

He straightened up, his heart light and his eyes stinging. "Dad?"

There, in the glowing light, stood his father. At first Javeen wanted to run to him, to feel him again, but somewhere deep within, he remembered this was a dream. His father wasn't really in front of him; he was just a figment, something Javeen wished to be true. The strange part was that Javeen, even right after his father's death, rarely had dreamt about him. So why was he having this vision now? He saw that his father was wearing the same outfit he'd worn when Javeen had last seen him, before the hunting trip. His other scattered, hazy dreams involving his father had been memories of his childhood but never of the day he had left.

"Jav, my son, I'm so glad you came." His father moved farther into the light. "I don't have much time to tell you what you need to know."

Javeen took a step forward, ready to ask so many questions, but froze as the low light shone on his father's body. He thought he would see the robust figure of his father, as healthy as the last time Javeen had seen him. Instead, he was dotted with slits, the rusty color of blood outlining deep slashes across his torso. There were scratches on his face as well, clearly made by hands, but the cuts that riddled his father's body were smooth. Not made by beast or man but something else. Something sharp. The bleeding seemed to have stopped, but these wounds obviously were part of the message Javeen's father wanted to relay to him.

His dad's ashen face looked at him with pleading eyes. "I didn't leave you." He trembled, taking yet another step. "I wouldn't leave the family, Javeen. You know that. I loved you all too much to abandon you." His body was shaking, as if he were using all his energy to talk to his son.

"I know. I always knew. We...knew," Javeen whispered, mostly to himself.

When he looked at his father, a calmness seemed to settle over his face. He gave his son a small smile, almost one of pride, showing that he'd never lost hope. Perhaps, even in the place where Javeen's father's spirit lay, he needed confirmation that his family hadn't given up on him.

His father's expression suddenly grew stern. "You can see this was no accident. My disappearance wasn't by choice," he said, gesturing to the wounds on his chest. "Javeen, you need to know this was foul play."

Javeen nodded, wanting to ask so many questions. Who had been with him? How did it happen? Why would anyone want his father gone? But around them, the light was getting stronger, even though he felt the darkness of his dream hadn't yet left him. He knew he was beginning to wake up. Quickly, his father came to him, embracing him one last time before holding him at arm's length.

"We don't have much time. You must remember this: these marks and my face. Remember what you saw here." His bright-green eyes looked deeply into Javeen's, pleading desperately. "Don't forget this, my son."

In a moment, there was a blinding flash, and Javeen woke with a start. He sat up quickly, trying to regain his breath, placing a clammy hand to his forehead. His stomach churned, not as though he was going to be sick, but from the pain knowing the awful truth. Although it was a dream, Javeen felt as though his father, in the flesh, had stepped toward him. Something wasn't right about his disappearance, and for some reason, now was the time for Javeen to find out what that was. But why?

When he finally had calmed himself, he looked around and saw others beginning to stir. Somehow, he had made it through the night, and although the dream had woken him in an unpleasant way, he felt much more rested than he had in a few days. He felt as though the dream and his sleeping through the night had recharged his brain. And now there was even more of a fire in his belly, more energy, and a greater need to survive. He knew that here, in The Factory, he would to find out the truth about what had happened to his father. There was no denying that now.

A few minutes later, breakfast appeared. Buttered toast and an apple. And although Javeen's stomach had hurt yesterday, now he found it quite easy to eat, knowing the food was fueling the vigor he desperately needed. He glanced at Mae, who looked well rested too. Perhaps The Factory had put something in the air to help them sleep. Javeen wouldn't put it past this place. He was about to make his way to the edge of the cage to wave to her, when once more a distinctive ding rang out. Javeen didn't even need to hear the voice to know what this meant.

It was time for Stage Four.

Chapter Twenty-Two:
<u>Mae</u>

"Good morning, everyone. I hope you all slept well. We will soon begin Stage Four. In a few moments, you'll be released from your cells, six at a time, which will divide everyone into five groups. When you're released from your holdings, please follow the illuminated lines to your destinations, where you'll receive your instructions."

Slowly, everyone sitting stood up, and those already standing made their way to the front of their cells. Mae looked at Raya, who stared straight ahead, but caught her quickly glancing in her direction as well. Mae then turned to Javeen; his jaw was tight, his eyes glassy. He wasn't going to look at her, not now. And Mae knew why. Unless they were in the same group, they couldn't ensure each other's survival.

The cages slowly receded into the ceiling. One by one, groups of six made their way toward one of the many hallways annexed to the round room, which was nearly shadowed in blackness. Had it not been for the lights illuminating the floor, they would have been walking in pure darkness. As soon as one crowd made their way into the abyss, another set was released from their cells. Most of them walked in silence, some trying not to get too close to one another, but a few tried to chat, perhaps attempting to lighten the mood. Those few, however, were always met with disdainful eyes.

When Mae's bars began to recede into the ceiling, she slowly looked around to see who was in her group. From the corners of her eyes, she saw that Raya's cell also was beginning to disappear, as was Javeen's. She felt some measure of comfort, knowing she'd be with two people she was familiar with, even if Raya wasn't ready to admit she wanted to join Mae and Javeen. The redheaded girl was strong, and Mae wanted to feed off that as much as she fed off Javeen's optimism. It would make her just as dangerous to the others if they tried to push her around. Taking a deep breath, she looked around to see who else was with them.

She spotted a lanky, dark-haired kid who wasn't much older than her, perhaps a little younger than Javeen, who watched his cell disappear in front of him. Sadler something, she remembered. On that first day, his name had been called a few minutes after Raya's had. He was the apprentice to the bookmaker in town and looked to be the feeblest here. Now that Mae was really close, she was able to see how thin his arms were. If this was the physical challenge they'd all been waiting for, Mae wasn't sure he would come out alive, but then, as she looked at him more closely, she realized his beanpole body actually held some muscle. Perhaps it was better not to judge that book by its cover.

As Mae's head rotated, her stomach churned as the bars from Medusa's cell receded, and she involuntarily made eye contact with the woman. The bone-thin prostitute gave her a smirk. Mae knew right away this wasn't a lip twitch with any good intentions. A much more sinister meaning, which only Medusa knew, lay behind it. But Mae couldn't dwell on that; she had to focus on the task at hand. She looked to see who the last member of their group was. When the final set of bars receded, Mae wanted to scream.

It was the man with the ice-cold eyes.

His large body moved up and down as he tried to breathe steadily, but then he looked at Mae. The terror from her face must have had a calming effect, because soon his breathing slowed, and he gave her another one of his grimy smiles. This time, Mae didn't cover herself up with her arms, even though she felt violated by his eyes. Something about him didn't sit well with her, but she couldn't back down. She had to be strong, and even though every ounce of her blood in her body had frozen up, she remained determined to survive this next challenge.

The floor began to glow, and Mae watched as the light danced down another dark hallway. Even with the light bouncing off the dark walls, she felt as though the tunnel was even more ominous now. Together the group followed the light. Mae felt a tug on her elbow and saw that Javeen was holding her back so the rest of the group was in front. Raya lingered a bit as well, staying a few feet in front of them. As the neared they opening, Javeen leaned in close. "You have to relax," he whispered.

"I am…" Mae said, but even to her own ears she sounded weaker than she wanted to. She hated that The Factory's voice hadn't told them what was happening right away. She couldn't prepare herself, which made her uneasy. "I want to know what's going to happen." She sighed irritably. "I…I just don't want it to be a physical challenge…like fighting each other." That was her greatest fear when it came to these stages. Even compared to Medusa, Mae wasn't sure she could throw a punch, let alone kill someone. "I don't think I could win something like that."

"It won't be a fight. It never will be," Raya said over her shoulder. She turned her head slightly, her eyebrows raised. "Haven't you gotten that yet?"

Javeen's eyes hardened on her, clearly wishing she hadn't heard Mae. He took a large step toward her and hissed his annoyance in her ear. "What the hell do you mean?"

Mae had to give Raya credit. When Javeen was mad or frustrated, he was a force to be reckoned with, or at least he seemed that way. His body was huge to begin with, but when he was agitated, he seemed to become larger, and his eyes lit up as if they were ablaze with the fires from below. Mae remembered how scared she'd been in the courtyard as he looked down on her, like he was doing with Raya right now. That first day, Mae had thought Javeen might actually kill her.

"Raya, what do you mean?" She tried calmly, but Javeen and Raya continued to scowl.

Instead of cowering, Raya rolled her eyes. She took a step toward Javeen and gave him a smile that resembled a dog baring its teeth. "Because that's not what The Factory wants. It doesn't like cleaning things up. No messes in this place. Not intentionally anyway." She lifted a finger to her temple and tapped it. "The worst damage that can be done to a human, while still keeping The Factory clean, is all in here. The mind is much more fragile than anyone thinks, and it's easily manipulated. The Factory wants us to suffer *mentally*, not physically."

Her wide eyes told them she'd been harboring this truth for some time. "We're in cages because The Factory wants us to believe we *are* animals, even when we aren't," she continued. "But it can mentally screw with us and turn us into the most feral of creatures. There won't be a physical challenge. The Factory is going to scramble our brains with every stage." She looked them up and down and whispered, "We'll only become animals if we don't watch ourselves. So, you two better stay strong." With that she spun around and entered the dark hallway.

Javeen stopped, taken aback by Raya's response, and although Mae hated to admit it, so was she. As she followed the bodies into the ever-darker hallway, she considered how right Raya was. None of the challenges had been about physically fighting someone. The stages had only turned out that way because people had become desperate, like the man who had knocked Mae over during Stage Three. All the stages had been some sort of mental challenge that you had to escape. If you didn't, you died, simple as that. But if you did survive, you still had scars—mental ones. Mae remembered her nightmares over the past few nights. The man burning next to her in a dark cell, her parents' decaying figures, the people who had fallen into the furnace as the last levers were pulled. These images would haunt her forever. Raya was right—The Factory didn't like messy games. It wanted to play with its victims from within. The more The Factory scratched and pulled at the minds of its captives, the stronger it became.

Mae's thoughts came to a halt when she realized she was at the end of the hallway and the group was entering a long room. In the space, which was much larger than any bedroom she had seen, stood a large, oval, black table that matched the black walls. Mae knew she was going to resent the color black for the rest of her life if she got out of here. Around the table were six chairs, two on either end and four on the sides. However, in the middle of the table was something that looked out of place. There, right in the center under a glass case, was a blinking red button. She had a feeling this button would be the difference between life and death.

The door closed behind them, and the ding rang out once more.

"Hello. Welcome to Stage Four. Please take a seat."

Mae sat next to Raya, who appeared extraordinarily calm. She gazed across the large black slab and was happy to see Javeen on the other side, though he looked like he was thinking hard about something besides this room. Unfortunately, Medusa took the spot next to him, her eyes trailing him up and down, as she moved her chair much closer than it needed to be. Sadler took the seat closest to the door, while the man with the icy eyes sat at the end.

Once they were all seated, the voice returned.

"In this stage, you must solve a crime. There is a murderer in this room. It is your job as a group to decide who that person is and dispose of him or her. When you've reached a consensus as to who the culprit is, simply lift the glass case and say the person's name. Then press the red button. If you choose the correct individual, they will be sent to their death. However, if you choose the wrong person, then everyone in the room will die. You have one hour to complete this task. The timer is on the wall, to the right the entrance. Begin."

Click.

Chapter Twenty-Three:
Javeen

Javeen wished there had been a moment of silence after the voice had disappeared. He hoped the group would sit and think rationally before the accusations began. But right as the timer started, some members of the group pushed their chairs back, not wanting to be near whoever the murderer might be. Eyes scanned the room, perhaps hoping to pick something up, but no one said a word. Javeen knew it was only a matter of time before fingers started to point, and then The Factory would begin to play its twisted game.

As he'd expected, Medusa was the first to speak. "Well, of course we had to be stuck in here with a crazy murderer." She stood up and began to pace, her dirty shirt sliding off her left shoulder, as she began scrutinizing the group with sharp eyes. Her pacing brought her to Sadler, who sat still, although his eyes appeared calculating.

"All right!" Medusa yelled, slamming her palms on the table. Sadler's focus was disrupted as he jumped in his chair. "Which one of you is it?"

Raya let out a scornful laugh. "Yeah, like the culprit is actually going to confess. Are you actually that stupid? You know what…don't answer that." She stood up and started toward Medusa. "We have to figure it out—that's the point.

We have to start asking questions or notice things. Maybe things in here or things that happened in town. But whoever it is isn't going to come out and say 'Yup. I'm a murderer.' They're a killer, and they'd rather see us all die than die on their own."

Medusa looked Raya up and down, clearly considering her words as truth, but not wanting to admit the girl was right. The tension in the room thickened as Raya's words floated through the air. The person they were looking for wasn't going to step forward; they had to work together to find him or her. If they succeeded, then five of them would walk out. But as Javeen scanned the faces in this group, he wasn't sure they'd be able to.

"Well, we can narrow it down. It's not Mountain Man over there," Medusa said, pointing to Javeen. "He's always at the market or his stupid farm. And he has, like, a family or something to take care of." Javeen was about to speak when the woman continued. "And bookmaker here is too weak. I mean, a strong wind would break his bones."

Sadler's face scrunched in frustration and anger, Medusa's words seeming to cut into him. It seemed that it wasn't the first time he had heard that he was an underdog. Javeen had even began to wonder exactly how he was still here. He wasn't outwardly strong. Javeen thought he heard the apprentice whisper, "Just because I'm not muscular, doesn't mean I'm not a threat here." His words were not menacing, but more of a promise that resonated back to Raya's words. Sadler didn't have to be strong here, he just had to be smart.

Medusa ignored the rest of the group and turned back to Raya, her shirt dipping even lower as she dropped her shoulder in arrogant confidence. "Besides, I already know who it is." She crossed her arms as a smug look washed over her face.

"Oh, of course you do. What's your IQ again? Seven?" Raya spat. She looked as though she wanted to punch Medusa in the face just to get her to shut up.

Medusa threw her hands up and looked at the group. "Isn't it obvious?" She extended one of her thin arms and pointed to Mae. "She's the killer."

Silence filled the room as everyone turned their attention to Mae. She was still sitting, watching Medusa the whole time, but her demeanor changed the second that bony finger jutted toward her. Javeen saw the color in her face rise, but she remained still, trying to take in what Medusa had just said. Then, as it registered, she exploded. In an instant, she jumped up and raced toward Medusa. "You stupid bitch! You think I'm capable—"

Javeen was up too, ready to get between the two as quickly as possible. But just as he moved, Raya stepped in front of Mae, blocking her from Medusa's path. "Are you kidding me?" she snorted. "Honestly, you're proving my point about your IQ. Why would Mae kill anyone? She lives by herself and barely survives. I think the food she's had in here is the most she's had in years. And to top it off, no one in town even wants to see her." Quickly, she turned back to Mae, who was now at her shoulder. "No offense."

"It's not offensive if it's the truth," Mae said easily, but she wasn't looking at Raya. Her eyes narrowed at Medusa. "You don't know what you're talking about. I wouldn't kill anyone."

Medusa scanned the room, ignoring the two girls standing in front of her. "Think about it. The town doesn't pay attention to her. That's the perfect situation in which to kill someone. No one would notice, and even if anyone found out she killed someone, they wouldn't do anything. No one wants anything to do with her."

"No, they want me gone. If someone knew I was a murderer, I'd already be dead from the rope," Mae hissed. Her eyes were wild, her hands curled into fists. "Here's the real question. Why would I want to kill someone? I have no issues with anyone in town, seeing as they don't speak to me."

"Maybe you were desperate for attention," Medusa said simply, raising an eyebrow.

There was a loud huff, and Javeen looked Raya, who'd clearly had enough. "Well, obviously, it didn't work. Because no one has noticed her still, so your point is invalid. At least you attempted to use your brain—and you didn't hurt yourself too much in the process. But you're wrong. Nice try, though." Raya gave her a sarcastic thumbs-up then turned back, guiding Mae back to her chair.

"What about you?" Medusa snapped.

Javeen watched as Raya's shoulders tensed, her hand gripping Mae's shoulder as she slowly turned around, her hazel eyes on fire. "What the fuck is that supposed to mean?"

Medusa's face danced with pleasure. Clearly, she wanted this exact reaction from Raya. "Exactly what it sounds like. Nasty scar on your face there. How'd you get it?"

"Dog attack."

"Bullshit," Medusa spat, her face turning vicious, a grin of venom plastered on it. "It's clearly a defensive wound. The cut is too clean for a dog. You got sliced while you were killing someone. Don't you lie. It was a final attempt someone took to save their life, a protective slash to the face, and boy, did they get you. She was probably your accomplice." She nodded toward Mae. "You two might as well admit it."

Placing a hand on Raya's shoulder to calm her, Mae rolled her eyes. "Out of anyone here, you should be the one we should consider."

Medusa's nostrils flared as her head whipped toward Mae. "You little shit. What the hell are you talking about?"

"No…no, she's right!" Raya yelled, pointing a finger toward Medusa with a crazed enthusiasm. "You have more reason than any of us to kill someone." Raya walked toward her and began to circle. "What was the reason? Someone didn't pay you? Or he got too physical for your liking? What happened, Medusa? Come on, tell us the truth. I'm sure the life you live isn't pretty, and there are many ways you can kill a man without getting any blood on your hands. You think I don't know the innkeeper isn't willing to help you out of the sticky situations you get yourself into?"

Medusa paled, almost looking guilty, then quickly said, "Why the hell would I kill my clients? I need to make money, you know."

"Maybe someone tried to stiff you. Seems like a motive to me," Mae snapped.

Javeen sat and watched as the women went after each other. How much time had this bickering cost them? He glanced at the timer and saw they only had some thirty-eight minutes remaining. Although he wanted to agree with them, and it seemed Medusa had the greatest motive for killing someone, something about her told him she was telling the truth. Mae couldn't kill anyone, as she'd almost rotted from the inside thinking she had killed her parents. And Raya, although sharp-tongued, didn't seem like the murdering type. Just a verbally abusive assassin who would wear you down slowly. And an occasional fist thrower. Still, they had a right to be cautious. A killer would lie, like Raya had said. It would be better for the murderer to let the whole group die rather than fess up.

The clock continued to count down.

"Enough!" a booming voice bellowed. The three women stopped arguing and turned their heads toward the voice. There, at the other end of the table, Ice Eyes had his feet propped on the table, his arms crossed as he stared at all three of them. "You ladies seemed to have gotten your howling out of the way. Now why don't we cut out the pity shit? We need to stay calm and figure this out." Medusa's and Mae's body posture shifted as they both deflated, avoiding his striking eye contact.

Raya, however, started in on him right away, placing her hands on the table and leaning toward him. "Oh, really? And what now makes you in charge?"

Ice Eyes shrugged. "Thirty-five minutes, doll face. We don't have time to make wild accusations. We need to find some facts. None of this senseless yelling. So why don't we all calm down and try to figure this thing out with some human decency?"

Javeen felt an air of unease cascade over him as he looked at Ice Eyes. The man was too calm for a room filled with such tension. But maybe the room needed someone level headed, or at least that's what he tried to tell himself. Ice Eye's reached into his pants pocket and pulled out a knife, to which everyone gasped. It was the last thing they'd expected in this already edgy room. He must have had it on him when his name was called, which meant he had every right to bring it. No one had been patted down upon entry; therefore, the knife was fair game. Ice Eyes scanned the group and chuckled, their frightened faces somehow making him to even more composed.

"Oh, calm down. If I really wanted to, I would have used this thing days ago." He played with the handle, keeping the blade inside. "Having it out helps me think."

The rest of the group seemed to relax somewhat, although Mae, Raya, and Medusa were still standing at the end of the table. But Javeen didn't notice them as he watched the man turn the knife over in his fingers. The handle was made of dark wood and was attached to a silver blade. A switch knife…a hunting switch knife. Something about it being in his hands didn't seem right. Not that he was going to use it…but it didn't belong there. Slowly and cautiously, Javeen asked, "Where did you get that?"

Ice Eyes rolled his eyes. "Look, sonny, I already told you, I would have killed you by now if I was a killer. And we can bring in whatever is on our person. Therefore, this knife is completely—"

Javeen shook his head, not wanting to believe what he was seeing. "No. That's not what I meant. Where did you get that knife?"

"I…it's mine." Ice Eyes faltered, as if he hadn't expected to utter such a foolish statement. "Now do you have any more stupid questions before we continue this search?" He continued to flip the knife, this time around his knuckles. That was when Javeen saw it and understood. It was only an instant, a quick flash, but he couldn't deny what he'd seen.

"You liar!" Javeen roared.

Ice Eyes looked up at him, the harsh look in his eyes fading. He stopped flipping the handle and gripped the top of the knife harder than before. "What did you just call me?"

Javeen's fists balled up, anger rising in his chest. "I said you're a fucking liar. That's not your knife."

Ice Eyes laughed. He lowered his feet from the table and glared at Javeen as though he were trying to talk sense into him. "All right, boy. You think I stole it. That's great. But we're looking for a murderer, not a thief. If we were, little Blondie over there"—he pointed to Mae— "would have been in the pits minutes after we walked in." He continued to stare Javeen down, his eyes harder than ever. "Now you'd better start focusing at what's at hand."

Heavy silence filled the room as everyone waited for Javeen to back down. Javeen finally stood and, through gritted teeth, hissed, "Then give me *my* knife back."

Everyone in the room took a sharp inhalation. Ice Eye's face fell, and Javeen stood his ground. The battle between the women was forgotten as a new clash began. This tension was the last thing the group needed, and Javeen knew that facing a man down with a knife wasn't the best idea. But he also knew what he had seen.

"What are you…" Ice Eyes retorted, standing up, trying to meet Javeen's height.

"That's my knife. It has my initials on it. Right there on the base. JCN."

Ice Eyes looked up at him, wide-eyed. He tried to hide the lettering by moving his hand over it, but it was too late. Everyone in the room had seen the initials before he clamped his hand over them.

"He's right," Mae whispered. "I saw them. Gold letters."

Mae and Raya were now on the other side of the table, cornering the man. Whispers erupted around the table. The timer continued to click, but Javeen took no notice. Instead he looked at the man who now stood before him. But this time, he *really* saw him as an image flashed through his mind—an image he'd almost forgotten.

Ever since Javeen had seen him in the courtyard, he knew this man looked familiar. That image passed through his mind, followed by the image of his father leaving the house for the last time. Someone else had been there. Javeen remembered the shadow stood in the doorway, the one who called his father away. The guilt from years of torment had disappeared, and the hunting party came back as a head rush. He couldn't forget his face now. It was Ice Eyes. But he had a name.

"You were there that day," Javeen almost whispered. "You went hunting with my father, Tharin."

Everyone stared at Tharin, who frantically looked around the room. His eyes were wide with fear, perhaps because Javeen had said his name or because he now remembered him. "Look you don't—"

"How did you get my father's knife, Tharin?" Javeen spat, taking a step toward him.

Tharin threw his hands in the air. "We got separated. I found it in the woods and picked it up, but I never found him." He was about to put the knife back in his pocket. "Now are we really going to worry about this damn knife?" He pointed to the timer on the wall. "We only have twenty minutes."

It all came together for Javeen. Sweat dripped from Tharin's brow, and he no longer wanted anyone's attention on him. Then there was the dream Javeen had had about his father the night before. Those wounds had been clean, like something a blade would make. His father had been stabbed multiple times. Finally, the words his father spoken before Javeen had woken up echoed through his mind: *You need to know this was foul play.*

"It's you," Javeen whispered. He looked Tharin right in the eyes. "You're the murderer."

"Oh, yeah?" Tharin sneered, challenging him. "And who did I kill?"

"My father."

There was a long moment of silent, and then Tharin switched the blade and raced toward Javeen, his once-cool manner turning wild. Javeen braced himself for the blow, ready to fight back, when Tharin stumbled and fell to the side. Javeen watched as Raya's leg moved back in place. Mae and Sadler grabbed Tharin's shoulders, forcing him into a chair. In a millisecond, Mae had taken off her belt and latched it around Tharin's broad shoulders, tethering him to the chair. The man seemed strong, but in this moment, he looked like a wounded animal.

"Take the knife from him," Javeen ordered the girls, his voice stern.

Tharin spat at Mae and Raya, who were trying to get the weapon. He held the knife tightly to his body, using it to keep them at bay, until Raya made her way around him and pushed a pressure point near his neck. Tharin howled in pain and dropped the knife. Mae snatched it, flipped the switch back, and handed it to Javeen. He remembered the smoothness of the wood and ran his finger over the two sets of initials. His and his father's. Before he could stop himself, he turned and punched Tharin, the hard wood of the knife's handle slashing his cheek.

"Why did you do it?" he screamed, his hands shaking. Tharin spat blood and a few teeth onto Javeen's boots and laughed. He knew these were his last moments, and still he was being cocky. Javeen grabbed him by the throat. "Why did you kill him?"

"A lady, my boy," he managed to get out in choked breaths "It's always about a lady."

Javeen let go and stood back. "What sort of confession is that?"

Tharin laughed once more and looked him in the eye with a crooked, bloody smile. "I had a lady once, you know. However, we had an issue in our relationship. She was married, you see."

Javeen's stomach soured. He couldn't be talking about…no. There was no possible way this man was telling the truth. He felt a body next to him, and he heard Mae whisper, "Don't. Don't listen to him. Just get rid of him." She sounded like she was pleading. "You don't need to know more. We only have fifteen minutes. Javeen just get rid—"

"We started up the affair right after the older girl was born," Tharin said, drowning out Mae's voice. "I guess your father wasn't enough anymore. She was looking for more of a man, and lucky for me, I fit the bill. We stopped for a bit, which was a good call; otherwise that little one might not be as related to you as you might think. It would've been mighty awful if she was born with these blue eyes."

Asha. He was talking about Asha. Her eyes were as green as their fathers had been. She was his sister through and through. But the thought that this vile man could be her father… "Answer the damn question! Why did you kill him?" he yelled even louder, the mention of Asha fueling him to fight.

"Your ma said she was going to leave your pa. But after that small one was born, well, she kept pushing it back. I got sick of waiting. That hunting trip was just the excuse I needed. Good thing you didn't come with us." He must have seen Javeen's breath hitch because he ran with it. "Yeah, that's right. I remember how badly you wanted to go. If you did, well, boy, this wouldn't even be a problem for you in the first place. You'd be lying right next to your pa."

Javeen was about to hit him again when Mae grabbed his arm and whispered, "Ten minutes." Her fingers dug deep into his skin, but he didn't even feel it. Right now, Javeen felt nothing.

But Tharin wasn't done, not yet. "Ever wonder why she never leaves that chair, you dumb oaf? It's because she knew what I did. I brought the knife back to show her we could be together. Wait the proper time then finally get hitched. But apparently, that was too much for her. The guilt, the cheating, everything. She's just as much to blame as I am."

"Yeah, but she's not in this room. And you just confessed," Raya snarled, her face filled with shock and pity. Without looking at the group, she whispered, "So we all agree. Tharin is the murderer."

Although there wasn't a single sound in the room, as no one could muster it, everyone's heads went up and down. Tharin took one last look at Javeen and flashed him a smile. "If you ask me, which you won't, if I'd do it all again, I would…" His bloody teeth grinned a sinister scowl. "But I'd make sure you came with us."

"Five minutes," Medusa said, her voice shaking, her arms looking as though they were the only things holding her together.

Javeen took a moment to consider what to do. Tharin was going to die. He would make certain of that, but he needed him to feel the fear his father must have felt in his last moments. The plan gradually came together. He turned to the group and gave the directions.

"We need to bind his hands," he said.

Mae placed a hand on his shoulder. "Grab the belt."

"But it was your father's—"

"We need something, and this is all we've got. Besides," she said, giving Tharin a disgusted side-glance, "this is far more important than sentiment." Quickly Sadler and Raya tied up Tharin with Mae's belt, and then Javeen told Mae what to do next.

"Mae, when I tell you to, say his name and push the button, but only when I say so. Do you understand?" Mae nodded, and Javeen hauled Tharin to his feet, making sure he was eye to eye with him. Even in his last moments, Tharin maintained a pompous look on his face. Javeen smirked back, knowing what was to come, certain the man's grin would soon disappear.

"Say it, Mae."

Mae flipped the glass as the timer showed two and a half minutes remaining. "We believe Tharin is the murderer in our group." Her voice quavered, and her hand shook over the button before she pushed it firmly.

Before the hatch under Tharin could open, Javeen grabbed the front of his shirt. He felt the weight of the man drop, but Javeen was strong enough to hold him close to his face. There was a blast of sudden heat as the flames of the furnace danced below them, but Javeen didn't focus on that. Instead he took in Tharin's terrified expression. Javeen's hard, knowing eyes glared at Tharin.

"Javeen!" Mae yelled, taking a step toward him, but he didn't listen. He was on a mission.

"You remember this face, you worthless excuse for life," Javeen roared. Tharin's eyes bulged, and his breathing quickened as his eyes darted from Javeen to the furnace. "I won. I beat you in a game you thought you'd never lose. I figured you out and you were caught."

"A minute and a half!" Raya screamed.

Javeen nodded, but he had one last thing to say. "I'm glad you're dying in the furnace and my hands are guiding you in. Feel the flames, Tharin. Then do me a favor and burn in the hell you deserve."

As he let go of Tharin's shirt, a final wail vibrated through the room. The man whose icy eyes had once stirred fear in all of them was now gone, melting beneath their feet.

The hatch closed, and the timer stopped with forty-five seconds to go. Everyone waited, hoping they'd made the right choice. After a few moments, with no other trapdoors taking them under, they all were able to breathe easily. Seconds later, the door through which they had entered opened.

Everyone stood still, waiting for someone—specifically Javeen—to move. They all watched him, their eyes full of fear. Mae, who stood next to Javeen, glanced at him with pity and terror. Sadler was breathing heavily and trying as hard as he could to avoid making eye contact with him. Medusa took a step back, her hand on her chest, calming herself. Even Raya was staring at

Javeen as if he had transformed into a monster. Javeen observed all of them then realized he couldn't take one more second of this. He wanted out of this room now. As he turned and marched toward the door, Mae quickly jumped in front of his path.

"Javeen…" she tried, but he didn't listen. He pushed her aside with a swipe of his arm and made his way back to his cell. As his feet carried him, he shook his head, trying not to think of everything he'd just learned. And, more important, what he'd done.

Chapter Twenty-Four:
<u>Mae</u>

The rest of the group made their way toward the door the moment Javeen had

trudged into the dark hallway. Mae pushed herself out of the room, trying to

follow him, but his long legs were taking him back to his cell faster than she

could keep up with. She wanted to yell after him but knew it wouldn't stop him.

Right now, Javeen didn't want to understand or listen to anyone, and he was

pushing himself farther and farther away from those who actually cared.

"You'd better hurry up." Medusa sang, her pace matching Mae's

quickening stride, "or I'm going to get the cell next to him. He needs a little

happiness, don't you think? And with the cells being two feet apart, maybe less,

from each other…well, it isn't *that* far apart, is it?" She gave her a wink and

took one more step farther than Mae. "I'll keep his mind off things tonight."

A white rage blinded Mae as she thought of Medusa touching Javeen,

trying to "comfort" him. Worst of all, imagining him going to her filled her with

a fury she hadn't felt in years. Before she knew what she was doing, she

grabbed Medusa by her dead hair and pulled her back with all her strength.

Medusa fell to the floor, her sickly body hitting it with a crack that echoed through the hallway. Before she had a chance to get up, Mae had rounded back on her and placed her shoe on her chest.

"Listen here, you worthless sack of skin." Her teeth ached as she clenched her jaw, resisting the urge to knock out Medusa's teeth. "You leave him alone. If you touch him, I'll make sure you fall into the furnace faster than you can say 'Factory.' In fact, let's change that. Don't even *look* at him, or I *will* find you, and then I'll make you wish the furnace had taken you instead of me leaving your almost lifeless body behind me. Got it?"

Mae continued to glare down at the woman. Her voice had been loud and strong, and she increased the pressure on Medusa's chest, proving she wasn't joking about her promise. She'd clearly shown this woman she was done being her play toy. Mae took a deep breath as Medusa's eyes flared with anger and hatred. Although Mae waited for her to spit some sort of remark back, the woman said nothing. They stared at each other in a stalemate until Mae was certain the slimy creature had gotten the point.

The others in the hall had stopped, and Mae felt a tug on her shoulder. Raya was pulling her back by the shoulder. "Let's go. She gets it." Mae nodded, removed her foot from Medusa, then turned and continued to the cell room. Raya gave Medusa a smug look of satisfaction before following Mae. There were a few moments of silence while they continued down the never-ending hall, and then Raya grinned. "He's still not your boyfriend?"
Mae shook her head and glanced at her, not returning the joke. Raya's face fell

for a moment, as even her wit couldn't fix this problem. Mae sighed. "You saw what he just went through. He doesn't need any more filth in his life. And right now, he's so desperate to forget that he might just do anything." Raya nodded in agreement as the two finally stepped into the manufactured light of the large circular room.

When the two scanned their surroundings, they saw an entire room of empty cells, something neither Mae, Raya, or any of the others were used to. It meant only one thing. They were the first group to make it out of Stage Four. The holdings were back in the circular format they'd been in when they'd first entered The Factory. Javeen was already in his cell, the bars locking in place. Sadler was on the other side of the room, staying as far away from him as he could, perhaps afraid Javeen might throw him into the fire with just a flick of his fingers. As they got closer, Raya grabbed Mae's shoulders and pushed her hard toward a cell next to Javeen's.

"What the hell are you doing?" she whispered, digging her feet down defensively.

"Something stupid, I'm sure," Ray huffed. She continued to push, her raw strength making Mae's feet slip. "But you need to talk to him."

"He doesn't want to."

"He *will* talk," Raya grunted, and with a final shove, Mae was standing in her chamber. Raya dusted off her hands as she continued. "And when he does, you're going to be the only person he'll listen to."

Raya stepped into a nearby opening and waited for the bars to drop. Once they did, Mae glanced at the amount of space she and Raya had. All she had to do was reach a little, and her entire arm would be in Raya's cell. It reminded her of what Medusa had implied, and the anger rose so quickly that Mae had to push it down. She shook her head and wondered why the hell Raya wanted her to talk to Javeen. When their cells were locked in place, Mae walked over to where Raya now stood, leaning against the cage.

"Okay, let's say he talks. And then what? What do I tell him?"

Raya shrugged, trying to look casual about it, but Mae could tell she was thinking hard. This stage had changed the way others perceived Javeen, and if he wasn't careful, he'd end up alone due to his actions. What that group had seen in that room wasn't the Javeen she knew; rather, he had been pushed to it. Tharin wanted to torment Javeen until his very last moments. He wanted to make sure Javeen remembered every syllable that slipped from his lips, wanted his words to haunt him forever.

Finally, Raya spoke. "You lost your parents."

"Not like that…" Mae whispered, taking a glance at Javeen's cell. He was in the corner, not facing anyone in the room. His shoulders were hunched, and his face was buried in his knees. The only movement came from his quick, uneven breathing. Mae knew that position—a mirror from her past—as she had done the same thing after her parents had died.

"No, that's true," Raya said. "He wants to say something, but he doesn't know what. So instead of talking, he's shutting down. And you, more than anyone, know what can happen if you shut the world out."

Mae's head whipped back to her; she was amazed that Raya was able to call her out on actions for which she had blamed herself for so many years. Raya understood that the reason the town didn't notice her was partially her own doing, due to the fact that she also tried not to notice them. Mae knew she couldn't let Javeen do the same to her. Not when their lives were at stake. She tilted her head to the ceiling, a headache forming, and finally nodded. "Fine. I'll talk to him."

Before she could make her way over, however, a few other groups had come out of their rooms. Mae stopped to see who had made it and who had turned to ashes. As everyone else counted as well, she saw that three other groups had succeeded, as five members of each group were heading to their cells. Everyone waited for the fifth group to make their way out. But as the minutes passed, the gruesome reality of the situation settled in. That group had failed. The original thirty survivors had now been reduced to twenty-four.

Once everyone was in their cells, lunch she thought it was, arrived, but Mae wasn't focused on that. She looked at the sullen figure in the corner and tried to muster up the courage to approach him. Yet her legs stayed still. Mae knew she had to talk to Javeen, but getting through to him wouldn't be easy.

Lost in her thoughts, she was brought back to the present with a hard shove in the shoulder from Raya. "Go. Now."

Mae nodded and headed to the other side of her cell, to the farthest corner, as close as she could get to him. If she sat, perhaps he wouldn't see her as pestering, rather just a person to talk to. As she lowered herself to the floor, she knew Javeen had felt her presence, as his head picked up and tilted to the side. His shoulders relaxed before immediately tensing up again. Quickly he stared at his knees once more. "Leave me alone, Mae," he said. "I'm not talking about it. Just go away."

It was blunter than she'd expected, but she wasn't going to back down. Mae rolled her eyes, feeling as though she were talking to a child, but tried to remind herself of everything that Javeen had gone through. In a span of ten minutes, he'd discovered why his father had died and also had learned his mother had been unfaithful. No way he would display his typically bubbly personality. She took a deep breath to steady herself, then said, "You need to talk about it, Jav. Please…I'm trying to help. I know it's hard, but—"

His head snapped back, fire blazing in his green eyes, which stared her down. "Oh, do you? Do you, Mae?" he sneered. Mae tried to keep her composure, but this face reminded her of the one she'd seen that first day in the courtyard. Fueled by fury and pain.

"My parents died too. Remember? I know what it's like to lose…" She heard the anger in her voice rising but tried to keep calm.

Javeen was up in an instant, striding over to where she was sitting in the corner, and stood above her, gripping the bars of his cell. "They weren't murdered," he snapped. "And your mom didn't lie to you for half your life. So why don't you do me a favor and leave me the hell alone?"

He was about to walk away when Mae grabbed the cuff of his pants. Her grip held firm, and she wrapped her arm around his leg. She wasn't going to let him walk away, and she sure as hell wasn't going to let him talk to her like that, no matter how hurt he was. Javeen stopped and looked down at her, the fire still there, but he didn't resist.

"You're right," Mae said. "My parents weren't murdered, and they didn't lie to me for years, at least not that I know if. But that doesn't change the fact that I've suffered pain just like this. And more important, I know what you're doing." She stood up to face him, and although he loomed over her, she stared right into his eyes to prove she had a point to make. "You're building a wall to keep everyone out and your emotions in. A wall that'll never come down if you keep building it. You'll make that wall even stronger if you pity yourself. If you don't talk about what happened in there, Javeen, you'll rot from the inside. All this guilt and anger will eat you alive, you ass."

Javeen pinched the bridge of his nose in frustration and started to move back to his corner. This time Mae grabbed his shirt, pulling him against the bars. There was no longer time to be polite. His shoulders slammed against the steel, and he looked at her in amazement. She wasn't going to let him leave without a fight.

"You're being so senseless right now," she continued. "I did exactly what you're trying to do now. I built a wall after my parents died because I thought I had something to do with it. Then I built it higher because I believed the town had something to do with their deaths. Each brick was layered by me or the people in the village." The more she spoke, the more her tone softened. "Slowly I stopped coming to town because my decaying soul told me that if I went there, I'd face a town of murderers. But that wasn't my only demon. Every time I looked in the mirror, I cried, for the same reason, because I too thought I'd killed my parents. I broke every damn mirror in my house after a while. Some people think the town abandoned me, and that's true, but you know what? I was also partially responsible for my isolation. I built a barrier too high to let anyone in, and because of that, I started to die on the inside." She took a deep breath and went on. "Until—and this is irony at its finest—I came here. You and Raya showed me human decency. You showed me that maybe I was wrong about the people in town…at least some of them."

Mae felt a tug to glance behind her at Raya, as she realized her voice had carried louder than she'd expected. She looked over her shoulder and saw Raya staring at her, her eyes wide and soft. Maybe she wasn't as strong as Mae had thought, and perhaps she needed to hear this too. It seemed Raya was determined not to let anyone in, because at some point in her life, Mae now realized, she had built that same fortress. The one that killed from within. After just hearing that she and Javeen had given Mae hope, perhaps that wall was crumbling a bit, just as Mae's had. The three of them needed one another, and the only way to ensure their alliance was by making sure Javeen was mentally and emotionally stable. With hardening eyes, Mae turned back to Javeen, ready to tell him the truth if he continued to build a wall around him.

"Why are you pushing me away, Javeen? Out of everyone here, why me? What have I done to hurt you? Nothing. Absolutely nothing. In fact, I actually saved your ass. Just a little reminder. But I can't stop you if this is the path you choose. You can go ahead and build that wall. Do it. But you'll be dead by the next stage. And you know why? Because you were too idiotic to figure out that all I'm trying to do is help. After all we've been through in here, all we've seen, are you willing to block me out so you can grieve in the corner? Don't be stupid. If you continue your pity party, you'll be useless to me. I don't want or need someone to push me away. I've already been through that. So figure it out, Javeen. Do you want to live or die?"

They stood there for a moment, eye to eye. Mae was breathing hard, her face red with heat, her eyes stinging as she held back the tears. She didn't want him to leave her, but it really was his choice. There was nothing she could say once he chose his fate. But she would stand by her word if he didn't stick with her. She couldn't endanger herself if he was just going to wallow. They needed to survive, and if Javeen couldn't get past his grief for the rest of the challenges, he would be deadweight.

Javeen's face had softened somewhat during Mae's speech, but she still wasn't sure he would talk. His breathing quickened as his eyes frantically darted from her to the floor. At first Mae thought he was going to have some sort of fit, or maybe he'd just tear himself away from her. Finally, he slumped to the floor and buried his face in his hands before curling into a ball and rocking back and forth. Mae slowly knelt and placed a hand on his shoulder. She felt Javeen shudder and knew he was crying, but if was a soft sob. The pressure he was holding within was slowly releasing. It was what he needed, so Mae let him cry, waiting for him to finally open up to her.

Minutes later he finally raised his head, his breathing still unsteady. Javeen wiped his nose and rubbed his eyes, trying to hide the fact he'd been crying. His eyes were red, emphasizing the green vibrancy they always held, and then he looked over at Mae. "I killed a man today," he said, still shaking. His face was pale and haunted as he continued. "I'm a murderer. I'm...I'm...no better than Tharin."

"No, you're not." Mae said, but she watched as he continued to shake his head. "Please listen, Javeen. You aren't a murderer. Tharin made you do what you did. He used his words to manipulate you into your actions. You didn't kill a man who didn't deserve to die. You got rid of someone who didn't deserve to breathe air on this earth. You avenged your father's murder. Besides,

Tharin was going to die anyway, regardless of whether you let go of him. He confessed to his crime. Are you hearing me? You're *not* a killer, Javeen."

He looked over, his eyes still pink, tears brimming at the edges. "It's not just that, Mae. I know you're right. But it's not just the fact that I threw him into the furnace. It was…what he said…why he did it. Mae, my mom…"

Mae had tried to tell him not to push Tharin into talking, as she knew nothing good could come from it. But at the same time, she understood why Javeen had questioned him. For years, he hadn't understood why his father had disappeared. Then once the truth was revealed, he needed answers. But he never had suspected the reason behind his father's death lay within his own house. "I know. I know it's hard to find out something like that," Mae said.

Javeen shook his head wildly, as if trying to clear the thoughts from his head. "I can never trust her again. Not after this. I might not even love her anymore. I don't think I could look at her without wanting to hurt her." He let out a deep sigh. "And if I get out of here, I might just kick her out. She's always been a burden since his death. And now that I know the truth, I don't want her in the house." He grunted, a grimace crossing his face. "Although it all makes sense now. Why she's sat there for years and done nothing. Once I tell my brother and sisters—"

"You can't do that," Mae interrupted. She waited for his wrath as the silence grew for a moment.

Javeen tilted his head toward her, confusion enveloping his face. "Why not? My siblings have the right to know. It's not fair for them to think she's some sort of grieving widow. And she'll never tell them. She's had six years to tell me what happened, and instead she's just been sitting in that damn chair of hers, rocking in her own guilt."

He's partially right, Mae thought. His mother should have told him she'd been unfaithful to his father, but that didn't mean his siblings needed to know. "I know you're filled with anger, but think about it. She can't be abandoned, Javeen. You can let her know what happened—let her know you learned her secret—but don't isolate her from the rest of your family. It could tear them apart. She didn't actually kill him…"

"She might as well have."

"But she didn't plunge that knife into him, and she knows what she did was wrong. Let her punish herself for the rest of her life, and allow your family continue to live in ignorance." Mae placed her hand on his. "I know it'll be hard, but I'm not saying you have to forgive her. I actually don't think you can. So don't. Just let her…let her die from her own guilt, I guess."

They sat there while Javeen let everything sink in. He remained still, his brows knitted, while he considered what she had said. Mae knew he wanted to keep his family together, and if he told everyone the secret, it would in fact tear them apart. That was his greatest fear, and if he understood what she was saying, then by not telling them, he could prevent that from happening. Slowly he nodded, turning his hand to hold Mae's and giving it a tight grip. His breathing steadied as he kept nodding. He gave her a pained smile. "You're right. Damn it, Mae, you're right." He sighed. "I won't tell them."

A few moments later, the bedrolls appeared, telling everyone it was time to turn in for the night. Mae wondered if their group would be able to, after all they'd witnessed today. She recalled the terrified look on Tharin's face, the bloody smile he kept flashing at Javeen, his screams as he fell into the flames. She headed over to her bedroll, pushing those images out of her head, when she saw Raya, her back turned toward her, her breathing choppy. She looked as if she were having a breakdown.

"Raya?" Mae asked, taking a step toward her.

"I'm fine," she quietly replied, and Mae knew Raya had heard everything she'd said, watched everything that had happened. But there was more to it. Mae could feel what was occurring. Raya's barrier was weaker than it had been before; perhaps she was having a panic attack. "I just…I just…look, go over to him. He's going to need someone to keep him company…someone other than Medusa." Mae smiled, knowing Raya would have thrown a wink at her if she wanted to.

Without another word, Mae dragged her bedroll to the corner and sat down. Javeen gave her a faint smile as she reached into his cell, patting the ground. He needed comfort, and honestly, so did she. Soon he was next to her, and slowly the drain from the day took hold of him. He drifted off, Mae watching to make sure he didn't have any fits, but he was sound asleep. Slowly she let the darkness take her as well, and once more, a sort of optimism filled her soul. However, it didn't come from her; it came just from Javeen. For the first time in a very long time, Mae felt confident in herself. She felt she now had the strength to get out of The Factory.

Chapter Twenty-Five:
<u>Javeen</u>

They sat in their cells for two more days. Javeen found it a tad amusing because those who remained had begun a regular routine. Either they walked in their cells all day, until it was time for food and rest, or they sat and sporadically got up and moved, only to sit once more. He tried to keep his body moving, and he knew moving was for the best, because the more he counted his steps, the less he thought. But still, what he had done to Tharin burned in his mind.

He was a murderer now, or at least that was how he saw himself. Tharin's horrible face, with his icy eyes, bore into him as he slept, reminding him of what he had done. He had killed a man, and even though Mae had tried to alleviate his pain, Javeen still felt guilty. He also couldn't stop thinking about his mother's role—voluntary or not—in his father's death. If she'd just stayed faithful or worked things out in her marriage, perhaps he'd still be alive. But Javeen would never know now.

As he paced, he glanced at Mae's cell, and his heart warmed at the sight of her. She had saved him by refusing to let him build the wall he so desperately wanted to surround himself with. When he had begun to create it, he felt a certain comfort in his solitude. And although he had argued with her and tried to push her away, she had stuck with him. She was right about how similar they were. They both had lost parents—not in the same way, but still the pain was there—and Javeen was comforted by the fact that she hadn't left his side. Although they continued to converse, keeping it casual and trying not to talk about what had happened two days ago, it didn't stop the thoughts that haunted him.

Still, he wondered if Mae really did care about him or if she merely pitied him. Yes, her parents had died, and yes, she had blamed herself for it for years, but she hadn't killed them—an illness had taken over their bodies. Javeen's father, however, had died by the hands of another, and Javeen had killed that man in return. Those two situations were vastly different. Did Mae really worry about that wall she'd preached about, or was she just feeling sorry for Javeen and telling him everything he wanted to hear?

His thoughts were broken with the familiar ping the survivors had all begun to fear. Javeen sighed heavily, closed his eyes, and waited for the next stage. A few moments later, that dreaded voice spoke once more.

"Good morning, everyone. I hope your days have been going well, as you've had time to rest. Later this afternoon, we'll begin Stage Five."

Javeen and Mae, who now stood closer to him, exchanged quizzical looks. Why was The Factory giving them advance notice about the next stage? A stage that was meant to kill them? Javeen, however, knew there was a reason; there always was. He remembered what Raya had said about the stages being mental challenges. Letting them fester and think about what was to come was just another mind game. Javeen remembered the second stage and wondering why the pills were being dispensed at different intervals, as The Factory had told them they would be, as well as the screams that followed. The Factory knew what it was doing, and Javeen knew not to question it.

"In a few moments," the voice continued, "you'll each receive a glass vial. Each of those vials will contain a hint that will help you survive the next stage. You'll have time to review that hint. Stage Five will begin in ninety minutes, at which point you'll receive further instructions." The voice ended with the standard click, but its cheery echo filled the room.

Seconds later, a tile in the corner of each of the cells buckled and lowered, then rose back up, producing a small vial. Many of the survivors stood in their cells, staring at their vial, wondering if this was some sort of trick. Slowly Javeen walked over, knelt, and gingerly picked up his vial. As he examined it, he saw a small bit of brown parchment coiled up, with some sort of writing peeking through. He uncorked the top and removed the contents. Carefully, he unrolled the paper.

In red ink was a rhyme, some sort of riddle. Javeen's face screwed up as he read it, trying to make sense of the words.

"*Though piercing through, or cutting thin, this object makes a sick man grin. But do not look at the silver shine; your safety lies where metal binds.*"

Again and again, he read the words, trying to piece them together. He had to look for something silver; that was clear. But where or what that silver object was, Javeen had no idea. He glanced at Mae, who looked just as confused as she stared at her slip of paper. He made his way over to their corner, smiling slightly as Mae rubbed her temple. Even though she was frustrated, her charm, unknown to her, captivated him. She looked up, catching sight of him, and shook the parchment in her hand.

"Does yours make any sense?" she whispered.

Javeen shook his head and nodded toward her paper. "What does yours say?"

In a dramatic fashion, Mae brought the parchment up to her face and tugged it tightly with both hands, then read it aloud.

"*Giving comfort after a long day's labor, this object is made for your body's favor. But do not consider its cloud a lining. Your safety lies in an object shining.*"

She dropped her hands and let out a quiet, aggravated huff. "A crock of shit if you ask me."

Javeen nodded; Mae was in the same situation he was. She had no idea what her hint meant or what it meant for the stage itself. The Factory was now pulling out all the stops; this challenge clearly would be more difficult than the previous ones. Javeen let out a grunt and glanced at his clue again. "Fitting that they would write it in red." He waved the paper about as he snickered. "Since, you know, we'll probably pay with our blood."

Mae raised an eyebrow, and Javeen thought she might have decided he'd finally gone insane. She looked down at her parchment then back at him. Finally she said, "What are you talking about?"

"The ink," Javeen said bluntly, not understanding her confusion. He showed her his paper. "It's red."

Mae looked at his small sheet then down at hers once more. "Mine isn't." She showed him the blue ink on her parchment.

Javeen leaned forward, looked at her paper, then back at his again. *Red and blue, blue and red*, he thought. There had to be a reason the inks were different. This wasn't an accident, because The Factory was smart, and it never made mistakes. Perhaps this stage had more than one aspect to it. Slowly a thought came to him as he continued to glance at the papers. "There are two clues," he whispered.

Mae moved in closer, analyzing his parchment. "You think the colors are another clue, huh? Not just what's written on the paper."

Javeen nodded. "The first clue, the written one, its something we need to look for. Something that will guarantee our safety, obviously. What that is, we aren't sure yet, but whatever we're looking for will be these colors." He pointed to his strip of paper. "Whatever my safety is will be red, and yours will be blue.

I have a feeling that if we take anything that's another color, it won't protect us."

"And into the furnace we'll go." Mae sighed, acknowledging that Javeen probably was right. With a sharp inhalation, she straightened up and jerked her head toward Raya. "I'm going to tell her…"

Javeen rolled his eyes and rubbed his forehead. This was getting ridiculous. Why did Mae trust that girl so much? He didn't want anything to do with her. Something about her made him not trust her. And besides, she wasn't someone he wanted to protect. The pact was between Mae and him; that was it. He was just about to say that when Mae got close and whispered, "I know you don't trust her, but I do. She helped us in the last stage. She stuck up for me."

"Only because it was in her interest," Javeen snapped back. "You know it's true, Mae. If she didn't help us figure out who the murderer was, she would have died too, along with the rest of us. Stage Five is an individual challenge. Everyone will be out for themselves. Just like with the levers. Are you sure you aren't setting yourself up to have her turn her back on you and send you into the furnace?"

Mae's blue eyes faltered for a moment as she considered Javeen's words. He was trying to warn her, not only for her sake, but also for his. If for some reason this stone-cold, scar-faced girl caused Mae's death, Javeen never would forgive himself. But Mae looked back up at him and nodded. "I'm sure.

You have to trust my decisions. It's gotten us this far. I know she'll be useful. Please." She reached into his cage and grabbed his forearm, giving it a squeeze.

Trying to argue was pointless. Mae was strong-headed, in a good way, but also in a dangerous one. Once she had an idea in her head, there was no altering it, no matter how hard Javeen pleaded. She was convinced that Raya was worth trusting, and perhaps Javeen should just go with it. Still, though Mae was right about Raya helping in the last stage, the girl had more to prove in order to gain his trust. Sighing, he dropped his shoulders in defeat and rubbed the back of his neck. "Fine." He cut his head in Raya's direction. "Now hurry up and tell her before I change my mind."

Mae grabbed his hand. "Thank you." With a smile—a real smile—she turned and made her way toward Raya's cell. A twist in his stomach remained as he wondered about this new alliance Mae was trying to form. He watched her back defensively, knowing he had to in order to protect her.

But as he watched her walk away, Javeen wondered what Raya's actual intentions were. Did she truly believe in Mae, and think that working with her would get them both out of here? Or would Raya use Mae's trust in her as a way of getting rid of one more person and securing her spot in the final six? Until Raya proved her worthiness, Javeen could only believe that Raya had one true motive.

To kill Mae.

Chapter Twenty-Six:
Mae

As she walked toward Raya's cell, Javeen's words bounced around in her head.
Could Raya really be trusted? Something inside her told her Raya had a
determination to win—the same determination she and Javeen had—but to what
levels would she go to in order to secure victory? And although Mae hated to
admit it, Javeen was right about her actions in the last stage. The lives of
everyone in that room had been in danger, and perhaps Raya only had cared
about saving herself. Something in Mae's gut, however, told her Raya was a
decent human being, unlike Medusa, who would watch others burn with a
wicked smile on her face. No matter what Javeen said, Mae was going to have
to trust her.

The girl with the fire-red hair was standing in the corner of her cell,
leaning against the bars and reading the words on her parchment. Mae watched
as her eyes constantly moved; she was rereading the clue over and over, like
they all were. The Factory had made this stage more difficult than any of the
others, proving Raya's claim about how it was all a mental game. There was
something odd about these clues, something Mae couldn't put her finger on. But
for now that could wait. Mae knew one thing about this puzzle and was willing

the take the chance to tell Raya. When she finally approached her, Raya gave her a quick glance, a nod, then went right back to reading. Only seconds later did she throw her hands down and let out an exasperated breath.

"Well, here we go again." She sighed, finally deciding to give up on her clue and face Mae. "What's going on?" When Mae said nothing, her eyes narrowed.

"What does yours say?" Mae blurted.

Raya's face went hard, and she looked as though she were about to take a step back and take up a defensive position. Her grip tightened around her piece of parchment. "And I should tell you because...?"

Mae shrugged, at the same time lowering her stiff shoulders and giving Raya an indifferent gaze. She wasn't going to fight with her, and she needed to show that. Either Raya would accept her help, or she'd be on her own. There were no other options, and Mae couldn't force a choice on her. It was the same thing Javeen had allowed her to do—make her own choices about what to do and whom to trust. "Maybe I can help you figure it out." She gave Raya a weak smile. "You look a little lost."

Slowly Raya stepped toward Mae once more, her hold loosening on her slip of paper. Her jaw relaxed as she returned the grin. She threw her head back toward the other cells, letting a little chuckle out as she did. "I look lost? Well in case you didn't notice, so does everyone else in this damn place. I don't think anyone knows what the hell this all means." There was a pause, and then she said, "Well, maybe not *everyone* is lost…" As her intense hazel eyes locked onto Mae's, she realized Raya was reaching for her help. She didn't just need it; she wanted it.

"Go ahead," Mae urged.

Both girls pushed as close as they could to the bars of their cells, making sure no one around them was paying attention. Mae watched the beads of sweat dripping off Raya's skin, dancing around her scar. Now that she was this close, it didn't look as frightening or intimidating. In fact, it was sort of intriguing and mysterious. What had happened to her? But before she could think about it anymore, Raya whispered her clue to her.

"Time to relax and sink in deep. This object many wish to keep. But do not look where water's clean. Your safety lies where it is never seen."

In silence they pondered the clue. Then the craziest thought popped into Mae's mind, and she let out a little laugh. Raya looked at her, questioning Mae, wondering what could be so funny about this. After all, they most certainly could die if they didn't figure out what these clues meant. Mae put her hand up, trying to tell Raya that she wasn't going nuts; the thought she'd just had was quite funny. It was so ridiculous that she almost shouted it as she tried to calm herself down.

"It sounds like a bathtub." She giggled, eventually getting enough breath to realize how insane it was to even consider.

When she looked up, Mae expected Raya to join her in her moment of entertainment, thinking how ridiculous it would be to have a bathtub in The Factory. After all, more than a week had passed, and none of them had seen a hint of something to clean themselves with. But Raya's face lit up. Her eyes darted to her parchment, looking once more over the words, moving faster than before and with much more intensity. As they did, her hard-lined mouth began to turn up. The more she read, the more she smiled. Mae cautiously poked her through the cell, hoping Raya wouldn't rip her hand off. "Raya? You...you okay?"

She dropped her arms, her smile still illuminating her face. "Mae, you got it! That's the clue. I have to look for a bathtub!"

It was hard not to look at Raya as though she'd hit the breaking point. Slowly Mae said, "Raya, there are no bathtubs in The Factory. You know that, right? This isn't a home."

Raya's smile didn't falter as she threw her hands in the air. "You don't know that! No one knows how big this place is. Who knows what they have in here? They could have a fake house or something... I bet they do!" Her voice rose as she moved her body up and down, trying to contain her excitement. "They have to! It makes perfect sense. I bet all the clues are about household objects."

Raya could tell Mae was still hesitant, so she continued. "Okay, okay, I know. But think about it," she said, enthusiasm dripping from her voice. She ran her finger under the lines of text on the parchment. "'*Many wish to keep.*' Bathtubs are so rare in town that they're usually the first things to go into a will besides money! And I mean, come on… '*Sink in deep*'…it all makes sense." Once more she read it, pointing at one line in particular. "Ah! Here's where I have to be careful. See, my safety isn't in the tub itself. '*But do not look where water's clean. Your safety lies where…*'"

"'*It is never seen,*'" Mae finished. She closed her eyes and imagined the few tubs she'd seen in her life. Water came out of a spigot, and the water was clean…but where was it never seen? Then it hit her. She looked up, finally understanding the clue. "Whatever you're looking for, it's in the drain."

"Yes! Yes, you're right! Alright, what does yours say?" Raya almost yelled, her optimism getting the better of her judgment. Others in the cells looked around, including Medusa, who glared at them. Raya gave her an obscene gesture, which told her to mind her own business, as she turned back to Mae.

Mae read hers aloud, trying to think of what might be in a house. "*Giving comfort after a long day's labor, this object is made for your body's favor.*" There were lots of things in a house that a body would find comforting, so that didn't narrow it down much. It could be oils, drinks, anything really. Then she read the second part. *But do not consider its cloud a lining.* There was only one thing in a house that looked like a cloud, and bodies loved it. Mae felt a smile cross her face as she exclaimed, "It's a mattress!"

Raya, nodding, then quickly reminded her, "But don't forget the trick." She pointed at Mae's paper. "That's not where your safety lies. *In an object shining?*" She rubbed her head. "I can't think of anything on a bed that would shine."

But Mae didn't care anymore. The pieces were all falling together, and she couldn't stop smiling. "That doesn't matter. I know what I'm looking for now. Or at least where it might be. Something shining on a bed or in a bedroom." In her moment of happiness, she remembered the person behind her. Mae paused and looked at Javeen, who was still glaring at the two of them.

"What? Mountain Man still doesn't trust me?" Raya spat, her sarcastic tone lingering in the air.

Mae let out a laugh. "Oh, how can you tell?" and gave Javeen a little wave, hoping his face would soften. When it didn't, she turned back to Raya. "His name is Javeen. And he's getting there." She then whispered, "I think."

Raya huffed and glared back at him. Mae wondered how long the staring contest would last. Just then Raya, not looking away, asked, "Do you know his clue?" The acid in her voice had disappeared. Mae raised an eyebrow in her direction, and Raya gave a dramatic sigh before finally breaking eye contact with Javeen. "I mean, *maybe* we can help him."

Mae tried to recite Javeen's clue, but she messed up most of it, except for, "*This object makes a sick man grin.*" After she'd uttered that line, Raya and Mae jerked up, facing each other. The two of them knew The Factory was cruel and wanted to play mental games with all the survivors, but this was wrong. This was clearly more than a coincidence. Javeen's object was…well, it was very real to him now.

"It's a freaking knife," Raya growled, no longer able to look at Javeen. "Right after all the shit he just went through too. His father was killed with a knife. *His* knife. And what happens? This place goes and gives the Mountain Ma…Javeen's safety in the form of a knife."

Mae felt her stomach curl, knowing she'd have to tell him what his clue meant. She just wanted to forget what the rhyme was about, but Javeen probably would figure it out anyway. He was smart, and it was better to get this over with now, rather than pretend she didn't know what it was. Mae was just about to head back when she remembered why she had come over in the first place.

"Oh! Javeen figured out something else," she said, watching Raya's face fall in frustration.

Raya groaned as she stared at the ceiling.

Mae motioned with her chin toward Raya's paper, a smirk creeping up on her face. "What color is your ink?"

"Why does that—"

"What color is it?" Mae said more forcefully.

Raya looked down and said, "Green."

Mae flipped her clue over to show Raya the blue ink that had stained the brown paper. Raya took a step forward, looking from Mae's clue to her own. Mae watched as the realization set in. Raya looked back at her. "You think that has something to do with our safety?"

Mae nodded. "Javeen's clue is written in red ink. Whatever we're looking for, the color of our clue is the color of our safety." She glanced at the rest of the cells. "Look around. Some people have black parchment. That must mean their ink is another color, one that won't show up on regular paper. Like white or something."

"That means, if we take something that's the wrong color..." Raya wiggled her fingers and made a whooshing noise before saying, "We go into the fire."

Mae was taken aback by the bluntness of her comment, along with her outlandish hand gestures. But then again, she should have been ready for something like that. At this point, Raya wasn't beating around the bush. She was determined to get out, and they couldn't leave a place like this by dancing around the facts. Also, Mae realized, humor kept them from going crazy in a place like this.

"I guess we figured it out?" she asked, giving Raya a side-glance. There was still no way to read what Raya was thinking or if she really did trust Mae.

"Yeah. I think we've got it." She turned to face Mae. "When the cages are raised, make sure Javeen stays with us. If we work together, we can get out of this."

"So you trust me?" Mae said, sounding a little too hopeful.

"I didn't say that," Raya sneered, then made her way to the middle of the cell, nibbling on a hunk of bread she must have saved from this morning.

Mae watched Raya read her clue again, then sighed and headed toward Javeen. Her heart began to ache for the girl, knowing there was so much more to her than perhaps she'd ever know. There was a reason Mae had been so hard on the outside, even if it was partially her own fault. But she wondered what had made Raya so untrusting of other people. It had to have been something traumatic. Something that had made her weak on the inside and strong on the outside. With one quick glance over her shoulder, she looked at the scar that lined Raya's face and knew it must have changed her somehow.

When she approached Javeen, she immediately explained what she and Raya had come up with. How, in some way, all the items were something that could be found in a house. In what way that was even possible was still a mystery to her, and Mae waited for Javeen to shoot down the thought right away. To her surprise, though, Javeen didn't find the idea as crazy as she thought he might.

"You never know with this place." He scanned the room. "We don't know how big it is. There could be a version of a house in here," he added, echoing Raya's thought.

Mae went on about how they'd figured out that Raya had to look in the drain of a tub and that Mae's clue had something to do with a mattress. As she told him all this, Javeen read over his paper again, this time with new eyes. They narrowed then widened in a moment. Then, in one quick move, he threw his arms down and stormed off toward the other end of the cell, nearest to Sadler, and slammed the bars with his fists. Sadler flinched but relaxed when Javeen walked back to Mae. Javeen's eyes were wild, but with a deep breath he calmed himself and whispered, "So mine has to do with a knife?"

Mae had no choice but to agree. With a sad smile, she attempted to get a laugh from him. "Kind of ironic?" she said with a shrug, hoping it might relieve the tension.

As Javeen looked at her—truly looked at her—Mae thought she might have gone too far. She waited for his eyes to spark with anger or frustration toward her. Then she saw the small pull on his lips and knew it had worked. Mae had made a bad joke, but somehow it had made Javeen feel better. His eyes were still on her, not looking through her, as if he were thinking about the task at hand, but at her. Looking at her as if trying to memorize every aspect of her. From her six braids to the freckles on her nose. Normally she would have backed away, but right now Mae didn't mind it at all. She felt a warmth inside, something she hadn't felt in years.

Javeen's arm slowly made its way up, almost reaching her face, when the ping came.

"Stage Five will begin momentarily."

Chapter Twenty-Seven:
<u>Javeen</u>

Quickly dropping his arm, Javeen looked up at the tall ceiling, where the voice had come from, and awaited The Factory's instructions. While he stood there, he reprimanded himself. *What the hell was I was thinking, almost showing my emotions for Mae?* But there was something in that moment, when she had made him laugh, regardless of where they were, that had created a feeling of home. No longer was their connection one of survival; rather, it was a sort of relationship. But when the ping for the next stage had rung out, he was reminded of where he was; the situation he was in was purely based on survival, both hers and his. He could worry about his feelings for her later. Right now, he needed to clear his mind and focus on the next challenge.

The voice, once again filled with glee, echoed through the room with simple instructions for the group.

"In a moment, you will be released from your cells. Follow the arrows from your cells to the appropriate hallways. When you reach the correct room, you will receive your final instructions for this stage."

After the click, everyone waited for their cages to recede into the ceiling individually, as they had earlier. Last time, Javeen had refused to look at Mae, fearing they'd be separated, but not now. Not after the moment they had just shared with one another. He looked at Mae, who gave him a nod of determination, then watched as she turned her head toward Raya, who returned her curt headshake.

Javeen felt a pull in his stomach once more about Raya. There was something off about her. He wasn't sure whether it was the hard exterior or the fact that the scar on her face made her seem more treacherous than she might be. Javeen knew that judging her by her appearance was wrong, but that nasty scar definitely didn't make him think she was a good person. Regardless of any of those factors, one thing was clear: the trust between them still wasn't there. They made quick eye contact, with Raya's eyes fixing on his, but neither acknowledged each other in any other way.

There was a grinding noise as Javeen's bars dislodged from the floor. He looked to see who would be joining him, but every other cage was rising as well. His gut curled once more as everyone was freed from their holdings. Did this mean the twenty remaining people would all be in this together? If they were, his job of protecting Mae—and watching Raya—would be much more difficult.

As he continued to think, there was a sudden flash, and arrows lit up in front of his feet, leading him to his destination. They were red, the same color as the ink on his parchment. When he looked at the other colorful arrows that lit up the floor, he assumed everyone's arrows must have matched their clues as well. His mood lightened when he noticed that Mae's and Raya's were going in the same direction as his. As he watched the other lights, he realized everyone wasn't going down the same hall. Others, like the town drunk, were headed in completely different directions. Javeen now knew the twenty survivors were going to be split up, causing the ache in his chest to lighten. As he began to walk, he felt Mae move up next to him, her steps quickening. But to her side was another set of feet, ones that weren't so quiet.

"So what's the plan?" Raya's demanding voice hissed as everyone followed their markers.

Javeen glared at her then looked at Mae, who seemed to enjoy the tension between the two. The smirk on her face didn't leave room for him to think much else. Raya's eyes bore into him, demanding an answer. He sighed loudly to show his disdain toward Raya's presence, then said, "Sticking together will get us killed." He rubbed the bridge of his nose. "I can't believe I'm saying this, but we need to split up."

He waited for a cackle from Raya, or an eye roll from Mae, but neither made it his way. Instead, both girls nodded in agreement.

"If we stay together," Mae said, "we're sitting ducks."

"I mean, people can think we're friends," Raya whispered, "but they'll never tolerate an alliance."

Their voices were soft, but Javeen noticed another figure hurrying to catch up. Nothing good could come from what he saw marching toward them.

The long stick figure pushed her legs harder than Javeen thought possible. Her wiry white hair was starting to weigh down from natural oils due to lack of bathing. Medusa was close enough to them that Javeen knew he had to end the conversation there.

"When we get in there, we can figure it out," he said, stopping to let Medusa pass before they continued. He thought he'd been speaking quietly enough, allowing Medusa to move ahead without giving any indication that they might be working together. But as Medusa sauntered by, a wicked grin flashed across her face. She stopped, slowly turned around, and made long eye contact with Javeen.

"Oh, you silly, silly boy. I don't think that'll be an option for you." She looked at Mae and Raya, then gave them a small laugh and continued down the hallway.

At first Javeen had no idea what she was talking about. Perhaps Medusa was just trying to get into his head or inside Mae's. There had to be a game behind her malicious look. But when he turned to Mae, whose face overflowed with anger toward white-haired figure, and then to Raya, his mood changed. Not because of Mae's darkening eyes toward Medusa, but because of Raya, who was glaring at the floor, followed by quick spit.

"Well, shit," Raya muttered.

Javeen followed her gaze and saw that his red arrows were now taking him down a different hallway, while Mae's blue arrows and Raya's green arrows were headed down the same hallway Medusa had disappeared into. Their plan had been foiled. The Factory was splitting them up.

Mae took a second before looking down at the lights, then inhaled sharply. "Couldn't have said it better myself," she muttered, grabbing her six braids and wrapping them around her fist in frustration. She looked up at Javeen, her eyes begging for some sort of answer. "What do we do?"

"You have three minutes to get to your halls," the voice from above chimed in.

Panic set in as Javeen tried to come up with a reply. He would be on his own, and for him, that would be easier. He only had to worry about himself and finding his object. But Mae would be with Raya, and his confidence in her protecting Mae was tenuous. His promise to keep Mae safe returned his mind once more, and for a second, he thought his worry for her might be so great that he wouldn't make it through this stage.

"Stick with the plan," he said firmly. "Split up and find your objects. And remember…" He looked closely at both girls, who, beneath their hard exteriors, looked terrified. "Stick with your color. Don't chose an object that's a different color. Even if it's right in the open. Stick with blue and green. Got it?"

Both acknowledged that they understood just as the voice came back on. "Two minutes."

"We'd better get going." Raya sighed, jerking her head toward the hall. "Otherwise we might miss our bonding time with our *favoritest* person on earth…" She rolled her eyes to the ceiling and muttered as she walked on. "Good luck, Javeen."

The mention of his name instead of "Mountain Man" threw him off for a moment, but he quickly regained his composure. He tried to think of a witty yet casual retort, but Raya already was headed down the hallway. As he turned to Mae, who was just about to walk past him, a surge of panic and impulsiveness rushed through him. He grabbed her by the shoulders and brought her close.

"Listen to me, Mae. We've made it this far. The two of us have been through a lot. This is the first time we won't be in the same room. You…you have to be careful in there, okay?" He swallowed hard. "If you don't come out…" He shook his head violently at the mere thought of it. "No…no, you need to come out. Finish this stage alive. Get out of whatever hell they have in there for you." He paused, and then the words slipped out before he could contain them. "Get out of there alive for me."

Javeen felt it all on the tip of his tongue. All right there, ready to fall out like a waterfall. He wanted to tell her everything, about these last few days, how he had felt for her for so long. In this moment, this last moment they might share together, he could tell her every last ounce of what he felt. But his mouth was stuck, the cascade of words blocked by a dam, so all he could do was repeat himself one last time.

"Mae. Get out for me."

Mae looked into his eyes, and for a moment he considered telling her everything. Her blue eyes were wide, as if understanding that something could happen in this moment. Wide with fear or anticipation, Javeen didn't know. And he'd never find out as she wiggled out of his grasp and placed a hand on his shoulder. "I will, Javeen. I promise. But promise me you'll get out too." Mae looked at him for a moment longer before racing toward the hall. "I'm going to need you after all this," she called after her. With a shrug, she added, "Who else will I talk to? Medusa?"

Letting out a soft chuckle, Javeen watched her go, then quickly realized his time was dwindling. He once more ran through a shadowy hallway, illuminated eerily by his red arrows, and into a dark room. Around him he heard voices, coughing, and the wheezing of a few people he thought might be afraid of the dark. Or The Factory. At this point, it didn't really matter. Fear and anxiety were now an immortal parasite in their minds, and they knew nothing else.

As they stood for a few more moments, Javeen thinking about Mae once again, when suddenly the lights came on.

Chapter Twenty-Eight:
<u>Mae</u>

The darkness in the room was almost too much for Mae to handle. She couldn't see a thing. But right before the door had shut behind her, she had seen where Raya was standing and positioned herself next to her. Every now and then, either she or Raya brushed hands to make sure they were still next to each other in the blackness, reassuring themselves that The Factory hadn't taken them away in a covert way. Then, with a burning flash, the room was filled with bright yellow lights.

After the initial adjustment of her eyes, Mae looked to see who else was with them. Medusa stood at the far end of the line, staring forward. But there was a quick moment, almost a burst, where Mae saw the woman's eyes glance over and give her a devilish grin. As the anger boiled her blood, Mae had to cool herself down, so she started by looking at the other survivors. She couldn't remember the names of anyone else standing close to her, except for one. Sadler, the bookmaker's apprentice, had made his way into the group. Mae was surprised to see him, as his lanky frame, although it somehow had some muscle, suggested that he wouldn't have made it as far as he had. But then she remembered what Raya had said. The Factory was all about mental strength, and it seemed Sadler's brain was more powerful than his body.

Suddenly another bright burst flashed in front of them, catching everyone by surprise. Still they couldn't see, as the lights were so bright, and Mae squinted as Raya covered her forehead to shield her eyes. When the lights eventually dimmed, Mae couldn't believe what she saw. More accurately, she couldn't believe that she and Raya were right. There, in front of the group, was a house.

The term "house" was an understatement for the monstrosity that stood before them. It was a mansion, even bigger than the mayor's house in the village, which was something to be admired. But that was as far as the resemblance went. While the mayor's house was ornate and well kept, this building looked as though it might fall apart at any moment, grasping onto life by an inch. The windows were broken, and the front door was missing. The roof sagged under some sort of weight, and Mae could see through the broken windows that some of the furniture was turned over. It was the perfect place to hide something.

She turned to Raya, whose eyes were wide with amazement. She had said they didn't know how large The Factory was, but the thought that it could contain an entire mansion was beyond comprehension. Mae then remembered her separation from Javeen and how other survivors had gone in different directions. There probably were *multiple* mansions here, not just one. Exactly how big was this place? And did Mae really want to know? As they all stood in complete awe, the ping rang through the room, and the woman's voice returned.

"Welcome to Stage Five. As you know, you all received clues that will help you survive this stage. What you are not aware of is that the ink from those parchments has injected a poison into your skin. Within this house, you will find the antidote that will save you from death. You have one hour to find your safety vial and remove yourself from this house in order to proceed to the final stage. Best of luck. You may now begin."

Once the familiar click echoed through the room, and there was a moment of pause, chaos ensued. Everyone ran toward the house, some even jumping through the broken windows in order to find their vials and get out. Raya and Mae were the only two to stay behind, watching as Sadler calmly strolled inside. Although there was something odd about his walk and his calm demeanor, Mae had no time to worry about him. As she and Raya slowly marched toward the house, they calculated their plan, sticking to what Javeen had told them.

"Okay," Mae said, as they worked their way up the wraparound porch, "you're looking for a bathroom, and I'm looking for a bedroom. Simple enough."

Raya snorted. "Have you looked at this place? It probably had twenty bathrooms and at least forty bedrooms."

"Then we'd better get started. We know where our clues are; others might not. So just look in every bathtub drain you can. But try to look like you're confused. We don't want anyone catching on that we know the way this stage works. I'll try to figure out what the hell that stupid shining thing means, and we'll meet up here in forty minutes, okay?" She grabbed Raya's arm and whispered, "And remember, you're only looking for something green."

Raya nodded, and the two entered the house. The madness they walked into was beyond comprehension. They no longer saw that same feeling of purpose or drive to survive. Everyone was enveloped by a sheer desperation to live. Some flipped the already turned-over furniture. Others kicked the walls, hoping their clues were in there. Mae could tell by their crazed expressions that they'd lost their minds, looking as though they might foam at the mouth at any moment. Their glazed-over eyes and bared teeth scared her as she backed up toward the staircase. A man lashed his hands toward a woman's face as she took a step in his general direction. The only person Mae saw walking around calmly was Sadler, his eyes squinting meticulously as he headed up the stairs.

Raya nudged Mae and gave her a crooked grin. "We'd better get started. We don't want to end up like them." She sprinted down the hall as Mae followed Sadler upstairs.

Upstairs, Mae combed through every bedroom in sight, looking for anything shining. Each room had a huge bed, rotting head and footboards holding them together. Objects, like books and ornate oil lamps that had long strings with pronged ends attached them, were sprawled on the ground. Some of the bedrooms had bathrooms attached to them and large closets, however the clothes were long gone. Many times she noticed there was paper hanging from the dingy walls, mold covering the exposed areas. In every room she went into, however, she was drawn to the mattress, hoping perhaps the clue was wrong. But Raya's voice in her head kept reminding her not to look there. She had to search for something shiny. And a mattress was the furthest thing from that.

Mae looked at the tables in front of each of the twenty-two bedrooms she was able to find, hoping her vial was in a lamp or a fancy piece of metalwork. But each table was empty, and if there was a lamp, it lay shattered on the floor. Nothing in the rooms shone. When she heard the announcement that thirty-five minutes had passed, she already had made it through the bedrooms a second time. Her heart beat wildly as she wondered if she'd ever find what she was looking for. In a moment or pure frustration, she kicked a footboard, causing it to creak and sending a searing pain through her foot. She hopped up and down, cursing quietly, the shadow of the lanky bookmaker's apprentice walked by. Finally, she decided it was time to head to her meeting place with Raya.

Raya was standing at the bottom of the stairs, a vial of green liquid in her hand. Pride radiated from her face, and she was smiling—that is, until she saw Mae had nothing in her possession. "What the hell happened?"

"I don't know what it is!" Mae yelled in frustration. Anger was eating

away at her. It would figure that Raya would find her cure, and Mae would be

left ripping her hair out, trying to find hers. "I couldn't find anything shining on

a bed or near it. Nothing at all! I think this place is screwing with me. I looked

at the side tables, the lamps, everything. *Twice.* I have no idea what the hell I'm

looking for." She sighed and once more felt the pain in her foot. Looking down

and wiggling it, she huffed, "And I think I might have broken some toes from

kicking a footboard."

She shook her head and went back to pitying herself as she looked up.

When she returned her glance to Raya, she no longer saw fear in the redhead's

face. Her smile had returned and had a sneaky aspect to it. "Mae! I know what it

is. What you're looking for. The shiny thing isn't an object we'd see in a normal

house. This place is fancy…or at least it used to be. Mae, it's a footboard or a

headboard!"

Mae's raised an eyebrow. If this girl was playing a joke on her, this

wasn't the time. "You might want to take that vial, Raya," she said. "I think the

poison has gone to your head."

Raya grabbed her arm. "No, listen. I went through all the bathrooms

upstairs. That's where I found my vial. A bathroom is attached to each of the

bedrooms in this place. You must have been too focused on finding a certain

object. This house…I don't know who lived here, but they had a shit ton of

money. The bathtubs are huge and deep. And the headboards in some of the bedrooms are really fancy. Like super fancy. I mean, one of them had this *huge* diamond-looking thing…" She stopped midsentence and looked up at Mae.

"Something shining!" Mae yelled, and bolted up the stairs. Behind her she heard Raya's footsteps, the stairs sounding as though they might break at any moment. When they reached the top of the stairs, they heard the fifteen-minute announcement. There were so many rooms that Mae wasn't sure they had enough time. She turned to Raya, who now stood next to her, panting. "Which room?" Mae asked.

Raya closed her eyes, her forehead lined in deep thought, then shook her head. "I don't remember which room, but it's around here somewhere. I'm positive it's on this floor." She pointed to the right. "You go that way and I'll go this way. If I find it, I'll scream. Or I'll do something that'll get your attention."

She was just about to dart off when Mae grabbed her arm and held it firmly. "Listen to me. I'm literally trusting you with my life right now." She squeezed harder to show she was both scared and serious. This was the time for Raya to show who she was. "Don't screw me."

When she let go, Raya gave her a sincere glance of sympathy. "I'm going to get you out of here." She gave Mae a quick salute before taking off.

Mae raced through the bedrooms, looking at each headboard and footboard. They were finely decorated, as Raya had said, but none of them had a diamond. Most of them were made of wood or rusty metal, with nothing shiny about them. Knowing the timer was ticking, she moved faster, peering into the rooms rather than actually searching through them. If there was a headboard with a large diamond, she would see it. Not hearing a call from Raya, Mae continued down the hall as her stomach lurched with anxiety. In the second-to-last room, she finally saw it. A footboard with two giant diamonds embedded into it.

"I found it!" she shrieked. "Raya, I found it!" Her voice echoed through the hall. Before she could hear what Raya had to say, she sprinted into the room and fumbled while unscrewing the first diamond. Nothing was there, so she knew the next one had to be her key to survival. Fortunately, this diamond was loose, and she easily removed it. She tossed it aside, but as the diamond hit the ground, so did her heart as she peered into the opening.

There was a space for something inside, a small thin space, but it was empty.

"Looking for this?"

Mae's heart nearly stopped. It was all coming together now, why it had been so easy for her to remove that diamond when she had to unscrew the other one. Someone had beaten her to the punch and taken what she needed. Slowly she turned to the voice, although she already knew who it belonged to. Normally she'd feel a rush of heat as she looked at her—a searing, uncontrollable anger. But not anymore. Mae inhaled sharply as her insides turned to ice when she saw Medusa holding her vial of blue liquid, a vicious sneer on her face.

"Looks like you're in a bit of trouble."

Chapter Twenty-Nine:
<u>Javeen</u>

After the voice gave the instructions, Javeen was so unsure of what to do that he stood frozen in place. The house before him was so large that he was overwhelmed by what might be in there. Many in his group pushed their way into the broken-down mansion, while others were thrown to the ground as distress kicked in.

Javeen took a deep breath and a moment to remember what he was looking for. A knife. There wasn't much more to say about it. But he still had to look in a number of places. The kitchen was the obvious choice, but some people kept knives by their beds for protection. Contemplating where to search first was foremost on his mind. Was it better to stick with the easiest choice, or should he take a chance and run around the house like the rest of the panicked figures he could see running about? Javeen realized that he had been standing outside now for almost three minutes. Three minutes of precious time. Javeen knew he had to get started, even if he was still utterly confused.

When Javeen entered the house, it looked as though a pack of wolves, not humans, had ransacked the place. The already disheveled house had become a dumping ground of objects and debris from the people inside. A man was ripping apart the cushions of a couch, the springs cutting into his hands, blood dripping to the floor. Another was breaking apart the railing of the staircase, looking into the support columns then tossing them over his shoulder, not caring if they hit someone. An older woman was tearing into the wallpaper, her nails breaking, fingers bleeding, finding only wood behind the shredded pieces.

Suddenly a man stood in front of Javeen, a vial of gold liquid in his hand. Quickly he opened it and drained the contents. He flashed a smile of satisfaction at Javeen, as if his safety was ensured, but his grin quickly disappeared. In an instant, he doubled over and fell to his hands and knees, his back arched and shoulders shaking. His breathing grew labored, and his eyes bulged from his head. He chest heaved as though he were trying to cough, but nothing came out. The man stuck his finger in his mouth to vomit the contents, but the foam that cascaded from his mouth proved it was too late. Finally, after he convulsed for another few seconds, he collapsed, his body displaying no signs of life.

Seeing a slip of parchment next to the man, Javeen knelt and picked it up, shaking off the foam. A rhyme was written on it in black ink. Javeen didn't even have to read the clue to realize what had happened. He looked once more at the paper, then at the body on the floor, and shook his head in pity. This man had grabbed the first vial he could find. Javeen stood up quickly, vindication and sadness filling his soul. He'd been right about the vial colors, but in order for him to see the proof, a man had to die in front of him.

Javeen knew he had no time to pity this man, as he had to find his vial

before someone else made the same stupid mistake. During all this madness, he

decided the kitchen would be the best place to start, and if he couldn't find the

knife there, he'd run upstairs. He only hoped he had time to find it. As he heard

the forty-five second announcement, he raced to the kitchen, hoping it would be

filled with multiple objects for him to rummage through. However, when he

walked in, there wasn't much there except for a table and a few wooden spoons.

Still, Javeen felt this was where his clue was; he just had to examine the room

closely. The Factory clearly wanted him to work to save his own life. He began

his search once more.

There were drawers all around, and he pulled them open, tossing them

aside as he did so. They all produced a hollow sound as they bounced off the

floor, proving there was nothing inside. Next, he jumped onto a small table and

opened all the little doors above him, hoping he would see the shine of a knife,

but once more, he saw nothing. He looked inside a tall white box on the other

side of the room, opening both the top and bottom doors, but all that came out

was the stench of rotten food. He turned his back and stared at the kitchen he

had destroyed, breathing heavily as panic sank in.

The knife wasn't here. There was no way it could be. Javeen gone

through every inch of this room, twice, and still he couldn't find it. He ran his

fingers through his hair, grabbing it in frustration. Perhaps he had enough time to go upstairs, and he'd find it in a nightstand. He started to make his way through the exit closest to the stairs, when something shiny caught his eye.

A chair lay knocked over in the corner of the room, one he had ignored earlier. But he remembered how orderly the kitchen had been before he had turned it over. There hadn't been a single person in the room, so the chair had to have been like this since the beginning of this stage. As Javeen thought harder, he realized the chair had been strategically placed this way. Once again, he looked through the kitchen doorway at the stairs, knowing his options and knowing his time was limited, but turned his back and made his way to the chair. The closer he got, the more his heart pleaded that his hunch was right. There was a reason this chair was lying here. He knelt and moved the wooden chair aside. That was when he saw it. A knife.

Carefully he picked it up and looked at his parchment, which he'd desperately held on to since he'd left his cage. *"But do not look at the silver shines; your safety lies where metal binds."* The blade of the knife shone in the dim light, but he couldn't understand how a vial of liquid could fit inside it. It was so thin; there was no possible way. Unless the blade itself was filled with the antidote. Javeen studied the knife then held it in a defensive position, as if ready to attack someone. That was when he felt it. He knew how a knife was supposed to feel, and there wasn't supposed to be a wiggle between the blade and the handle. He looked back at his clue. "Where metal binds," he muttered.

His vial had to be inside the handle.

He grabbed the dull end of the knife, and with one quick motion, he pulled. The handle came off easily, and within it Javeen saw the cork of the vial and a glint of red inside it. He had found his antidote, and his heart leapt as he reached for it. Then everything changed as Javeen noticed a shadow behind him. He tried to get up and attack, but in a flash an arm gripped his throat, pressing on his windpipe.

"Give it up, kid," the raspy voice hissed against his ear.

Javeen froze, knowing this man could kill him in an instant. He caught a glimpse of the man's forearm and saw how thick it was. One quick turn of the neck, and Javeen would fall dead to the ground. And this man's voice echoed with the familiar sound of despair. He would do anything to stay alive, even if he had to kill someone half his age. Javeen looked down at his hands; he still held the blade of the knife. As swiftly as he could, he brought the knife up to the man's arm and cut deeply, feeling the blood run down the front of his shirt. The man let out a howling scream, let go, and backed away.

Javeen was up in less than a second and turned to face his attacker, the knife now held in a protective position. He wasn't sure he was ready for a brawl with a man twice his size, seeing as he had his own cure in his hand. Even so, Javeen knew that no matter what, if he had to, he would kill this man to stay alive. Prepared for the dark stare of a man ready to maul him, Javeen straightened up when he saw the man crying.

At first, he thought it was from the cut on his arm, which was bleeding profusely. He had to be in pain, yet Javeen didn't think it was enough to make a man cry. But then the man spoke…or at least attempted. Walking toward Javeen, he moved his hands about, blood dropping everywhere, while his mouth spewed unintelligible nonsense. He continued to try to get his words out, but the blubbering that came with his tears masked anything he was trying to convey. When he looked up and saw that Javeen had no idea what he was saying, he slowly pulled a slip of black parchment with gold ink out of his pocket.

Now it had become clear, and Javeen felt pain in his heart for the person standing in front of him. Javeen had seen that gold vial earlier; the dead man had downed its contents. The man in front of him had no antidote, and therefore, he knew he was going to die. They both looked at each other, compassion etched into Javeen's face as the man coiled up. He hunched over and hugged himself tightly while trying to calm himself. Javeen stood, allowing him the time he clearly needed. He had something to say, and the least Javeen could do was hear him out. But at a safe distance.

After another minute or two, the man took a deep breath and finally composed himself. "I don't want your vial," he said, his voice still shaky, his eyes bloodshot. Javeen cocked his head to the side as the man extended his hand. "I want your knife."

"Why?" Javeen said slowly.

Once again tears welled in the man's eyes. Javeen saw fear and the familiar sense of desperation, but this face was different. This was the man's final wish. "I want to leave on my own terms. Not the way this place wants me to."

Trembling, Javeen knew that if he did this, it would be the second death he had facilitated. Still, this was different. He looked down at the knife and knew he couldn't stop this man from doing what he wanted, nor was it his right. The man had a plan, which Javeen found admirable. It was as if he wouldn't allow this place to change him. Not even when it came to his death. Javeen nodded but knew he had to set some ground rules for his own safety.

"I'll give it to you. But first I'm going to take my vial, and then I'll leave the knife on the table. When I'm out, it's all yours. Understood?" Javeen's voice was unsteady, but he tried to remain strong. The man agreed, a sad smile crossing his face.

"Thank you, my boy."

Javeen reached in, and sure enough, the vial in the handle held a red liquid. Though the moment was tense, he felt a lightness in his heart, knowing he would make it out. He quickly uncorked it and drank the contents. As promised, he placed the knife on the table and backed away slowly. He looked at the man once more as he reached the exit and said, "I'm so sorry."

The man had made his way over to the table and gave Javeen that heartbroken smile one last time. He took the blade and walked away from

Javeen, showing him he had nothing to fear. "Don't be. You've given me the freedom that this place took away. I can't thank you enough." He looked at the blade and back at Javeen. "Get out of here, boy. Trust me, this ain't something you want to witness."

Javeen turned and raced toward the door in front of him. However, when he heard the loud thud behind him, he couldn't help turn around. The man was lying on the floor, his head facing away from Javeen. But the pool of blood forming around his throat was enough to tell him that he had taken his own life before The Factory could. Although he reminded himself that this was what the man had wanted, a sick feeling in his stomach accompanied him as he sprinted out of the kitchen.

That was when he heard the ten-minute announcement.

Chapter Thirty:
<u>Mae</u>

As the ten-minute announcement echoed through the house, it vibrated through the bones of the structure and through Mae. But she heard none of it as her tunnel vision focused on the stick figure in front of her. Medusa stood there, her eyes wild, her oily hair plastered to her sweaty face. Mae continued to stare at the woman, who looked like a rabid animal. Her hands shook as she took cautious steps toward her. "Medusa…"

Medusa raised the vial and put her finger on the cork. "Take another step, and I swear to whatever is above us that I'll drink this right here and now." She was serious; that much was clear now, as her hand danced above the cork.

Slowly raising her hands, showing she was trying to make peace, Mae gently said, "You can't do that. Medusa, please don't drink that. It'll kill you. You have to…"

"Drink the one that matches the color of my ink?" she spat, her voice quavering. "Yeah, I know that," she whispered.

That was when Mae truly focused the crazed person in front of her. Medusa's typically strong posture was now deflated and defensive. She obviously was scared. Her hair, which was a mess before, was sticking out in all directions, as if she'd been tugging at it. But why? Then Mae looked deep into her eyes and realized they were red and puffy. Mae shifted back, standing straighter as the reality of Medusa's situation sank in.

"Did someone already drink yours?"

Medusa's eyes fell for a second, and Mae saw pain and fear behind them—a dead giveaway that Mae was right. Medusa had lost her vial to someone else, and now she knew she was going to die. But in another moment, she was back to her ferocious self, not wanting any sort of pity from Mae. "Well what if they did? *So what?*" she shrieked, letting her voice resonate through the room. "You think that would have changed anything? Even if I'd found my vial, I still would have tried to find yours. Yours and the one that belongs to that stupid redhead bitch. Before this challenge began, I wanted to send you both to the furnace."

Mae realized how dangerous the situation was becoming, because Medusa had nothing left to lose. If Medusa had taken her antidote, Mae perhaps could have negotiated with her, explained the worth of life. She could have even fought Medusa, tried to scare her away. But Medusa had nothing to fear. If she wanted to take Mae down with her, she now had that power. She had gained it the second that someone else had taken her antidote. Even so, Mae knew she had to at least try to reason with her, though doing so would be nearly impossible.

"Medusa…this isn't fair. I didn't do—"

"Don't lie." She chuckled, a laugh bubbling with anxiety and frustration. "Don't you dare say you *didn't do anything*, you lying bitch. You threw me to the ground and threatened me. And the things you've probably said about me? This is the least I should do."

Mae knew she was right. Ever since she arrived here, she'd had a feeling that one moment of unclear thinking might come back to haunt her, but never in this way. She watched as shadows of the other remaining survivors raced behind her. Didn't they see what was happening? Didn't they care? And where the hell was Raya? She should have been here by now, at her side, trying to get the vial away from Medusa. Mae felt a stone form inside her as she wondered if Raya was one of the shadows. Maybe Raya had seen her in this room and had run, only looking out for herself.

"Medusa, please don't do this." Mae tried to take another step, but her feet wouldn't move. "This won't make anything better. I'm sorry you're going to die...I really am. But why take me with you?" Although Mae didn't want to sound as though she were pleading, she heard the panic in her voice.

Medusa's eyes went dark as she took a single step toward Mae. "Because I'll be a hero."

Confusion flooded Mae's mind, and she shook her head, trying to make sense of what this woman was saying. "You're panicking. Medusa, think about it. No one will know what happened in here."

Medusa bared her teeth into something that resembled a smile or perhaps a wince; Mae wasn't sure which. "You don't get it. I mean, really, this is a simple concept, and you can't comprehend it. You're so stupid, which is funny because everyone thinks you're one of the cleverest people here."

She took another step toward Mae, her smile growing more savage.

"This place…this place chose you, Mae. Don't think it didn't. We all know what it's capable of now and how smart it is. You weren't a random pick from a hat. Oh, no. This place was dying to bring you inside. And it chose you for one reason only." She stood up straight, knowing her next words were the final blow. "You aren't needed in this damn town. No one wants you around."

Mae inhaled sharply, trying to keep herself calm. She knew this already, so why bring it up? But then she understood. Time was running out, and Medusa was stalling; her speech was one of hopelessness. Still, even though Mae had known this from the beginning, the prostitute had pulled her in. Medusa was pushing her to believe that not only did the townsfolk want her to disappear, but they also wanted her dead. She had poked at a wound inside Mae that hadn't yet healed. The more she thought about it, the more truth rang out from her words. The townsfolk probably *were* happy she had entered The Factory. The villagers must have been thrilled when they heard her name, because there was a chance that she would die, and they'd never have to see her again.

Medusa continued as Mae stared at the floor. "That's right. And you know it's right, you human trash. No one in town wants you there, ever since the day your parents died. They've just tolerated your existence because of what happened. But they're so sick of you and the constant shadow of death you carry around. Do you know how many smiling faces I saw when you headed toward the gate? Half the town looked like they were going to throw a party. If you died here, it would be a damn annual holiday for this place. They'd probably build a monument to me or The Factory for getting rid of you!"

Anger flushed her face and Mae couldn't stop herself as frustration made her spew, "Oh, I'm sure they'll be thrilled that the prostitute died in here too. You really think anyone will miss you? You're just as much human garbage as I am. Think about what you do for a living! You just lie on your back for money."

Medusa faltered but quickly regained her composure as she crossed her arms. "True. That was my job. But I'm not trash like you. Because I was able to do something you never did. Ever. I brought happiness to people lives. Even if it was for one moment, that person was some sort of happy. Whereas you..." She pointed a dirty finger at Mae. "You did nothing but remind the town of horrible things. You brought sadness with you wherever you went and coated the town in it. You're worthless, a parasite that sucks the life out of people—a parasite that needs to be removed." She held up the vial and snickered, "And now I can do that."

As Mae heard the five-minute announcement, her eyes burned as Medusa's words sank deep into her skin, beyond any protective layer she had built over the years. The woman was right. The town didn't need her there. What good did she do for it? Mae remembered all her visits to the marketplace and how everyone looked away from her, as if she were a monster that took away the pleasures of life. Would her death allow the villagers to live the lives they wanted and not the ones they had to tolerate with her being there? Mae's breath became ragged as she realized Medusa had taken away her will to fight by providing her with a truth she hadn't wanted to hear.

"Clearly, we're done here," Medusa taunted Mae, who continued to stare at the floor. "And I'm glad I was the one to tell you. Before you die, remember this: you're worthless, nothing more than garbage. In fact, if the townsfolk had to choose whether to come into this place or keep you around, there would be a line out the door. No one wants you or loves you, and no one ever will. And most important, when you're dead—"

A loud yell and a sudden crack made Mae's head jerk up, her eyes brimming with tears. Medusa was lying face down, her arms sprawled out. The vial lay unbroken near an outstretched hand. Medusa's white hair was soaked with blood, her eyes wide open. Her nose was bleeding, and a few teeth had been knocked out. When Mae noticed a pair of feet standing behind Medusa, she knew she wasn't alone. Her eyes traveled up the legs of her savior to see a familiar face.

Raya was glaring down at Medusa, holding a broken chair leg in her hands. The end of it was covered in blood, and a few strands of white hair were woven into the splintered wood. She was breathing heavily, as if she had put all her energy and anger from the last few days into bashing Medusa's head. Raya stared at the body for another second, then took a few steps and kicked the motionless Medusa. They both watched her for a moment longer and noticed that her chest wasn't moving. That was when Raya gave a small shrug and threw the chair leg on top of her body. She looked up at Mae. "I told you I was going to kill that bitch."

Mae stood frozen, her eyes darting from the body to Raya. She couldn't comprehend what had happened. Everything in those moments was almost too much. She could have died. She *should* have died, but suddenly Raya had saved her. The redhead was motioning toward the vial, and Mae took in a few breaths and nodded. It was as if everything were happening in slow motion as she picked up the container. She tried to get the cork off, but her fingers fumbled. Raya quickly opened the container and poured the liquid into Mae's mouth. Then she opened up her own vial and downed it.

Mae looked up at her, a tear or two slipping from her eyes. "I thought...you weren't... Thank you." The tears fell faster now, and her breathing grew more rapid as she realized what had happened. She thought she was alone and Raya had given up on her. In an instant, Mae had given up on Raya and everyone else. But Raya hadn't left her, as Mae had assumed. Instead she had come back, and she had saved her life—because until Raya had killed Medusa, Mae had been willing to die. She had given up and thought she would be sent to the flames with Medusa. Worst of all, she had accepted that fate. But Raya had returned and killed someone so Mae would make it out alive.

Mae's tears continued to fall as she repeatedly thanked her, shock still settling in. Raya looked sharply at her, and Mae waited for her defense. How she was only doing it because she hated Medusa. How she always said she was going to kill her, and this was the perfect opportunity. But instead she put her hand on Mae's shoulders and said, "I trust you, okay? Listen to me. I have since you first approached me. I knew you had a fire in you. And with you and Javeen, I know we're going to win. But Javeen and I can't win without you." Mae looked into her eyes and knew she was telling the truth. Her eyes held a smile that showed her optimism, and Raya even gave her a small, pure grin. Raya's barrier had broken down, and now there was nothing left for her to do but join Mae's alliance with Javeen.

Then Raya gave her a snide smirk, one only she could get away with. "Besides, I told you I'd get you out of here. If I didn't, Javeen would kill me. And that's not even close to a joke. I think he actually would murder me if you didn't get out." She pushed her toward the door. "But I do have to get you out of here to keep my promise…*Now move*!" She grunted as she gave Mae another strong shove.

Mae's feet were dragging as the thirty-second countdown began. They were still on the second floor and would have to sprint in order to get out. She quickly shook her head, ridding herself of her demons for the moment, and pushed herself, turning the corner and bounding down the stairs with Raya right behind her. They both jumped the porch steps with ten seconds left. They ran over to the two others, found spots next to Sadler, and waited for the last three seconds to end.

Mae and Raya had both thought that a door would open behind them to bring them back to their cages, but clearly The Factory wanted to show them who was in charge. The floor beneath the massive house creaked and slowly opened up. A sudden heat filled the room, and a smoldering wind rushed past their faces. Like a sinking ship, the house began to go under, engulfed in flames. All they could do was watch, knowing that two of them were still in there and would never see the outside world again.

When the tortuous descent finally ended, the floor closed once more. Mae hadn't realized that she and Raya had been clinging to each other, and Raya was leaning on Sadler for support. The lanky apprentice, put an arm around her, and Mae felt his fingers touch her shoulder. The assurance was calming but only for a second. Sadler stared straight ahead, as if knowing this would be the end result. Everyone stared at the emptiness in front of them, remembering that The Factory was in total control. A door behind them creaked open. As the others made their way out, Mae and Raya stood frozen, contemplating what would have happened if they had stayed inside the house a moment longer.

Finally, Raya gave Mae a shove with her shoulder. "Let's get the fuck out of here."

The two sprinted down the long dark hallway, refusing to take one last glance at the room that had almost taken them both.

Chapter Thirty-One:
Javeen

Javeen made his way back to the room of cages, the rest of the survivors from his group in tow. When they reached the large room they'd called home for the past week—perhaps almost two now—he counted who was left. Only twelve people had walked back out of their hallways. The end was clearly nearing, but only six would make it out. Half these people would die before he hopefully would see the light of day again.

When he saw Mae clutching onto Raya, staggering in the circular room, his heart did a flip. Even though he wasn't pleased that Raya was with her, he was overjoyed that Mae was still alive. Mae looked ahead, Raya's arm draped around her shoulder, steering her toward the cells. The redhead's face was close to Mae's, her lips moving quickly, her hand lightly moving up and down her back in a comforting motion. Mae's face was grave, and there was no emotion to it as she stared blankly into space. She trudged inside her cell and sat in the farthest corner, hugging her knees.

Javeen was trying to understand why Mae was acting so strangely. He stopped, contemplating whether he should run over to her or give her space to think. Before he knew what was happening, Javeen saw Raya rushing towards him. Her eyes were filled with anger and fear. Javeen was so confused, that when she grabbed his arm and pulled, he followed his ease. She started to drag him towards the empty cell next to Mae. Javeen dug his feet into the ground suddenly, not trusting Raya at all. She quickly got behind him, and with all her might, shoved her entire body into his back, continuing to slowly push him forward.

"Get. In. There," she hissed.

"Why?" he said, glaring over his shoulder at her. Raya kept pushing him, but then she looked up and gave him a scowl back. Javeen just wanted to push her to the ground and storm away. Just because Mae was alive didn't mean he had to start liking or trusting her.

"Well, if you move your mountain man ass a little faster, I can get into the cell next to you and tell you. But that might not happen if you don't pick up your damn feet!"

Javeen finally looked down at her and saw that Raya's face was full of anger and some sort of determination. But that look wasn't one of someone who was trying to survive, but someone who wanted to help. With what, he didn't know, but he finally headed into his cell, and Raya hurried into the one next to him. The thought of Mae's troubled face as she walked into her holding crossed his mind, and he wondered if it had anything to do with Raya suddenly becoming interested in him. After a moment, the cells were closed, and they were back in captivity.

Javeen glanced at Mae, who was still huddled in the corner of her cell. Her back faced everyone, and her knees were so close to her chest that Javeen thought they might disappear into her body. The more he looked at her, the more worried he became. Something clearly had happened inside the house that she and Raya had been in. It must have been worse than her hallucination in Stage Two, because Mae seemed like just a shell of who she had been before she had gone in. He could feel the truth even though he couldn't see it. Mae was retreating from him and their mission.

"Get over here," Raya snapped, her eyes cutting into him.

Javeen turned his head and stormed over to her, wanting to reach into her cell and grab her by her shirt, demanding to know what she had done to her. Raya had to have done something to Mae; there was no other way. But Javeen became even more afraid when he looked at Raya's face. She was worried too, staring over his shoulder at Mae. When he finally reached her, he didn't even have a chance to respond when Raya whispered, "I can't... There's so much..." She finally sighed. "You have no idea."

Javeen looked her up and down, still trying to figure out what she was telling him. He was ready for the best acting he'd ever seen. Finally, Raya let out a huff and gave him an exasperated look. "Okay, I get it, Javeen. You don't trust me. And honestly, I'm surprised you're trying to trust anyone in this game." She stuck a finger right in his face, her voice demanding to be heard. "But you need to listen to me. What Mae just went through, what happened to her in that house, was one of the worst things that could have happened before the last stage."

Javeen said nothing for a moment. He tried to look at Raya with a critical eye, attempting to gauge her intentions. Then he looked over at the sad excuse that was Mae. He glanced back at Raya and sighed heavily. It was time to bring himself back to reality. Raya was right; something had happened to Mae. He knew that the second he saw her. It was time for him to pull his wall down with this scar-faced girl, if only for this moment and this moment alone. "What happened?" he finally asked.

With a deep breath, Raya began her story, detailing everything they'd gone through in the house, up until the point when Raya had heard Mae yell. She had raced toward her, hoping Mae had found the antidote. When she got there, she saw Medusa holding Mae's vial, threatening to drink the contents. She told Javeen all the horrible things Medusa had said to Mae, trying to stall her for as long as she could. But what scared her the most was that Mae had begun to give up on trying to survive the more Medusa belittled her.

"So how did Mae get the vial?" Javeen said, looking around for Medusa, ready to lash out at her for everything she had done. He spiraled around his cell, looking at the others, but didn't see her. Confusion rushed over him as he wondered where the lanky woman had gone. When he looked back toward Raya, a haunted expression had washed over her face. Javeen understood right away, but he also knew she needed to say it out loud in order to help herself.

"I saw them standing there, but I knew if I went into the room, Medusa would have downed Mae's antidote it right there. I had to think of something, so I went into the next room to see if there was any way to sneak up on them. That was when I found an adjoining bathroom. I saw Medusa standing at the entrance to the other room. I knew this wouldn't be pretty, and I had to surprise her in order to save Mae. Before...before going in there, I broke a leg off a chair." She took in a shuddering breath and looked Javeen straight in the eyes. "I hit her over the head, breaking her skull, I guess. I didn't mean to...or at least I don't think I meant to. I just wanted her to pass out. But the next thing I knew, she was dead on the floor. Fortunately for Mae, the vial didn't break when Medusa dropped it." When she looked up and saw Javeen's wide eyes, she gave a mock, wicked grin. "Didn't think I had it in me, did you?"

Javeen stared at her in amazement, taking in everything she'd said. Yes, mostly the story about Mae and her encounter with Medusa, but also the underlying story. He was seeing Raya in her true form. In that moment of watching Medusa and Mae in a standoff, one that looked like a stalemate, Raya had the chance to run away and save herself. Before, Javeen would have bet anything that Raya would have left and never looked back. She had no reason to stay behind and help Mae. And yet she had. Raya had taken valuable time— time that could have killed her—and used it to save Mae. The distrust he had built toward her exploded in front of him when he realized he was completely wrong about her.

As his barriers turned to dust, Javeen gave Raya a sincere smile, something he never thought he'd do. Then he slowly extended his arm toward her, palm out, as a peace offering. Raya smiled back, as if she'd been waiting for this for some time—for Javeen to show, in his own time, that he actually trusted her. She quickly pulled herself together and took his hand in a firm grasp. Their eyes met with a intensity that told Javeen one thing: Raya was going to walk out of this place with them, and they both knew that now.

"Thank you," he said weakly, knowing that without her, Mae would be dead.

As Raya let go of his hand, a small smile remained on her face. She shrugged, trying to brush off the compliment as if it were nothing. "I like her. And I tolerate you." She winked at him. "And somehow you two make an amazing duo that has outlasted everything this place has thrown at you."

"Don't forget. You're still here too," Javeen reminded her. She wouldn't be standing there right now if she didn't have the wits; Javeen knew that. Raya seemed to have this place figured out more than all of them combined.

Raya nodded, looking at the floor. "Yeah, I know. But I did it on my own. I thought that was the only way to do it. But then I watched you two. You don't just work together; you make sure the other person knows what you're doing. More important than any of that, you *talk* to each other, keeping yourself as sane as you can be in this place. The two of you are actually fighting this place together, which I'm sure The Factory isn't used to. Dare I say it…you might even be pissing it off. And with that, I have to admit I'm beyond honored to say I was able to stand by your side."

"Well, I think you'll be even more pleased when you leave this place with us. We can have a party. Hell, after what we've been through, we can even have a few drinks…you know, with some friends." Javeen smiled once more, his heart now opening up to this strong-willed girl.

Raya pushed away the thought. "Eh, my mom works at the The Blood Broth as a waitress, and I've been helping out for the last four years. Because of that, well, I've already dabbled with all the bottles they have. Unless you want me to drink you under the table, then I recommend we do something else." Her face suddenly grew serious, and she dropped his hand. "But right now, we have more pressing matters to attend to." She nodded her head at Mae then looked back at Javeen.

The eye contact said it all. Raya wanted him to somehow fix whatever had happened in that house. Now he understood why she had wanted him in this cage so badly; she wanted him between her and Mae. He opened his arms up. "Oh, come on! What am I supposed to do?"

"Medusa's words messed with her head. Badly. I think she basically turned it into mush," Raya said, glancing over Javeen's shoulder at Mae. "She said some pretty nasty things."

Although Raya had told Javeen some of the things Medusa had spewed in her final moments, he had a feeling she had masked how dark the woman's words truly were. Medusa knew she was going to die, and if she couldn't kill Mae, at least she could inflict some sort of pain on her. Mae was fragile, even though she'd never admit it. Some of the scars in her mind and soul might never heal, no matter how much time passed. And from the look of her—she was curled up in the fetal position—Medusa had dug in deep, not only reopening those scars but also letting it bleed her out slowly.

"I already tried to talk to her and got nothing," Raya said. "You have to be the one, Javeen. She was there for you when you needed someone. She brought you back from an emotional state I'd never seen before. Without her, your mind would still be clouded with whatever hell you were living in after what happened with Tharin. Hell, you might not even be standing here right now." She placed a gentle hand on Javeen's shoulder and nodded toward Mae. "It's your turn to be there for her. She needs you and...I think you're the only person who'll be able to save her."

Javeen felt a sense of pride as Raya bestowed this honor on him. Perhaps he really was the only one who could bring Mae back. But his pride was quickly replaced with fear. Raya was right. Javeen had escaped being devoured by his dark thoughts only because Mae had pulled him out of his hole of self-pity. If she hadn't been so determined to get him back, Javeen might not have had the energy or willpower to have gotten through this last stage. He couldn't sit here and hope she got over whatever Medusa had said to her. After all she'd done for him, he had to bring her back to the real world, away from the monsters that inhabited her mind. They'd planned to get out of The Factory, and damn it, they would, especially now that Raya had joined their ranks. As he took a step toward Mae, Raya forcefully pulled him back.

He had expected her eyes to be dark. Maybe she'd give him quick pep talk, saying if he didn't get this right, she'd set him straight. Instead, he saw they were soft, softer than he'd ever seen them. She was breathing quickly, anxiety emanating from her face. She didn't just want him to bring Mae back. She was thinking the same thing he was: Javeen *needed* to get her back. He watched as her tough and cocky facade melted in front of him. Her fingers deep into his shoulder as she gave him a sincere smile.

"We *are* getting out of here. The three of us." The confidence in her voice matched what Javeen now felt in his soul. "I'm not leaving here without the two of you next to me."

"Me neither," Javeen said, the truth in his statement bringing light to Raya's face. "But first we have to get one of us back."

Nodding, Raya let go of him, and he felt her watch him as he headed toward Mae. For the first time in a while, Javeen was glad he was wrong. Especially about Raya. She had seen something in Mae that had pushed her to save her life. And now, though she hadn't said it, she'd probably do the same for Javeen. They were all going to protect each other. As he reached the corner of his cell, the weight of the situation fell upon his shoulders. *This has to work,* he told himself. *I can't fail.* He let the heaviness push him down as he sat in the corner of the cage. Slowly he turned his head and made quick eye contact with Mae, whose head popped up as she heard him approach. Although she looked away, Javeen knew she had seen him.

He placed a hand in her cell and said, "All right, Pox Face. Get over here so I can tell you how wrong that bitch was."

Chapter Thirty-Two:
<u>Mae</u>

Mae had heard Javeen walk toward her and call her over, but she pretended not to. She didn't want to move. This was her safe spot in this nightmare she'd been living in for the past two weeks or so. And after what just happened, she never wanted to leave. Sitting with her knees held tightly to her chest was the only thing keeping her from falling apart. This wasn't the time to cry or sob or anything like that. And she knew if she went over to where Javeen was sitting, she would fall to pieces like a small child. Like she almost had after Stage Two.

"You know I'm persistent," Javeen continued, and from the corner of her eye she saw him settled into the spot he was sitting in. "I'll stay here all night calling you Pox Face until you finally get your ass over here." His shoulders went up and down. "It'll probably piss some people off, but I'll keep it up until you do it."

Still Mae sat, digging her face even further into her knees. She wasn't going to let him win. She wanted to be like this. She felt her knees leave imprints on her cheeks as she tried to burrow deeper. After her parents had died, she didn't know she was letting herself go into the darkness. But now in this cell, she felt it dancing around her as it moved into her soul, and she willed it to take her with it. The darkness was the only thing that kept the pain away because it was nothingness, and that was what she needed. To feel nothing, to know nothing, to be nothing. She pulled her knees in even closer as she continued to breathe shakily.

Javeen let out a snort then whispered, "Come on, Mae. Don't be like this. We need to talk about what happened. Remember the talk you gave me? Well, now it's my turn. Get over here so I can help you. Please *let me* help you." He paused. "This isn't the time to be stupid."

Mae's head lifted slightly as those last words echoed through her head, but in her own voice. A familiar memory flashed through her head. Those words. She'd heard them before. She'd said the same thing to Javeen when he had finished off Tharin. When he had begun to shut himself off from the rest of the world. Mae had told him she knew what he was doing, giving up on himself, and he had to get out of it. She looked down once more at her posture and realized what she was doing. This way of sitting, she had done it before. For months after her parents had died, Mae had sat like this, trying to hold herself together. But mostly to shut herself away from the world, so that the nothingness of her life could consume her with guilt.

With a shuddering sigh, Mae turned her head slowly and moved on her hands and knees toward Javeen, still not getting up and still refusing to look at him. She inched her way slowly, her arms sliding her sideways as she got closer. As she felt the weight of everything from the last few hours begin to build, she pushed away the tears forming in her eyes. When she reached the corner, she expected Javeen to try to reach out to her, and she was ready to recoil. But by this time, he knew better than that. She had to approach him.

Without looking at him, Mae told him everything. The story of how she thought she was going to die in that house because she couldn't figure out her damn clue. How she and Raya had discovered the truth behind her riddle and searched frantically through the house, while the timer ticked down. The moment her stomach plummeted when she saw Medusa holding her vial in her hand, with that revolting grin on her face. Medusa was going to die there no matter what, and she had told Mae she was going to take her down with her. Mae had known she would have to fight her if it came down to it, but all that changed when Medusa began to talk.

When Mae began to recall what Medusa had said, slow hot tears fell from her eyes. Every word she repeated set a drop free, and she felt each one, reminding her it wasn't all a dream. She knew the pain that came with them was something Javeen might never be able to understand. How could he when'd he never felt useless and unwanted? Even now, as she recited what Medusa had said, word for word, the invisible knife Medusa had wielded in that bedroom dig deeper and deeper into her heart and mind. Out of all the challenges so far, this was the one Mae knew would stick with her. If she survived this place, Stage Five would haunt her until her death—that is, if she even wanted to try to survive anymore.

When she finished her story, she finally gained the courage to look up at Javeen. "I know I shouldn't, but I'm starting to believe her. That my death would be for the overall good of the town." Before he could protest, Mae put her hand up weakly. "No. She was right—somewhere in all that she was right. I really don't think I was chosen in some random way. I think I'm here because the town didn't want me there anymore and needed an excuse to get rid of me. I know Medusa said it to upset me, but she might have been onto something. Perhaps it's not an accident I'm in here." She looked back at the floor. "This town hates me. They despise everything about me, and no one can deny that."

"Well, 'hate' is a strong word," Javeen said.

"Fine then." Mae sighed, exasperated. "They don't hate me, but I don't bring a pleasant feeling when I come to town. I notice people and everything about them. Instead of looking at me, they look in front of me or behind me, because looking at me directly would stir up some sort of pain in them. They look away, as if I'm a creature that might attack at any moment. Children even run away from me when I get near. The villagers must have made up some sort of ghost story about me or something. I'm not stupid, Javeen. I pretend I don't care, but…sometimes I do." She scuffed her foot on the floor, letting the last of her thoughts spill out. "Maybe I should've just stayed in that house with Medusa. It would've made the town happy."

There was a moment of silence as both Mae and Javeen took in her words. Then Javeen whispered, "No. The town wouldn't be better without you."

Mae, her eyes stinging, rolled them and gave him a sad smile. "You know that isn't true. Those people have been waiting for me to die ever since my parents died."

Javeen's checks were red as he turned to look at her. It reminded her of that first day in the courtyard, when she had bumped into him. When he had threatened her. But this time, it was a different anger, one she wasn't sure she wanted to face. He opened his mouth then closed it, only to open and close it again. His face scrunched up, as if he were trying to figure out what to say. The right thing to say.

"No. It's true. Mae, you don't even... The town... I..." He stared at the floor and pounded his fist into it. Mae was taken aback. Why was he hitting the floor? Did the thought of her not being in town anger him? He clearly was trying to say something, but the words wouldn't come out. Finally, his anger subsided, and he continued, a sharp look in his eyes.

"Who cares what the town thinks? Honestly, I mean that. They're a bunch of gossips, and you're a perfect target for them. That's all it is. Yeah, they feel bad, I'm sure, but at this point, you're the only entertainment they have." He put his hands up in defense as Mae tried to confront him. "Yes, I know how terrible that sounds, but it's the truth. Nothing happens in this damn place. It's the same routine every day. Before you, everyone talked about The Factory. After it closed, they needed something to chatter about; otherwise they'd be bored out of their minds."

The fire of anger and disgust in his eyes transformed into optimism as he turned his body and grabbed her hands. "You know what? Keep them talking, Mae. If they want to talk about you, let them. But make them talk about how you beat this place and became a survivor again. How you walked out when no one thought you would, with more fire than anyone has ever seen. You have to show the whole town that you're much stronger than they thought. If you can take down The Factory, then what else can you do? Make them wonder." He squeezed her hands and pulled himself closer. "But most important, *make* them look at you, Mae. That's what you need to do."

Mae nodded, letting Javeen's words cover her like a warm blanket. He was right, and of course he would be, she now realized. He was always at the market, so he knew the people and had heard the gossip. He understood the public better than any other seller there—that was why he did so well. And Mae could tell from the look in his eyes that he was telling her what he'd seen every day. What the town would never admit to: that they just needed a story. But above all, he gave her hope. If she got out of here, if they were able to get out of here together, then the town would have to look at her. Especially with the plan she had brewing in her head. A plan that would surely have everyone talking about her in due time.

She was going to tell everyone what happened in here. She refused to be one of those people who sat around and did nothing. The villagers had a right to finally know what went on inside these metal walls. But she had more in store.

Mae had a plan for this place, a plan to take it down. She hadn't put all the pieces together yet, but she knew with the help of Javeen, and now Raya, they would have everything they needed to make sure no one suffered any longer. The Factory had to be destroyed.

Slowly Mae looked up at Javeen, his green eyes staring deeply at her. The warmth of his words stopped her from shaking, but the look he gave her ignited her soul. She stared back, her breath now trembling. His hands, his large calloused hands, held her, not just physically but mentally. At this moment, she realized how important he'd been to her during this journey. But this feeling within her—well, she knew she was getting close to a line, a line she never should cross in a place like this. Still, she couldn't stop looking at those soulful eyes of his.

Suddenly she heard a cough in the background, and Javeen quickly dropped her hands. He gave her a sheepish grin as he rubbed the back of his neck, while looking anywhere else but at her. His face…was Javeen blushing? But in that same moment, Mae realized her face also burned. *I can't be blushing, can I?* she thought. She shook her head and looked at him once more, then whispered, "Thank you, Javeen."

Javeen grinned, finally looking at her again, and ruffled her hair, her six braids batting the back of her neck. He got up slowly and said, most sincerely, "I'd do anything for you, Pox Face."

As Javeen walked over and spoke to Raya, Mae's heart lightened as the two interacted. They seemed to have relaxed and were exchanging friendly glances. At one point, Javeen even laughed, and Raya gave him a playful punch on the arm. What had happened while she'd been moping in the corner? Had the universe changed the tides so everything would work out for her? Mae's spirits soared even higher. Now that the two of them were finally getting along, they had a much greater chance of getting out of here alive.

Mae sat in her cell as dinner came and went, the bedrolls following shortly after. As she laid hers, a huge shadow headed her way. Javeen brought his bedroll over to their corner and slept nearby, if only to keep her company. As he drifted off, she looked at his outstretched hand and put hers close to it, without touching it. It had brought her comfort before, so why not try again? As Mae closed her eyes and listened to the soft sound of Javeen's rhythmic breathing, a smile crossed her face as fell into a deep sleep.

This time there were no flames in her dreams. No sounds of people falling to their deaths. Not even the sneering face of Medusa as she clutched Mae's vial. There was only the comforting darkness of nothing. And for this first time since she'd set foot in this iron version of hell, Mae was able to sleep well.

Chapter Thirty-Three:
<u>Mae</u>

Mae woke up more refreshed than she'd felt in days, perhaps months. As she stretched, she noticed Javeen's sleeping area was empty. Looking over, she saw him sitting by Raya, eating the bread that had been delivered this morning. They were speaking in quiet tones, and every now and then, they smiled at each other. Raya glanced over and saw that Mae was awake; she gave her a grin and a wiggle of her fingers as she continued to eat. When Javeen looked over his shoulder and gave Mae a tiny wave, Raya shoved him lightly. He turned his head back to her as he stood up and said something, to which she laughed, and then he made his way over to Mae.

When he sat down, Mae pushed aside her bedroll, which promptly disappeared, her food taking its place. She grabbed a hunk of bread and took a bite. When Javeen sat down, she leaned nonchalantly against the bars and tossed the remaining bread between her hands. "What? You two are besties now?" she snickered, and gave him a wink.

"What? Are you jealous?" Javeen retorted with a smirk, nudging her shoulder.

In reply, Mae tore off another piece of the bread then opened her mouth and showed the chewed food to Javeen. As he chuckled, Mae couldn't help laugh too. It was contagious—though she did almost choke in the process.

"She's actually a pretty cool person," he said. "You know, once you get past that whole tough-girl act. Raya's smart. More important, she knows what she wants."

"To get out of here," Mae said, knowing what Javeen had said was true. "But then again, we all do."

"No, Mae, that's not what I'm talking about. Raya has plans once she gets out of here—plans for…this place. She wants something done about it." His face went grave as he picked at his bread. He leaned in closer and whispered, "I think…I think she might be thinking about… She's wondering if this place is really worth it. I've wondered the same thing myself."

There it was. The question that had been floating in Mae's head for so long. Javeen wanted this place destroyed as well. Finally, he'd said it, and now Mae knew she was no longer alone in that mind-set. And Raya not only wanted this place taken down, but she also wanted to see it fall into its own ashes. Then, maybe just for fun, she'd stab it a few times with a dagger. Still, it was a daunting thought, as they were still trapped in here. And this place was so large and perhaps much smarter than they knew. But it made Mae happy that she wasn't alone and that the other two people in her alliance wanted the same thing she did: the end of The Factory.

Then it came. The final ping filled the room, and the remaining twelve stood, leaving whatever food they had left on the floor. No one made as single noise as they stared up at the ceiling, waiting for instructions. The air was still and filled with apprehension. A cold sweat covered Mae's body as her stomach twisted into knots. This was it, the final stage. Although she tried not to look at Raya or Javeen, she could feel what they were all thinking. Whatever this stage had in store, if the three of them remained calm and thought rationally, they could get out alive.

"Good morning, everyone." The voice's vibrations traveled through Mae's bones. "The final stage, Stage Six, is about to commence." Once again, the voice took a dramatic pause. "In a few moments, you'll be paired off. Once you have been, follow the arrows on the floor to a room at the end of one of the corridors. When you enter that room, further instructions will follow. And for the last time, good luck." *Click.*

Everyone exhaled, and Mae felt even more anxious as it all sank in. It made sense that they would be paired off. Only twelve of them were left, so that meant that if one member of each of the pairs died, then six would leave The Factory. Mae looked around, wondering who she would be paired with. Obviously, she didn't want to be paired up with Javeen or Raya. But at the same time, being separated from them made Mae queasy. She knew she didn't need them, but having at least one of them there had given her comfort. Still, even though she knew the challenge probably wouldn't be physical, she didn't want to end up in a standoff between the two people she'd grown to care for here.

As promised, Stage Six began a minute or two after the voice had left the room. One by one, the survivors were released from their cages, revealing to everyone who their partner was. Mae watched as the first two pairs headed down a hallway. The first two she didn't really know. It was an older man, round around the stomach area and balding at the top of his head. It was Graham Kiros, a thirty-year-old man who had lived with his mother, until her recent passing a few days before the names were called. With him was Catherine Pontis, the baker's wife, who many knew had multiple lovers on the side. Well, everyone but the baker.

After they disappeared, Sadler's cage lifted, and they saw he was paired with a small, thin man. She wondered if he'd be able to survive this last challenge, and then she remembered his calm demeanor during the last stage. Sadler might have looked weak, but something about him had gotten him this far, and Mae felt he might make it out. Sadler had beaten all the odds, and not through his strength but his wits. It was an admirable feat, and Mae truly wanted him to win, to prove there was more to this game then brawn. However, that thought was pushed it out of her mind as Raya was release from her cell.

She watched as Raya, once more displaying her stone-cold exterior, stared ahead as her partner was released. It was the Ripley, the drunk, who'd somehow made it this far in the competition. How was anyone's guess, as Mae noticed the man's shaking hands; clearly the withdrawals hadn't stopped yet. His haggard eyes here half closed, as if he had no fight left in him. When Mae looked back at Raya, she saw the smallest glint of sorrow in her eyes, knowing her freedom most likely lay between her and this sick man. But it was quickly replaced with a fire for self-determination, and Mae knew she would put all her money on Raya leaving.

Raya and the man followed the arrows on the floor before them. Mae wanted to keep staring forward, but she knew that as Raya passed, she would give her friend a supportive wave. However, there was no need; Raya slowed down as she passed Javeen's and Mae's cells and looked at them with sheer purpose.

"Get out of here. Both of you. I…I need you guys to get out." She gave them her signature smirk, with the added wink, and said, "See you on the other side." Mae watched as Raya disappeared down a dark hallway, just like everyone else had.

Mae heard a thud and knew what would follow. As the bars of her cell receded into the ceiling, she closed her eyes. This was the last stage, and she wasn't sure she was prepared for whatever lay ahead. Still, she had to be strong and make it out—if not for herself, then for Javeen and Raya. As she heard the bars of the other cell receding, she took a deep breath before looking to see who she was up against. When she opened them, none of the other cages were moving. Once more she closed her eyes, hard this time, then opened them and looked at the cell next to her, dreading what she would see.

Javeen was her partner.

Mae felt sick, the small amount of bread she had eaten forcing its way back up. *If this is a physical challenge...* But she pushed that thought away, even though it always clung to her brain. She knew it wouldn't be; that would be too messy. Raya had been right about how this place worked. The Factory was clean, and mental challenges kept it clean. Both she and Javeen had proved to be strong mentally, and as a team they'd be unstoppable. Even though they were paired together, Mae knew they'd both leave The Factory somehow.

Arrows lit up on the floor, showing them the way. Mae glanced at Javeen, who shrugged as they walked toward the tunnel. Worries were overtaking her mind, monsters making their way back to cloud her judgment, but then she felt a sudden weight against her shoulder as Javeen stood next to her. He was walking as close to her as possible, as if he were protecting her. Mae's fear began to melt, but some frozen anxiety within her remained. The Factory had plenty of tricks, and she needed to be ready for all of them.

Down the dark hallway they went, with only a few dim sconces on the walls around them and the light of their arrows illuminating the way. The sounds of their marching feet ricocheted down the corridor, reminding them how alone they were right now. Although Javeen stared straight ahead, Mae saw the worry in his eyes. But behind that worry, she saw the same conviction she had come to believe. Yes, they were be paired together, but the two of them were leaving this place alive and would see Raya on the other side. They were going to make it.

Eventually the arrows turned, and Mae and Javeen were in front of an outline of a door. It had no handle, so they stood there, waiting for something to happen. Their final destination in The Factory was now in front of them. Mae tried to keep her breathing calm as the time seemed to pass so slowly.

Finally, there was a loud noise, like the sound of a deadbolt coming free. The door slid into the wall, and a room appeared in front of them.

This is it, Mae told herself. *No going back.* This room was what they'd been trying to get to since they'd first arrived at The Factory. As Mae attempted to take a steady breath, Javeen's warm, rough hand wrapped around hers. Immediately her chest lightened, if only slightly. They didn't look at each other as his fingers intertwined with hers, but a feeling of ease was there. Mae felt it and knew Javeen did too. They gave each other one more squeeze as, hand in hand, they entered Stage Six.

Chapter Thirty-Four:
<u>Javeen</u>

Fear crept into Javeen's veins as they walked into the dark, ebony-tiled room. Four lights, one in each corner, illuminated the room. But still the darkness of the place had a haunting effect on him. Even with the light, he thought the room was darker than it should be. He felt it symbolized something, but he tried to shake off that feeling as he clasped Mae's hand. He had to be strong for her, as he felt her fear. He couldn't let her know he felt almost the same way. Silently the two went to the back of the room and lowered themselves to the floor, waiting for their instructions.

They sat there, staring at the outline of the door, the tension growing the longer they waited. Mae exhaled sharply as she lightly tapped her head against the wall. This wasn't sitting well with her, as she was now used to having someone to talk to or something to talk about. Before Javeen could offer any words of comfort, she said, "Do you think this was planned?" Her head turned lazily, her eyes looking up at him. "The two of us being stuck here together?"

Javeen wondered if perhaps it was. It was odd that they'd been chosen as partners, seeing as their relationship had grown during their time here. Throughout this whole ordeal, although they'd clearly communicated, they'd tried to keep their alliance a secret from everyone except Raya. Perhaps they hadn't hidden it as well as they'd thought. Javeen's brow crinkled. "I don't know. Maybe. The Factory is full of surprises. It wouldn't be shocking if it's been taking notice of us." The thought of this place watching over him like a hawk sent a shiver up his spine.

Mae nodded and turned her head back toward the outline of the door. "What do you think will happen?"

"We know it won't be a physical challenge," Javeen said. "Raya made that clear, and she was right." He gave Mae a playful shove. "As much as I hate to admit that." He pondered some more, really thinking about how a few rooms could reduce their numbers from twelve to six. Perhaps it wasn't just about outliving your partner. Maybe this mental game would be the hardest kind of challenge a human could face. That's when it came to him.

Finally, slowly, he told Mae his idea. "I think it's going to be some sort of solitary confinement. I think The Factory will keep us cooped up in here until something happens. Most of the people left are already pretty unbalanced already. Half of them almost lost it in their cages, where at least they could talk to someone. But being locked up in a room with little or nothing to do, and knowing this is the end, well, that might make them actually crack." Mae bobbed her head in agreement, although she wasn't too convincing as she chewed her thumbnail.

Javeen continued. "We just have to keep our heads on straight. In every other pair, one person wants to beat the other one and get out. But we're both here for each other. Just because two people went into a room doesn't mean only one is coming out. Someone might accidently kill another person, then off themselves. I know it sounds cruel, but sometimes that's what happens. You snap, and then you realize what you did, and well, you can't live it. How they would do it, I don't know, but it's a possibility." The gruesome turn of the conversation was starting to get to him, so he decided to end it. "All I know is we're getting out."

Again, the room became still as they waited. At this point, they were waiting for anything. Seeing an insect cross the floor would have been better than staring at these ebony tiles for another minute. Then everything was broken with a small giggle that turned into a laugh. Javeen glanced questioningly as Mae, who had burst into hysterical laughter. He nudged her, and she put her hand up as she caught her breath.

"I was just thinking..." she started.

"Oh, you do that sometimes?" he returned, and she playfully jabbed his ribs.

"I was thinking," she continued, "about the village, and then about the marketplace. I'd always go there whenever I could, and I'd always see your cart."

Javeen's stomach jumped as he realized she'd noticed him before all this. "You did?"

"Of course!" She smiled. "For two reasons…well, actually three. One, you were literally the biggest seller in the market. No one could miss those huge shoulders of yours. I mean, really, what the hell do you eat? Two, I always noticed how nice you were to people, no matter how they treated you. Everyone always made their way to your stand—all kinds of people—and you still had a smile on your face the entire time. And trust me, I saw some of the nastiest, ill-behaved people at your cart."

Javeen remembered the tomato man he'd dealt with two weeks ago. Had Mae seen that? He was more taken aback that she had noticed any of these aspects about him. He barely realized that he stood out in the marketplace. And rarely did he think that many people came to his stand. But the more he thought about it, the more he realized he did sell much more than the other vendors.

He was ready to thank her when Mae's expression turned smug. "And three, my dear, dear friend, is the main reason I'm laughing. Your cart was the easiest to swipe food from."

Javeen tried to hide his smile. "You stole from me? I mean, I know you stole from some of the carts, but you stole from mine?"

"All the time. I mean, really, Javeen. Every time I was there, I was able to take at least three pieces of fruit. Let this be a lesson to you. You need to install a better security system. Or at least notice when half your food is missing. It's almost like you wanted…" She stopped when she saw that Javeen now wore a smug look. He cocked his eyebrows toward her and gave a little snicker.

Anger, rage, and frustration bubbled up in Mae's voice. "You didn't. Javeen, tell me you didn't do what I think you did." He nodded, and she punched his arms. "You let me steal your food!" she yelled, but the smile was still there. "You put that food where it would be easy for me to swipe!"

Laughing at how ridiculous she was being, Javeen pushed her off as she continued to swing. "Of course I did!"

"I didn't want pity food," Mae said, sulking.

"It's not pity food when the person is practically starving," he said, looking down at her. Even though they hadn't received much food in here, Javeen noticed how she ate—as if it were her last meal. Her lean body already was looking healthier than when she had walked in.

Mae let out a huff as she rested against the wall. "I thought I was one of the best pickpockets at the market, and you went and spoiled that for me. You could have at least let me think I was sneaky!" She crossed her arms dramatically. "Well, now everything is ruined. The image I've created for myself has vanished." She gave him a small pout. "What am I going to tell my friends?" And with that they both howled with laughter.

When they'd calmed down, they still hadn't received any instructions, and Javeen knew that sitting in silence would only make things worse. He could already feel Mae getting twitchy again, and he knew her anxiety and frustration would only escalate. So, he turned to her and said, "Tell me a secret."

Mae rolled her eyes. "Are you serious? You think I have any secrets? Come on. The whole town knows everything about me. I'm an unwilling open book."

Javeen leaned toward her, wiggling a finger. "No, no, no. They *think* they know you. I want to know—*actually* know—something about you. Something you haven't told anyone. A memory of a crush or something stupid you did once that no one saw." He waited as she said nothing. "Come on."

He knew he had her when she uncrossed her arms and threw them to the floor. "Fine. But you have to promise not to laugh or anything."

Javeen crossed his heart, and then Mae said something. However, it was a mumbled whisper that he couldn't understand. He asked her again, and once more she uttered words he couldn't quite grasp. He leaned in even closer. "What was that? You need to—"

"I don't know the name of our village!" she yelled.

He jumped back and stared at her, trying to regain his composure. "You don't know the town's name?" he finally said.

Mae shook her head. "After my parents died, I didn't care about anything anymore, and I pushed anything that didn't have to do with survival out of my head. That included the name of the town. Why would I want to remember a place that had kicked me out? I knew the name for a few years, but now, after all the burying on my part, well, it's too deep to find. I don't remember it."

Javeen shifted, his long legs beginning to ache. "Do you want to know it?" he asked.

Mae looked conflicted as he waited for an answer. Finally, she shrugged. "I don't know. I guess...I mean, it won't hurt, right?"

He gave her a lighthearted laugh, and she glared at him. "Sorry. I wasn't laughing at you. But I do think it's important to know where you're from." He paused. "No matter what they did to you there."

Mae sighed and nodded. "All right, Farmer. Tell me the name of our town."

"Destaville," Javeen said, then laughed once more, this time clearly to himself. "Which is the most ironic thing in the world, seeing as 'Desta' means happiness. In like...I think Greek or African or something. I looked it up once in the bookshop."

"Irony at its finest." Mae grunted as she took in this new information. Then she threw her shoulder into his. "All right, big boy. It's your turn. Tell me a secret."

Javeen felt his breath hitch and hoped Mae hadn't noticed. This was a loaded question if there ever was one. Oh, all the secrets Javeen wanted to tell her. He had a whole book of them, and if he wanted to, he could confess everything to her. But he decided on one. One secret that might allow the rest of his secrets to come forward with much more ease.

"When I saw you coming into The Factory, I was afraid of you."

There was a pause as Mae stared at him, her eyes wide. Then the corners of her mouth began to twitch. In a sudden moment, a holler of enjoyment rose through the air as she slapped the floor. She turned to him, trying to catch her breath. "Please…please tell me you're joking." She pointed to her smelly, grimy shirt. "You thought I was scary?"

Javeen nodded, feeling the color rush to his face. "Yes. And I don't think it's fair that I can't laugh at your secret, but you can laugh at mine," he whispered, looking down at the frays that lined the hem of his shirt. That shut her up. Javeen fiddled with the strings as the silence went on. He felt a jab in his side, and Mae was still staring at him, clearly wanting him to continue.

He took a deep breath and explained, "You didn't see your face the day you came in. I mean, you're an average-size person, nothing to fear. But that face was one of a killer. That's why, on the first day I was so mean to you. At first I didn't know why I did it. But I kind of snapped when I saw you coming in. Then it hit me that it was because of the way you looked at this place. You had no fear on your face, like you were ready to take on whatever The Factory was going to throw at you. When you bumped into me, I let my anger, envy, and fear get the better of me, and I tried to push you around. I wanted to prove I could be just as tough as you were." He sighed. "And then…we got in here, and I proved to be a giant softie."

Javeen rested his head back and waited for something to come from her direction. Maybe about how someone his size should be ashamed, or perhaps Mae would burst into another fit of laughter. Instead he felt a weight press against him and saw Mae was resting her head on his shoulder. His heart beat faster as she whispered, "Nah. I think you're pretty tough. I mean, yes, you *are* a total softie. You got that. But you're tough too. You're not the other guy, though. The one I met in the courtyard. I don't think you have to be one or the other. Besides"—she looked up at him, her blue eyes glowing—"I like this Javeen better. The tough softie."

"So then, that face I saw when you walked in. What was that about? Were you that determined to come racing in here? Ready to show The Factory everything you've got?"

He regretted asking it, as Mae immediately sat up and picked at her fingernails. Her breathing became deep, and her eyes darted around the floor. She looked as though she were trying to figure out what to tell him, but it wasn't coming to her. Mae, still looking at the floor, began to open her mouth, perhaps to explain what she was thinking. Then suddenly her head shot up as a sound from the center of the room brought her to her feet.

Javeen slowly lifted himself, the blood rushing back through his legs. They both watched as a table slowly rose in the center of the room—a black table that matched the entire space. There was something on it—he could see that right away—but he didn't dare come any closer until the table came to a stop. Ever so slowly it inched its way up. Javeen's breath quickened, and Mae's body shook as the table finally halted. They exchanged a quick glance before cautiously making their way to the table.

Mae went around one side while Javeen took the other. As they reached it, Javeen saw that he was right. Something was waiting for them. Two objects actually. The first was a glass of water, simple enough. But what really caught his attention was a small bowl with a small oval-shaped object inside it. He moved closer, trying to get a better look at the mysterious object. His stomach dropped when he saw the red-and-blue pill. This pill was different from the pills in Stage Two. It had a skull on it.

Mae and Javeen looked at each other in pure horror as the truth sank in. Javeen had been wrong—very wrong—about what this stage had in store. It was clear from the beginning. There were twelve of them, and The Factory's math was always correct. Twelve people, separated into six pairs. And only one of those people would survive. There could only be one. There was only ever going to be one.

Then it came. The words they dreaded hearing.

"Stage Six has begun."

Chapter Thirty-Five:
<u>Javeen</u>

Click. No directions were given. None were needed. Their directions were on the table in front of them. The rules of this stage had become clear once the two of them had seen what was on the stand. Two in. One out.

Javeen's heart plummeted to his feet. Sweat built on his brow and upper lip. Around him, the world swirled into a mass of black that had no beginning or end. He could only focus on two things on while his world spun out of control: the water and the death pill. This wasn't how it was supposed to be. They...they were supposed to wait it out. They were going to leave together. That was what they had said just moments ago, as they leaned against the wall. But now everything had changed.

Javeen's thoughts raced faster than he could process them. Everything he knew—past, present, and future—flashed in front of him. He had a family to get back to. The thought of his mother holding the hatchet rushed to the front of his mind. He had to get out of The Factory to protect his siblings. He was the only reason his family was still together, why none of his siblings had run away. And what about managing the farm and going to the market? Jiro wasn't old enough yet to take care of everyone, or at least he didn't act like it. And it wasn't his job. Javeen wanted Jiro to live his life and not become trapped like he was. His mind then raced to another, darker thought.

He knew what his mother had done. Or what her actions had done to the family. Her behavior had been part of the reason their father was dead. Could Javeen really go back and pretend he didn't know what had happened? Go on with his life as if he didn't know the grisly truth behind his father's death? Another flash and another thought: he would always remember that he had turned into an animal in this place. Would his family understand what he had done to Tharin? Javeen, with his own hands, had made sure Tharin had fallen into the fiery pit, sending him to his death. Could he live with that? Mae could have sugarcoated it all she wanted, but he still had murdered that man.

And there it was. The name. Mae. Javeen had made a promise to her before Stage Two, one he never intended to break. He was going to get her out of here. It wasn't just a promise to her; Javeen also had promised himself. When he saw her walking through the gate that cold morning, he knew it would be his job to make sure she saw the light of day again. Javeen had made it his personal mission to protect Mae with everything he had. He thought back on all the stages, everything they'd done for each other. She had saved him too, multiple times. And he had a debt to repay her. Javeen remembered saying he might even pay it with his life. But as he sat here and stared at the table…

A voice woke him from his thoughts, and he realized it was his own. He was talking to himself the entire time he was thinking. He heard his voice coat the walls, floors, and the table as he recounted his trials and woes. Then he remembered he wasn't alone. Javeen slowly looked up at Mae, who had her knuckles in her teeth and was biting hard. She too was glaring at the table, her breath unsteady. Briefly they made eye contact. Javeen thought he saw pity in her eyes.

"Don't pity me now," he growled. It wasn't something he needed at this moment; it would hinder his thinking. Suddenly Mae shook her head violently, and Javeen looked at her again. He thought she was biting her hand as a thinking method, but she was trying to keep herself from crying. Mae was literally trying to bite the tears away, to stay strong in this moment, for both of them. Yet the tears still fell. She backed up against the wall, droplets flying off her face as she kept everything bottled in. When Mae finally took her hand away to take a breath, Javeen saw teeth marks on her index finger, along with drops of blood. Then, like a match to kerosene, she exploded.

"Damn it! Damn it! Damn it!" she screamed, pounding her fists against the wall. For a moment Javeen stood frozen as her fit continued, bruises already forming on her knuckles, which continued to strike the tile wall. She wasn't thinking rationally, and he needed to step in before it was too late.

Javeen took a step toward her. "Mae…It's going…"

"*Don't tell me it's going to be okay when clearly it's not!*" she bawled at him, her eyes wild with anger and fear. Tears continued to roll down her face, the whites in her eyes now pink. All they had to do was look at each other.

Javeen knew she was right; there was no longer a need to say that to her. Not anymore.

They stood in silence, staring at each other. Tension filled the air as the seconds passed. Javeen didn't know what to do, and they both understood that no one was leaving until one of them died. It was the ultimate standoff between morals and survival. Javeen knew neither of them wanted to die, as they'd made it this far, but to watch the other perish would be too much to live with. Mae's eyes continued to water as she stared at him, and slowly the pity Javeen thought he had seen was no longer there. Neither was the anger or fear.

"You're not taking this…" she started, her breathing beginning to steady.

A rush of frustration filled Javeen's body as he struck the table with his hands. A little of the water shook out of the glass, landing near his fingers. "Well, damn it, Mae…I don't know. I mean, really? What the hell are we supposed to do? Don't put this on me like I've already decided. We haven't talked about it yet and—"

"No," she said through gritted teeth. "I wasn't asking you." There was a pause as she looked down, took a deep breath, and grabbed his attention once more. "I'm *telling* you."

At first, Javeen didn't know what she meant, but then he saw her calm expression. Everything about her countenance told him they didn't need to talk about the pill anymore. Mae already had decided the outcome. She was in charge of her own fate; Javeen always knew that. He looked at the table once more and then at Mae and understood the grave reality of what she was saying. Javeen started around the table. "Mae…"

She backed away quickly. "No, Javeen. You won't talk me out of this. I've made up my mind. I'm not letting you die in this hellhole. You can't. You have so much more to live for than I do. You have a family. You have people waiting for you on the other side." Mae's tears continued to fall. "I have nothing out there. No one wants me back. If I walk out there, I'll walk into an in an empty house, with nothing but the bugs to talk to. In fact, Medusa was right…the town probably will throw a party if I don't return."

Slowly, once more, Javeen stepped toward her, trying to reason with her. "Mae…please. You aren't thinking."

But she was. He knew the moment the table had appeared, she was thinking. The biting of her knuckles, the fit against the wall. Javeen understood why she had yelled at him. Not because she was scared. It was because she didn't want to choose; she knew she would die for him. And then, amid all this tension, all this weighted air, Mae let out a small, soft chuckle. Javeen looked at her with concern and sadness.

"It's so funny," she said, staring at the table. "You were afraid of me when I walked into The Factory. You said I looked like I wanted to take this place on. I have to admit, at first, that wasn't the case. I just wanted people to look at me and talk about me as I walked past them. You know, notice me. So, I put on a brave face and walked through the gate as if nothing had happened.

"That all changed once those doors closed in Stage One. The longer I stayed here, the more I *did* want to fight back and make The Factory bleed. With death after death, this place has haunted my dreams, and it's fueled me to get out of here with you. I knew that with you, and Raya, we could do something. There was something about us that would be different than any other Leavings before us. We could be the change this town needed, and the strength it deserved. I wanted to see The Factory burn to the ground, like the countless souls that have already burned within it. I wanted this place…to be afraid of me."

Javeen tried to say something, but once more Mae suddenly moved around the room. She looked up at the ceiling. "You hear that!" she shrieked, throwing her fist in the air. "I wanted you to fear me! That's why I wanted to walk out of here. So that you, a place of fire and death, would tremble knowing I got out alive. My dream was for you to have nightmares of me!" She sighed sadly. "Me, a simple human."

Javeen watched frozen in amazement as she spoke, her voice filled with passion and anger. He almost forgot to breathe. Never in his life had he seen someone so determined. Her dream was to make sure no one would ever have to fear another list of names or tremble at the thought of what might lie inside The Factory's iron walls. And here was Mae, throwing all that determination away, just so Javeen could live with his family. His now dismantled family. He was still stuck in his spot as she slowly approached him and placed a hand on his cheek.

"You can still do it, Javeen. You and Raya. Go home to your family and be with them. Then figure it out. I want you to make sure this place shakes when it sees you two." She gave him a sad smile as she stroked his check. "I know you can do what I wanted to do."

Mae then strode to the other side of the table and, with a sigh, picked up the glass of water, her eyes focused on the pill. Then, with a shaky hand, she reached into the bowl. She did a few flips with the pill and gave him a weak smile before she moved it toward her mouth. Her hand seemed to travel in slow motion as Javeen stood there.

He looked at her one more time. Mae. The girl with the six braids, who had fought like hell through all the stages. The girl no one ever noticed, or so she thought. The girl who was probably the only person able to actually take down the Factory, and there she was taking poison. Worst of all, he was letting her. Then, as if someone had given Javeen a fire that lit up his soul, a bolt of energy surged through him. He stood for a fraction of a second as the pill was at her lips.

At that moment, Javeen lunged out and tackled her.

Chapter Thirty-Six:
<u>Mae</u>

Mae prayed it would be quick. Perhaps the poison would immediately attack her brain, allowing her to feel nothing. Her body would fall to the floor and that would be it. That way, Javeen wouldn't have to watch her suffer. Then the furnace would take her and he'd be free to go. Back to his family and a town that actually wanted him there. That was what she was thinking, just before Javeen's body slammed into hers.

In an instant, Mae was thrown to the ground, her head hitting the tile and the pill slipping from her hand. The sound of it bouncing into the corner was the last thing she heard before a ringing filled her ears. She felt the weight of Javeen atop her for a moment and then, quickly, he pulled himself off her and moved forward. Mae pushed herself up and tried to regain her bearings. Although she was disoriented, it took her only a second or two to figure out what Javeen was rushing toward.

The pill in the corner.

Anxiety and rage rush through her. This wasn't the plan. Hadn't she listened to what she had said? She was going to free him. She was going to give Javeen a life worth living. What the hell was he doing?

He hadn't made it too far, and she knew she didn't have much time before he was out of reach. She latched her hands onto one of his legs and pulled back as hard as she could. Fortunately for her, he was in mid-step and lost his footing; otherwise he would have just dragged her with him. He fell with a crash, his muscular body making the floor shake. Mae crawled over him, trying to get to the pill before he had time to register what was happening. If she was on top of him, then perhaps he would be locked down.

Just as she had pushed herself over his shoulders, however, Mae flew up in air, the collar of her shirt clinging to her neck. While she'd been focusing on putting space between them, she hadn't noticed Javeen had gotten to his feet. Now he was pulling her back to the corner where they'd they been laughing only minutes ago. With an underhanded toss, he threw her down, letting her body slide across the floor toward the wall. Not even waiting to see if she hit the other side, Javeen turned around and raced toward the pill. But Mae had gained her footing before she hit that wall. Once more she was up, and with a new fire inside her, she was much quicker than he realized. Even if he did let her take his fruit.

It took three strides for her to reach a launching point, and Mae then lunged herself at Javeen's back. As she crashed into a wall of hard muscle built by years of farming, she felt the air leave her for a moment. Javeen was caught off guard as he staggered sideways for a bit, but he continued toward the pill. Mae's plan wasn't working since she was so much smaller than him. To make up for her lack of size, she had to take extreme measures. Although she felt guilty about what was to come, she knew it was the only way. As quickly as she could, Mae clawed at Javeen's face with her nails. He shouted in pain as warm blood covered her fingers. Seeing that his neck was also unprotected, she sank her teeth in while continuing to scratch his face.

"You have a family!" she wailed before trying to take a bite of his ear.

They were dancing around the room as Javeen tried to bat her hands away. For a moment Mae backed off, thinking her words might sink in, but Javeen quickly found her face and arms and clawed at her. When he missed a few times, Mae noticed how clumsy his large hands were. She felt the sting, however, when his fingers opened five large slices on her cheek. Mae took one hand off his neck to react, the other still clutching Javeen with all she could. At that moment, Javeen bit her forearm, releasing a howl from Mae. She immediately fell to the floor but quickly bounced back to her feet, ready to fight again. She wasn't going to stop until he let her take that damn pill.

As Mae stood up, Javeen's back was turned, and she kneed him in the lower half of it. Javeen yelled out in agony as he arched and fell to his knees. Mae jumped over him, feeling his torso hit the ground as she did. Breathing heavily, she spotted the pill in the corner and Javeen on the floor. It was over, Mae knew. She had won, and when it was all said and done, he'd be happy that she'd done what she had to do. Mae headed to the corner and reached down to pick up the pill. Everything would be over in a few seconds.

Suddenly, Javeen turned on her. Up on his feet and stealthy as a fox, he grabbed her once more in a swift motion and pulled her in front of him. Mae's mouth fell open in shock as he carried her away from the pill. For a second, his eyes looked down at her with sorrow, not the anger she'd expected, which made her want to fight even more. *He can't do this*, she thought. *He has nothing to be sorry about because he's going to live.* Mae flailed her legs, trying to catch him somewhere, perhaps take him down for the last time, but it was too late. Before she knew what was happening, Javeen was holding her at eye level, one last look of despair on his face. Then, with more power than Mae thought possible, he took two giant steps to the back of the room and slammed her into the wall.

The wind within her vanished in an instant, and she felt as though she'd been rammed by an ox. Her head cracked against the wall, and when she opened her eyes, Javeen and the rest of the room spun around her. She tried to focus, say something, but only moans escaped as the world slowly began to reform around her. With a soft apology, Javeen let her go as she fell to the floor in a crumple, and then he headed to the corner. Mae leaned against the wall, quickly assessing the damage. The second she tried to inhale, she knew some of her ribs were broken. Each breath was more painful than the next, stabbing her like shards of glass. She'd be useless if she attempted another fight, but she had to try. She moved her arms and pulled herself forward, her legs too fatigued to be of any use.

"Javeen," she wheezed, as she crawled her way toward him.

He turned to her, the pill in his hand. He gave her a half smile and a light sigh. "You never give up, do you?"

As Javeen stood under one of the few lights in the room, Mae was now able to see the damage she had inflicted upon him. His shirt was riddled with holes and tears, the frays hanging down to his knees. His neck was raw and red and littered with bite marks. Cuts covered his face, including a rather deep one below his left eye. Although they weren't bleeding much, it was enough to make Javeen look as though a cougar had attacked him.

"You have a family," she tried again, knowing how important his siblings were to him. Mae had to do everything possible to make sure he handed that pill to her.

Javeen threw his hands in the air. "What does it matter? It's not worth it. Not with everything I know and what this place has turned me into. Everything I've done in here has made me a different person—and not for the better. You say I have a family, but do I really? I don't want to go back there and pretend everything is okay. That bond, the one that held my family together? It's gone. And it can never be repaired. Perhaps if you were there with me, I could make it work, but that isn't happening. I can't go out there by myself. And I don't want to."

Mae's breath hitched painfully. "Please," she pleaded again, pulling herself forward. With each move and breath, pain coursed throughout her body.

Javeen, clearly seeing she was no longer a threat to him, placed the pill on the table and walked over to her. His strides were long and strong, making Mae was nervous. *Why is he coming over here?* she wondered. *Is he going to make sure I don't get up? Knock me out cold?* She stared at the floor, the toes of his boots approaching her. Javeen knelt and lightly placed his fingers under her chin. She knew he wanted her to look at him, but the reality of the situation had paralyzed her. These were probably going to be their last moments together. When Mae finally mustered the courage to look at him, his eyes emanated a pure emotion, a feeling she hadn't witnessed since her parents were alive.

Affection.

Javeen smiled at her, a smile that somehow radiated light. "You know, it's kind of funny. You never knew this, but I had my own little mission in here too. My goal was to get you out of here. At any cost. And then, when you saved my ass a few times, I absolutely knew I had to make sure you saw daylight. And although I really, really would have liked it to have been the two of us, I *am* keeping my promise."

Hot tears stung the cuts on Mae's cheeks, but the pain was nothing compared to his words and the way he looked at her right now. "Don't. Please, Javeen, don't keep that promise. You have so much more for you out there. I'm…I'm not worth it." She felt as though she might pass out from the pain in her ribs.

Javeen shook his head. "No, Mae, you *are*. I can't even believe you think my life is worth more than yours. You want this place destroyed, burned to the ground by its own flames. Well, I felt moved by your speech. Just your speech, Mae. Imagine what you could do out there with your ideas and your actions. I know you'd be able to start something. You're so passionate about that goal; it would be reckless—evil, even—to let you die here. You think I could do take this place down? Without you by my side, I could never find that passion. The only person who can make that happen is you. You're the one who needs to get out of here and destroy The Factory. I just ask that you do two things for me. First, make sure my family is okay. I just need to know they're going to be all right. If you help them, I know everything will be as normal as it can be. But more important to me than anything else, Mae, is this: I want you to make this place fear you." He gave her a grin. "Fear a simple human."

Mae thought he was about to get up and leave her, but Javeen leaned in closer, and his eyes brimmed with tears as he continued. "And see, I never really told you my secret. I mean, I did, but not the secret I've been wanting to tell you for so long. You thought no one noticed you. You thought were just a ghost, with no one who cared about you. Well, you were wrong. Because there was one person. Every day you came to the market or walked through town, I saw you. From your braids to your worn leather shoes, I saw you." He smiled sweetly. "Something about you drew me to your soul. I never went up to you, afraid you'd scoff at me, see me as someone who pitied you. But I didn't. I wanted to know everything about you: the good, the bad, and everything in between. Your fears and dreams. What foods you like. Your favorite flowers. I wanted to be your friend and companion and show you I was there, in a town you thought had forgotten you. I noticed you and wanted to know the real you. You think you don't matter to anyone, but you do. Somehow, you finally made me say it after all these years. Damn it, Pox Face. You matter to me." Javeen took a shuddering breath then smiled again. "Better late than never, right?"

He cupped her face and kissed her. A rush of emotions surged through Mae's body as his lips touched hers. She closed her eyes, tears cascading down her face. In that one moment, everything happened. The kiss was tender and soft yet hard at the same time. It was a kiss of a wish come true, but also a kiss of goodbyes. They both wanted more than one, but knew that one was all they had. It would be their first kiss together and, sadly, their last, Mae thought. Slowly Javeen pulled away, tears falling from his face too.

He gave her one last smile, his hand falling as he rose. Mae tried to reach for him as he moved away, but pain shot through her side. Javeen walked over to the table, not looking back, and picked up the pill. For the last time, he turned to her, the glitter in his eyes somehow still there. "Keep your promises, Mae. That's how you'll remember me. Live a happy life, and keep your promises. It's all I ask of you." Then, before she could stop him, Javeen put the pill in his mouth and swallowed it.

His body fell as soon as it went down his throat. As he convulsed, Mae crawled over to him, screaming his name. She froze in horror and watched as Javeen's strong body tried to fight off the poison to no avail. Mae pressed on his chest, tried mouth-to-mouth, and even stuck her fingers down this throat to make him throw up. Anything to stop the terror and agony, for both their sakes. Perhaps she could get him back, and somehow The Factory would let them both go. But just as that thought passed through her mind, foam billowed from Javeen's lips. The same ones that had kissed her moments ago. Mae screamed at him, telling him not to give up, hoping he could still hear her. But finally, she felt his heart stop, his labored breathing coming to a quick halt. She collapsed on top of his torso and reached for his hands, clutching them in hopes that they would at least twitch. But they didn't. She buried her head into Javeen's chest and tried to listen for his warm heart to beat once more. Silence was her only answer, and then all Mae could hear was her own sobs.

Javeen was gone. The Factory had won.

Mae held on tightly to his shirt as she wept. Then, from behind her eyelids, she saw a flicker. When she opened them, an orange light was filling the room. *The Factory must be letting me out*, she thought. She grabbed Javeen under his arms, ready to drag him out with her, when it hit her. It wasn't the bright white light of the outdoors but an orange light glistening around her. Panicking, she looked down at Javeen's feet and saw that the floor had begun to open. Heat flooded the room the more the floor opened up, and the ebony tiles became even more sinister looking. The furnace was taking its last victim.

Closer and closer the fiery canyon moved toward Javeen's body. Mae watched in horror as his feet began to slide down, followed by his knees. Although the door below his body seemed to move slowly, Mae felt it was moving entirely too fast. When she felt the pull of his hand, she truly began to panic. Then, as she looked at his face, that panic transformed into purpose. This wasn't how Javeen would leave this earth, not in this horrible blaze. His family deserved a proper burial with Javeen's body. Not an array of ashes from who knew where. Mae had to try to bring him out with her in order to make things right. As she tried to pull Javeen toward her, his weight was too much for her broken ribs, pain hurtling through her body. Still she fought.

When his waist began to sink, Mae braced herself. If she could push herself up, injuries and all, she might be able to drag him away. Struggling, she moved her arms so they were around Javeen's torso and held on. As his lower body dangled above the fire, Mae felt the heat rising as it tried to take more of him. But when his waist finally gave out, she felt his body mass take over. She tried to push herself up, gritting her teeth through the pain, but her arms were sweating and her shoes had lost their grip. Just as she was about to stand, Javeen's upper body slipped through her arms. His body fell towards the fire, and Mae dove after it, chest slamming against the ground and lip of the widening gap. He was about to plunge, disappearing forever, when Mae reached out and grabbed one of his arms with both hands.

The searing pain in her ribs hit home quickly and she now knew she couldn't do it. Javeen was too heavy for her, and The Factory wanted him. She could fight all she wanted, but The Factory always got what it wanted. Even so, she had to try to do something. Anything for his family so they would know she had fought for him. Feeling the bubbling of blisters, she knew her arm was becoming severely burned as she continued to hold on. She was now leaning over the edge, as the floor had stopped opening up once Javeen had fallen in. Mae's eyes scanned everywhere for something that was important to him, and then she saw it. Right there, next to her reddening wrist. The twine bracelet he had shown her in the second stage.

It was only thing he had of importance in this damned place, besides his knife, which had to too close to the furnace by now. Mae could take the bracelet with her as a memento for his family. With tears still falling, she hurried as sweat loosened her grip and Javeen's fingers were beginning to slip through her fist. While struggling to hold on with one hand, with the other hand she transferred the twine from his wrist to hers. When she felt the scratchy material against her arm, she looked down at him one last time. His pants were burning, and there was nothing she could do now. Mae closed her eyes and exhaled slowly.

Then she let go of Javeen's hand.

She jumped up and curled herself into the fetal position, her eyes closed tightly as she clutched her red-hot arm. She refused to watch this place take Javeen and only knew it was over when the floor suddenly closed up. All that remained was the lingering heat of the furnace as it cloaked the room with the memories of what had happened. Mae sat there, her chest aching, her face stinging, her arm feeling as though it would never stop burning. She just remained there and stared into space. As a light color caught her eyes, she quickly glanced at it. It was one of her six braids. The tie must have burned off near the furnace, as now the braid had come loose and was no more. Six braids for six people, but now one of her six was gone.

Suddenly she heard a loud noise behind her, as if the walls were moving upward. Mae felt the heat rush out of the room as the winter chill sneaked in. Bright rays of sunlight bounced off the black tiles as a light wind rushed into the space. It was then that Mae knew the truth.

She had survived.

Chapter Thirty-Seven:
<u>Raya</u>

The sun was the only thing that warmed Raya as she marched back and forth near the gate, looking over her shoulder every few minutes. Almost three hours had passed since The Factory had released her. She was the first one out and had watched the gate open in front of her. After visiting a doctors' tent due to requirements, she had sprinted back to the gate to wait for Mae and Javeen. She watched as two others walked out, Sadler and that man who lived, well who used to live, with his mother, Graham. Sadler had looked at her when he walked by, and for a moment she though he might try and talk to her, but one glance kept him away. Raya was surprisingly happy the lanky apprentice made his way out. His wits were what kept him alive, and she had nothing but respect for that. As he limped his way past her, Raya turned her focus back to the open gates.

She kept pacing to keep herself warm and to prevent herself from going crazy. Raya looked down at her hand, still shaking, and brushed off the black power that still remained her right hand. There was a slight burn underneath, but the cold air added some comfort to it. She looked back at the entrance, rubbing her hands up and down her arms, calming herself and keep herself warm. Still she saw no sign of Mae or Javeen.

"Where the hell are they?" she hissed, her teeth chattering.

The clock tower struck two, and Raya glanced at the gate once more, wondering how much longer she would wait for them. Then, as if her thoughts had been read, she heard a crunch of snow behind the gate and watched as Mae walked out. She sprinted toward her, wanting to embrace her with the overwhelming joy she felt. However, she froze in place when she took a good look at Mae. Her face was teeming with cuts, some of which were still bleeding, and she was clutching her rib cage as she staggered out with a limp. Mae's hair was everywhere, as if it had been pulled, and one of her six braids had come loose. Her right arm bore a deep purple bruise, with the outline of teeth around it. Her left arm, which she was using to hold her ribs, was riddled with what looked like third-degree burns. *Exactly what shit did Mae go through in there?* Raya wondered.

Raya rushed to her friend. She wanted to give her a familiar face to smile at, something to bring her peace. Yet Raya sensed something was deeply wrong as Mae's hollowed face stared at the ground. Still she yelled, "Mae!"

Mae flinched and took step back, wincing as she did so. It was as if the noise of Raya's voice had scared her, not comforted her. When Mae finally did look Raya in the face, her eyes were bloodshot and glazed over, as though she were haunted by something. Raya couldn't deny it; Mae looked like she'd run into some sort of rabid animal and then made it back. Still, she ran over and wrapped her arms around her friend, guiding her toward the medics.

"Listen to me, Mae. It's me, Raya. You're out. You're okay. Everything's going to be all right…" She spoke in soft tones, waiting for Mae to respond in her own time. Raya didn't want her to go into shock like other Leavings had in the past. "I'm bringing you to the medics. I'll stand by the gate and wait. Then, when Javeen gets out, we'll—"

Mae's throat released a sob, and tears fell at an alarming rate. She clutched her side and clenched her jaw, but still she continued to cry. Raya looked her over once more, really taking in what had happened to her. Those cuts were defensive, along with that bite, as if Mae had fought someone. It looked like she'd been attacked from behind. Whoever she was partnered with had tried to pry her off. But why? The burns were a whole other story Raya couldn't figure out. To be honest, she wasn't sure she wanted to. And if Mae had survived, why was she crying? She should be happy she had beat out her partner in Stage Six. She had won and they had lost… Unless…

"Mae?" Raya heard herself say, her voice squeaking with fear. Everything was coming together as she stared at Mae's emotionless face. Raya stopped and made her look at her. "Mae…Javeen…"

"Javeen isn't coming out," Mae snapped, the tears continuing to fall. Raya felt her knees buckle and her heart sink. Before she knew it, the medics had hurried over and carried Mae into a nearby tent to tend to her injuries.

Raya stood in place, no longer feeling the chill of winter or the warmth from the sun. Javeen was gone. How could that be? The shiny iron wall caught her attention, and Raya looked at where The Factory stood looming, dark smoke still billowing out of the stacks into the sky. She had worried, thought it might have happened, but kept hope that they'd both leave. Still, Raya should have known. From the beginning, she'd understood The Factory was highly intelligent and could play with them however it wanted. It had seen the two of them and knew what they could do. Raya's fears and understanding slammed into each other when she realized the truth: The Factory had made sure Mae and Javeen were paired together.

Raya knew she had to be strong for Mae. She couldn't imagine what she'd been through or what had happened in that room. Shaking her head to clear it, and trying to stay focused, she ran into the medics' tent. As soon as she entered, anguished screams echoed through the area, while hushed whispers tried to calm Mae down. Raya quickly followed the noise, pushing past a crowd of medics. Eventually, she reached Mae, who was trying to fight off the town's small medical team. She was screaming at them, her legs flailing, her arms swinging, tears cascading down her face.

"Leave me alone! I don't want help!" she shrieked, throwing a pillow at one of the nurses.

Everyone was trying to calm her down, telling her everything was all right, but nothing seemed to work. That was when Raya saw it: a reflection of light, just enough to catch her eye. A woman was walking over with a syringe in her hand. Raya got there just in time, before the nurse could prick Mae with what had to be a sedative. She grabbed the woman by the wrist, squeezed it with all her might, and pulled her face toward her own.

"Let go of it." When the nurse refused, Raya moved in closer. "Fine," she hissed. "But here's a little warning. Prick her with that needle, and, I swear to God, I'll stick it so far up your ass, it'll take weeks for you to pass it."

The nurse looked at her for a moment, wondering if Raya was actually serious. There must have been something in Raya's fiery hazel eyes, because the woman stepped away slowly, her arms raised in defeat. Raya glared at everyone in the tent, challenging them to fight her. "Why don't you all leave her the hell alone until the shock wears off? Don't you have other patients to attend to?"

They stood frozen, looking at her with wide eyes.

"No? Well, maybe I can go break some faces so you can attend to those." Once more she glanced at the nurse with the needle. "What do you think of that?"

It took two seconds for the medics to find somewhere else to be.

Raya looked back at Mae, who was sitting on a gurney. She grabbed a fold-up chair, pulled it in front of her, and leaned forward. She clutched her friend's hands, which Mae first recoiled at, then melted into. Raya didn't say a word; she merely watched as Mae's entire body shook. After another few minutes of trembling and silence, Raya finally whispered, "You know, you really should have a blanket."

"I don't want one," Mae barked, staring at the ground.

"Okay, then," Raya said, leaning back in her chair. "No blanket."

Mae glanced at her, clearly relieved she wasn't pushing it. Although her breathing had calmed somewhat, she looked deeply troubled by whatever had occurred in Stage Six. Raya knew that whatever had happened, Mae would tell her in her own time. This wasn't the time to force her to relive what she'd just gone through. That time, oddly enough, was four seconds later.

As Mae began her story, once more the tears fell one by one, her voice hoarse and ragged. She picked at her fingers and refused to make eye contact, as if she were ashamed of what had happened. Raya listened as Mae told her about Javeen's original idea—that perhaps all they had to do was wait things out, and eventually they'd both leave. They'd laughed, telling each other secrets and tossing around friendly banter, before it all went to hell. She explained that she had planned to take the pill because Javeen had a family to take care of. There was no other way. Then Mae described the fight that followed. Raya's stomach tightened, knowing they'd both been willing to do anything to keep each other alive. She confessed everything Javeen had said, from taking The Factory down, to his feelings for her. She even told Raya about their kiss. As the last of her tears began to dry up, she explained how she had desperately tried to bring his body out of The Factory.

Now there was an explanation for the burns on Mae's arms. She must have held on to Javeen until his weight took him, the flames licking her skin.

Then Raya caught a glance of her wrist and the twine that hugged it. Javeen had played with it whenever another stage was about to begin, as if it might bring him luck. Mae followed Raya's eyes and nodded as she rolled the bracelet between her fingers.

"It...it was the only thing I could get," she whispered. "The knife was in his pocket, and I forgot about it until it was too late."

Raya nodded numbly. "He probably would have wanted it to go with him. It was his father's too. It would have caused the family a lot more pain you know? Could have stirred up too many questions." Mae nodded as well, and silence fell over them again.

They sat there, Raya still taking in what she'd heard, trying to make sense of it all. Mae was frozen, her eyes refusing to look anywhere but the ground. They both had lost a friend, but Mae had lost more. For the first time in years, someone had said he cared about her, truly cared about her, and he was gone. And yes, they'd only known each other two weeks, but knowing that someone actually noticed her—and always had—was something Mae had yearned for. Even Raya knew that. Now that hope was gone, and Mae once more believed she had nothing.

They sat there for a long time, neither of them speaking, just trying to figure out their next step. The silence quickly became too much for Raya. "There was nothing you could do," she said softly. "Javeen told me he was going to get you out of The Factory at all costs, and he really meant it. He was just as determined as you, Mae."

Mae sniffed but didn't nod. She just stared at her shoe as it made trails in the dirt. "I shouldn't be here." She inhaled sharply, her hands shaking. "Raya, I shouldn't be sitting here right now."

"There's nothing you can do at this point. You can't change what happened in there," Raya said, but she knew she couldn't change Mae's mind or alleviate her guilt. "Javeen was—"

"Can you just go?" Mae asked. It wasn't polite, but it wasn't a demand. She just needed to be alone, to think and mourn for a bit longer. Soon, Raya would come back with her condolences and help her friend see the light. But right now, Mae had every reason to want to be alone.

Raya nodded and gave Mae one more pat on the hands before standing up and leaving. As she walked away, she noticed the medics looking at her, then back at Mae. It was clear they were asking if they could finally tend to her injuries. Knowing they were waiting for her permission, Raya rolled her eyes at them and spat, "Give her five more minutes and try again. If she doesn't want your help, leave her." She two more steps then turned back. "And if I hear you used a needle on her, you'll regret it." They all nodded curtly as Raya marched out.

The sunlight blinded her as she pushed the tent fold back. She had to find somewhere to go, but where that was she had no idea. Raya decided to walk to Market Street and just allow her feet to carry her. As she glanced around, she saw the wide boulevard was teeming with people. Apparently, the entire town had heard the gate open when the first person—Raya herself—had walked out of The Factory. And since then, the masses had gathered to see who the Leavings were. There was no clapping when someone ambled out, no cheers of happiness. There were just whispers and the sobs of those who knew they wouldn't see their loved ones again. But there was really only one reason the masses had gathered there now: they were just curious.

As one more person shoved past her to see who the last two Leavings were, almost knocking her down, her frustration rose. She understood the families who had come to check and see if they had someone to wait for. Her own mother had rushed in with an embrace so huge, Raya almost fell over. But after Raya was determined to wait for Mae, she returned back to the house, hopefully preparing some sort of warm meal. Minestrone would be comforting right now. However, that was Raya's family member, which made sense. But these other people, those who knew no one in The Factory, were the ones who infuriated her the most. How dare these people come and wait here, staring at them as if they were some sort of creatures they'd never seen before. They had no idea what the survivors had been through, and the last thing any of the new Leavings wanted was to be gaped at like animals. They'd already thought that while they were in there; they didn't need to feel it back in the real world. She tried to conceal her rage and prevent herself from throwing the next person who ran into her to the ground with her fist.

Something else, however, was making Raya much angrier. It was that damn place. The Factory had put Mae and Javeen together for a reason. It had an intelligence, one Raya always knew it had. It must have noted how close the two of them were or possibly known about Javeen's feelings toward Mae. The memories unwillingly flowed back into her mind as Raya thought of the mountain man. She smiled slightly, remembering the way Javeen had looked at Mae. He wasn't very subtle, which was so funny to Raya. And still, Mae had been clueless about his feelings for her. If they'd made it out together, she was sure they would have been happy and done incredible things together. Perhaps they would have established the relationship Javeen had always wanted. But now he was no longer here. Their alliance was broken, the future bleak, and as Raya glanced back at the medic tent, she wondered if Mae would ever be strong enough to do what she knew they both wanted to do.

Scanning the crowd, Raya collided with a large figure and took a few steps back to catch her balance. She shook her head and started toward the man, her patience at an end. Whoever he was, he would feel her wrath. But when she looked up at the young man's face, she stopped mid-step.

That face…she had seen it before. Somehow familiar but also different in the same breath. His body was huge, hard as a rock from moving heavy objects or toiling through fields. Jet-black curls covered his forehead, almost falling over his eyes. It was those eyes that made Raya stop. Those nearly green eyes, with a hint of brown. They were almost the same eyes she knew, yet a slightly different color. How was this possible? Raya thought she was experiencing a dream come true. Everything that had been lost... But she knew the truth of the situation. This wasn't what she'd thought.

As the young man looked down at her, Raya knew she must have looked crazed. She was dirty and disheveled, and her eyes must have been wide with amazement. Still, she knew who this man was and how he would fix everything. Before he had a chance to push his way around her, Raya quickly looped her arm around his forearm and began to tug. He began to resist and was about to growl something at her, but then Raya grabbed him by the front of the shirt. She pulled him down to her level, making sure he knew she meant business, and whispered, "I know who you're looking for. Come with me, and I'll explain everything on the way there. Just follow me."

The young man looked into her eyes, and slowly she saw him let his guard down. He was looking for someone, someone she knew. And if Raya could give him any indication of where that person was, he seemed willing to take it. With one more tug on his arm, she made her way back the medics' tent.

Chapter Thirty-Eight:
<u>Mae</u>

"Dear, it's going to get infected."

Mae rolled her eyes and snarled while the nurse poked and prodded. She'd finally let the medics near her so they could take care of her wounds. They had cleaned them and bandaged the deepest cut after a ten-minute debated on whether it needed stitches. There wasn't much they could do about her ribs, but they did give her some sort of liquid that alleviated the pain somewhat. It didn't matter anyway; Mae's entire body was numb with guilt. After taking the tonic, all she wanted was to be left alone so she could wallow a bit more before heading home. But this insistent old woman wouldn't leave her alone about the burns on her arms. Although they hurt like hell, Mae didn't want them to be inspected or even for them to heal. She needed a reminder of what she had done.

"Good," she spat, ripping her arm away. The heat was intense, and some of the blisters were beginning to pop and ooze, but she didn't care. If she ended up getting some sort of horrid skin disease, it wouldn't even begin to make up for what she had done. What she had allowed.

"It'll scar," the nurse pushed.

That was too much for Mae. She threw her hands up in the air and snapped at the old woman. "I don't care! Let them scar and never heal. Don't you see? I don't want them to heal! Leave me the fuck alone and let my burns fester, you insistent old hag!"

The entire tent went silent as Mae's voice carried throughout it. The nurse said nothing and didn't look too hurt, since she and the rest of the medics were convinced Mae was still in shock. Still the woman held on to the bandages and ointment, ready for her patient to give in. Mae glared at the nurse, and the nurse glared back. They were ready for this standoff that would last all day if it had to, and they both knew one of them would win. Then a cough from the side of the gurney broke their eye contact as Mae looked to where it was coming from.

Raya stood in front of her again, but this time two others flanked her. A small girl with brown hair stood to Raya's right, while a young woman with the same hair, but a bit darker with red undertones, stood to her left. The little one looked at Mae with curiosity, her eyes wide with amazement and fear. Mae could only assume it was because of her outburst with the nurse moments before. The older girl was wringing her hands in her skirt, her eyes glistening. In fact, she looked as though she'd been crying for some time now, as Mae spotted salty outlines from dried tears. Mae knew she had seen her before, but in the haze of the last few hours, she couldn't remember where. Then a figure stepped forward from the shadows at the back of the tent.

Mae's heart jumped as the huge young man reached over and dragged a chair in front of her. His shoulders were wide, his chest muscular, his arms massive. As he sat down, his hair fell forward, and Mae stared at his dark curly locks, ones she had known for the last two weeks. *How is this possible?* she wondered. She had seen him go; she had let go of his hand. He couldn't be here now. Her heart continued to soar, until she looked at his hazel eyes staring straight into her. Her stomach dropped; she knew this had to be too good to be true. But still, she was confused. What was Raya doing, and who were these people?

Raya had stepped to the side and moved closer to the nurse, whispering something to her. Mae glanced up at her, asking with her eyes what was happening. But all Raya did was nod toward the group. As she did so, the young woman wringing her hands took a hesitant step forward. Then the memory slammed into Mae's mind, and she finally remembered where she had seen this girl before. Mae recalled Javeen saying she loved to come to the market with him. Mae almost had told him how much she had loved and envied her beautiful hair. Then she looked at the smaller girl, Asha, whose eyes brimmed with tears. She had given him the bracelet. She was the one Tharin had made insinuations about, angering Javeen so much he had punched him. Javeen had talked about all of them, and now they were here. Fury rising in her face, she turned to Raya. What was she doing?

"I'm Mami," the tall girl said softly, her eyes raw from crying. She was much closer to Mae now, as she also had pulled a seat up. Slowly she sat down and held Mae's hand, massaging it in a relaxing, comforting way. "We heard you...that you..."

"We heard you were there with our brother. At the end," said the large young man, whose name she couldn't remember. Mae reluctantly glanced up, still not wanting to look at him, but she couldn't help it. She was transfixed by how much he looked like Javeen. From his shoulders to his hair and even the way he sat, the two looked like twins. Almost everything was exactly the same, except for his eyes.

"Jiro, be gentle," Mami whispered, placing a hand on her brother's leg. Mae noted he seemed tense, but that was expected, considering what had happened to Javeen. He exhaled slowly and nodded, looking from his sister's hand back to Mae. Mae looked up and tried to smile, though there was torment in her eyes. She stared at Mami in wonderment and confusion. Why did Javeen's sister even care about her? After what had happened, she had no reason to think twice about her. Mami should have just moved aside and let Jiro attack Mae, ending their torture now.

Jiro leaned forward in the chair, his weight making it creak, reminding Mae how solid he was. He kept trying to make eye contact with her, although Mae was attempting to avoid it. Looking at him kept reopening the wound of Javeen and his death. Every time she caught a glimpse of Jiro, she felt she was looking at his ghost. After a long moment, he was able to lock eyes with her, and Mae gave up her fight. She sighed as he cleared his throat.

"Look…Mae, right?" She nodded. "Your friend Raya here kind of told us what you said and some of what she saw. She also told us about you and my brother. About how you saved him twice in there. She said you all became friends, and the three of you had some sort of system for getting out. And then she told us about the final stage. What had to happen and…the rules." He swallowed hard. "And she told us it was his idea to do what he did."

Mae couldn't keep it in anymore. She thought she had no more tears left in her, but now, with Javeen's family surrounding her, she let it all out. Tears she thought were dried up fell continuously as she tried to explain everything, her sobs sometimes making her unintelligible. She shook and pointed to her face when she explained how the marks on her body had come from her attacking Javeen to prevent him from taking the pill. She babbled about how she had told him she had nothing out here, while he had everything, and yet he still had done it. Mae even lifted her arm to show them she had tried to bring Javeen's body out with her. The only thing she refused to tell them was Tharin's role in it all. That perhaps Javeen thought he'd have no family to come home to after he had learned the truth. This wasn't the time or place for that, and Mae wondered if there ever would be.

After she finished telling her story, she shuddered and threw her face in her hands, trying to steady her breathing. Then she heard footsteps in front of her. Mae peeked through her fingers and saw Asha step forward. She was glancing at Mae's wrist, her eyebrows furrowed in concentration. "What is that?" she asked softly, pointing at the twine.

As Mae lifted her head, she felt her breath leave her lungs. Asha moved closer and took the string between her fingers. Mae looked at her while she studied the twine. She'd also been crying, as her eyes were pink all around. She seemed old enough to understand, but she also looked so young. Did Asha really know what this meant? What The Factory had done, and where her big brother was? Was she aware that yet another person in her family wasn't coming back?

Asha looked up at Mae. "This…this was Javeen's. I gave it to him. It should be…in the…" Her voice cracked when she finally managed to say, "You saved it?"

It was heartbreaking to know Asha knew the bracelet belonged in the flames. She clearly understood that Mae had taken it in order to make sure something of his survived. Asha stared at her, demanding an answer.

Mae nodded. "He…Javeen said it was one of his favorite things. I couldn't get him out of there, but I wanted to save something of his. I wanted to make sure some part of him, a part that was truly his, was returned to his family."

Slowly Mae removed the bracelet from her wrist before placing it in Asha's small hands. Her bright-green eyes looked up at Mae, first with sadness and then in gratitude. Mami and Jiro gazed at Mae too, their faces reflecting their sister's. They knew the hard truth: their brother wasn't coming back. But because of Mae's quick thinking and bravery, they at least had something that represented Javeen. As Mae took in their faces, Asha grabbed her, holding her around the middle. Mae rocked back, shocked by the gesture, then winced. Pain shot through her as her broken ribs shouted against the hug, but Mae let the little girl squeeze harder.

Asha finally pulled away, with tears in her eyes, but a smile on her face. "Thank you, Mae," she whispered.

Mami now came behind her sister and crouched down to her level. "Asha, you probably just broke her ribs more!" She glanced at the twine that was peeking out of Asha's hand. "Honestly, thank you, Mae. This small thing means more to us that you'll ever know. When…when we have the funeral, we'll make sure to bury it with his ashes." Once more she looked at Mae with appreciation and understanding in her tear-filled eyes.

As Mae looked at Jiro, a cold feeling drifted over her. Mami might have been wearing all her emotions on her sleeve, but Jiro had shown no type of feeling toward Mae at all, though his face had fallen in grief. Mae could tell he was mourning his brother, but he wouldn't show it through tears. Jiro wouldn't allow himself that privilege, as he was now the man of the house, and he needed to remain the foundation for the family. He finally looked at Mae, taking in the mess she probably looked like, and sighed. Then he stood up and extended a hand toward her.

"You probably should head home. Staying here will make you go crazy, make you stew in your thoughts." And then, shockingly, he smiled. "Besides, I think the medics will be able to relax more when you're gone, especially since your bodyguard is back." He jerked his head toward Raya.

The redhead let out a huff but knew it was true. The medics hadn't stopped staring at her since she'd walked in, some even shaking as she passed. Mae, on the other hand, was still trying to figure out what was happening. Jiro wanted to make sure she was okay? But at the same time, she knew what he'd said was true. Staying here would only make her feel worse. Slowly she reached her hand toward him, only to notice that her burns were now bandaged. As Jiro helped her up, she snapped her head to where Raya and the old woman were standing. That sneaky nurse smiled in self-satisfaction, while Raya's eyes twinkled with mischief. Mae sighed as she gained her footing. Of course. Raya knew the best time to bandage her up and had plotted with the nurse. They had waited until she was so distracted by her story and Javeen's family to finally bandage her burns. Mae gave the nurse one last glare, along with an obscene gesture in Raya's direction, then followed Javeen's family out of the tent.

The paperwork was agonizing. The head medic was trying to tell Mae something but could tell she wasn't listening. She just wanted to get out of there as fast as she could. He shrugged and told her all the information was in the documents. Mae didn't even read them, just to spite the man, knowing the only important things she needed were her signature and a witness. Mae quickly looked behind her, waiting for Raya to step forward, but her friend remained still. Perhaps a Leaving couldn't be another Leaving's witness. Seeing Mae's panic, Mami quickly pushed Jiro to the front, and the two grumbled as the head medic told them where their names were needed. After Mae and Jiro signed the paperwork, Mae was allowed to head home.

There was only a few stragglers left, the last few who wanted to see that she had made it. Mae quickly pushed past them, and up the main street, staring at the ground. After everything that happened, she felt as though the people who did look at her as she walked through town saw her as some sort of animal. A creature that did anything she could to get out of The Factory. And Mae knew she probably looked it. With all her cuts, her staggered walk from the broken ribs, and the bandage on her arm, she knew that she looked like an animal that had just lost a fight. She could feel the pity of the eyes on her, knowing they felt sorry for her. But this wasn't what she wanted. Mae didn't want people to look at her with that type of idea in their head. Poor child, she knew they were thinking. She was supposed to walk out in triumph, but Javeen was supposed to be next her. She lowered her head further, wanting to burry herself into the ground. Right now, Mae felt like she needed her old life of transparency back.

No one said a word as they trudged in the same direction toward the edge of town. The large crowd Mae had caught a quick glimpse of was gone now, as Mae was the last person to leave, and that was a few hours ago. The only noise came from Asha, who was kicking the same rock up the hill as a game. Raya followed the group, though Mae knew her house was right by the inn, which they'd long since passed. Mae realized Raya wanted to be there and make sure Mae was safe at home before she returned to town, and she couldn't blame her. Mae wasn't even sure how stable she was. Having her around was somewhat comforting in this awkward situation. The setting sun cast a yellow glow on the ground that reflected brightly off the snow, and the chill of winter was beginning to come back full force as they climbed the hill. Even so, Mae's forearms burned and throbbed under her bandages. She swore to herself, just to annoy the nurse, that she was going to scratch at them all the time so they'd eventually become ugly scars.

They all arrived at the fork in the road that separated Mae's side of town from the farming area where Jiro and his siblings lived. There was a pause, and then Mae quickly thanked everyone before she started toward her house. All she wanted was to get out of here and wrap herself up. She hadn't taken two steps before a hand gripped her arm. Mae stumbled forward but caught herself quickly. She turned to see Jiro, towering over her with a confused expression.

"Where are you going?" he asked, his voice gentler than it had been before.

She looked at him as though he were asking the dumbest question in the world.

337

Mae pointed down the dirt road toward her shack. "I'm going home. It's that way," she said slowly, wondering if Jiro wasn't aware of this simple fact.

"No. That's not where your house is," he said. "Not anymore." Just as he said that, Mae caught sight of Asha, who was pointing to the other road. The one that led to their farm. While Mae glanced at Asha, whose smile was now widening, Mami approached Mae on the other side of Jiro. She cocked her head toward Asha.

"Come on, Mae. It's time to come home."

Mae's heart rose and then sank as she realized what they were saying. They wanted her to live with them. Javeen's siblings were inviting her to stay with them, rather than let her live in solitude. She quickly shook her head, trying to find the words to say no. This couldn't happen. They were just trying to be kind, to show her they held no resentment. All she had to do was say no, and Javeen's family would let her go back to her run-down house. *No.* Although they were very simple letters, she couldn't find them. She continued to shake her head in protest.

Finally, she was able to say it. "I can't. Thank you very much, really. But I can't live with you. I'll just be a constant reminder of what happened." It was the truth. She didn't want to haunt them every day with her presence. Going back to her place would be best, for all of them. "Thank you. But no."

Mami shrugged, as if Mae's words meant nothing. "You're putting a lot on yourself. We're inviting you to live with us because it's better than living by yourself. We're not doing this out of pity. Besides, it would be better to have another body in the house, instead of an empty reminder."

Jiro straightened up and stepped forward. "Mae, we aren't taking no for an answer." When he saw the look of dread on her face, he put his hands on her shoulders and whispered, "Look, you tried to save our brother. We know that. But apparently, he had demons that even you couldn't save him from. Javeen always had a clear head, and when he made a decision, no one, including us, could change his mind. You might not have known that, but we do. It was his choice, not yours. Until you understand that, you can't live by yourself. You'll just sit in your guilt and who knows what will happen? Honestly, I think being alone will kill you."

Raya came to the other side. "The paperwork is signed. Technically, if you don't have anyone to go home to, you have to live with whoever picks you up at the medics' tent, at least for a while. And since you didn't want to listen to the head medic or read anything, you missed all that. Jiro wasn't signing just as your witness; he was signing as your guardian. The town records now show you're a part of their household. So really, you *are* living with them." Of course, Raya knew that. And now it made sense why she had walked so far past her home with them. She was there to keep the peace, in case Mae absolutely refused to move. Mae almost laughed at the irony—Raya keeping peace. What kind of world was she now living in?

"You've been through a lot," Jiro continued, his hand still on her shoulder. "More than I, or any of us, could ever imagine. And not just in The Factory. Even before you went into that place, you had to deal with more shit than someone your age should. But we want to help you with that. You need stability, Mae. You need to be with people who'll take care of you, even when you don't know that you want it. I'm not saying this situation is perfect. To be honest, it might feel uncomfortable for a bit. But time will fix that. And at least you'll have something close to what a family is."

Mae was about to protest once more, explain the inconvenience this would be for them, and then she closed her eyes. In that moment, she saw Javeen standing above her, but this time there was no pill in his hand. As she looked at him, he mouthed, *"Promise me."* When her eyes opened, she remembered her two promises to Javeen. The first was to take care of his family; the second was to destroy The Factory. It would be a lot easier to make sure his family was doing okay if she was living with them. And besides, they had been kind enough to offer her space in their house. If, over time, they didn't want her there, Mae could just leave. Slowly she nodded.

Asha wiggled her fists in happiness, and Mami smiled. "We're so glad you agree." She grabbed Asha by the hand and headed down the road. Mae was about to make her way toward them when Jiro, whose arm was still on her, held her in place. She looked at him, but the glance she received told her not to ask questions. Mami had moved a few feet when she noticed Jiro and Mae weren't moving. She quickly turned and called out, "Come on, you two! My breath is turning to snow."

"Yeah, just give us a minute," Jiro yelled. He waved his arm toward their home. "Go get Mae's bed ready and warm up that beef stew. Throw some of those rolls in too Mami. We'll be there before the stars come out."

As the two walked down the path, Mae glanced up at him. He clearly wanted time with her to say something he didn't want his sisters to hear. This was perfect for Mae as well, because she knew she had to tell him the truth. She had to tell him about her second promise to Javeen. As Mami and Asha disappeared into the dusk, Jiro's hand finally fell, and he turned to Mae, ready to speak. But Mae knew she had to go first.

"I'm taking it down," she stated, looking Jiro right in the eyes. He closed his mouth and crossed his arms over his chest. "I'm going to take down The Factory. It was something your brother and I talked about. Raya too. Before Javeen died, he made me promise I'd make sure The Factory burned, and I'm keeping that promise. I don't know how or when we're going to do it, but I'm sure we'll watch that place fall." She quickly continued, not letting Jiro speak. She needed to give him the option now. "You're the head of the family, and that's why I'm being honest with you. If my plan makes you want to reconsider my living with you and your family, I understand, and—"

"Raya already told me all this," he interrupted, his face serious.

Mae threw her head back and laughed as she glanced at her friend. Raya, standing off to the side, avoided eye contact with her as she twisted her toe in the dirty snow. Mae sighed. "Of course she did."

Raya's head snapped up and looked between the two of them. She threw her hands up in defeat. "What?" she asked innocently. "I thought it would take you a year to tell him. I thought I should let him know before he took you into his house. And besides, I didn't tell anyone else. Jiro's the only one who knows."

Mae looked back at Jiro. "Please. Just let me go back home, and I won't be a problem. No one will know I'm not living with you. This is a lot to deal with, beyond what you're already going through. If you let me go, I won't cause your family any more pain."

Jiro looked at both Raya and Mae, contemplating the situation. His stern eyes eventually stayed on Mae when he finally spoke. "I understand your mission. Really, I do. The Factory is a terrible place, and it deserves to be demolished. But it's so large, and no one knows much about it. Who runs it or how it works. Hell, I don't even think people know how to get inside once the gate is closed. I'm just confused by it, that's all." His face screwed up in consternation as he rubbed the back of his neck. "How are you going to do it without any muscle power? Besides..." And for the second time on this sad day, Jiro smiled at her. "...three is the magic number."

Raya looked as though she'd found out her birthday was coming early, and Mae's heart nearly leapt out of her chest. The two girls exchanged glances, making sure they both understood what was happening. Jiro nodded, which was all the confirmation they needed. He was in. Perhaps this was his way of mourning his brother's death, by fighting for the same cause. Whatever his motive was, Mae felt relieved. The more power they had behind them, the more reason to fight, and the better their odds were of winning.

The church bells rang, echoing all the way up the hill. Their heads snapped in that direction, and they watched as the last of the sun's rays covered the valley. Raya looked down and grabbed her hair in frustration. "Oh, shit. That late, huh? Well, I'd better get home before my mother thinks I'm in trouble. Or causing it." She flashed them a smirk. "But I mean, me? Causing trouble? Really?" As she passed Mae, she placed a gentle hand on her shoulder. "Don't worry. We aren't letting this mission go. Not till that place is gone and goes to hell. But it will. And we'll be the reason it burns."

Mae nodded as the girl with the fire-red hair and the mysterious scar headed back to town. Raya had so many secrets, ones she knew would come to life at some point. Right now, though, Mae was happy with the Raya she knew and would give her the time she needed to truly open up. She turned back to Jiro, who was breathing into his hands as the temperature lowered even more. Awkwardly she clapped her hands together, trying to figure out what to say.

"Well, I'm glad you're in," Mae said simply, before taking another step toward her home, but Jiro caught her again.

"Nice try, slick. I might look stupid, but I'm not *that* dumb. You're still living with us. Don't think your crazy plan has changed that."

"It's your crazy plan now too. Or did you already forget?" she retorted, but gave him a small smile. Although she was dying to go to her house, there was something about the way Mami had looked at her, telling her to come home, that made Mae happy. It was comforting to know someone wanted her to go to a warm household, one with actual food in it. Even if it only was because of a scam Mae had fallen for.

Jiro jerked his head toward the house, hands in his pockets, as he bounced on his toes. "Mae, I mean it. I'm going to fight with you. But you can't tell my sisters. I don't know where we are going to start. But we can do it. Just please, let it be the three of us." Mae nodded, knowing now that was why Jiro had sent his sisters away. He didn't want them to know anything about their plan, just in case they wanted to join in. Mae couldn't blame him either. Even knowing them for such a short time, the thought of losing another member of their family crushed Mae. She agreed to his terms.

They stood in silence for a moment, and suddenly a great wind caught them by surprise. Jiro let out a shivering breath and looked down at her again. "Can we go now? I forgot my gloves, and I don't want to come home to a cold dinner." Mae nodded. She hadn't even taken three steps, and Jiro was already halfway down the road toward the warm, inviting lights. If Javeen's family could take her in as one of their own, Mae knew this new chapter of her life might actually be…bearable.

She turned and looked at The Factory one last time. The massive iron structure jutted into the sky but was shadowed by the light, which was now retreating. The blood-orange glow of the setting sun behind The Factory was beautiful yet haunting. An array of emotions flowed through Mae as she stared at it, mesmerized by the building that had held her captive. The same place that had inflicted wounds upon her, ones that would scar her mind and memories for years to come. This wicked outline had taken away a person who, for the first time in years, had brought light to Mae's world.

As she stared at the darkening Factory, her sorrows and pain melted away, replaced by a surge of anger and determination. No longer was she a child, afraid of the simple shadow of this place. Mae was a changed person. The Factory was no longer her fear; it was her mission. She would make sure The Factory crumbled to dust, never to rise again. She, Raya, and Jiro would watch it burn, just like the countless victims it had taken. She stared up at the black smoke drifting into the sky. That was who she was fighting for. Those people, past and present, whose ashes had lifted into the sky because of The Factory. For the future that would fear a building they knew nothing about. And for Javeen. She would fight for them all. These emotions would fuel her, and with that power, she would reach her goals.

Mae would be remembered.

Everyone would notice her.

And The Factory would fear her.

The Factory continues to operate, ready to take more souls into the flames as spring draws near. While the smoke still covers the sky, Mae, Jiro and Raya must uncover the truth behind the impending structure. But as they begin to take a true look at the monster they face, they find there is not only a darker side to The Factory, but to everything they hold close.

Coming Soon:

THE MAINTENANCE

Acknowledgements

After two years of working of this, I honestly don't know what to say. To those of you who have read to this point, I cannot express how grateful I am that you read this book.

I know this is the time to create my laundry list of "Thank You's", but it's so difficult to do. Everyone who ever supported me in my creative writing process deserves nothing but praise. I know that sometimes I can be a tad…abrasive. From the constant nagging to ask how the plot was, to wondering who your favorite characters were, you stuck by me through and through. And to that I am extremely grateful.

The first people I must thank is my family, my mom, dad and sister. Mom, you have to know how important you are to me, and how you have shown me how strong women can be. Every female in my book has that sense of independence that you have always made sure your girls have had.

Dad, I have to thank you for not only being an awesome dad, but also for fueling my passion to read. Reading the *"Little House"* series together is a childhood memory that I will cherish. From there, I learned how amazing it was to not only read one book, but to then look forward for a story to be continued through multiple more.

And Haley, thanks for just putting up with me. You are the best little sister, and without you I wouldn't have really had the confidence in this novel that I do now. You were one huge reason this book even exists, since you told me to just write. I needed your honesty more often than you know, even though you did think I would have Mae bite Javeen's ear off... And by the way, I'm still sorry. But also, not.

I also have to thank my Aunt Michelle for her amazing patience and kindness when it came to this novel. I wouldn't have known how to make sure everything was in tip top shape without my you. Thank you so much for sticking with me when I was utterly confused on basic formatting of a document. And for helping me figure out exactly what I had to do when I wanted to get the amazing cover that I have.

As for the Fydo family and Mae, just thank you for being the second family I always needed. You are all amazing. Not only have you taken care of me and my family, but you have always been a good group to laugh with. I mean just look at every event we end up at together. And I'm still feeling a little guilty that Mae is constantly telling you she's a main character of a book, so thanks for putting up with that too!

Mae, you are in a book. It was what you wanted right? And just like Haley, thank you for pushing me to write this story with the magic words, "Whatever you write, make it about me." And don't ever lose those braids.

Finally, thank you for anyone who read my book in its early stages. Your comments, questions about plot and people, and other contributions are what made the novel you are now reading.

I would also like to thank tea. Calming tea, English Breakfast, Chai…literally all the tea that made this novel possible.

Made in the USA
Middletown, DE
20 December 2017